ARE MY ROOTS SHOWING?

ARE MY ROOTS SHOWING?

KAROLA GAJDA

Copyright © Karola Gajda, 2016

Karola Gajda asserts the moral right to be identified as the author of this work.

Apart from historical events, everything and everyone portrayed in this novel is fictional.

All rights reserved. If you have purchased the ebook edition of this novel please be aware that it is licensed for your personal enjoyment only and refrain from copying it.

For translation rights and permission queries,
please contact the author's agent,
Geraldine Cooke: geraldinecookmac@yahoo.com
www.geraldinecooke.co.uk

ABOUT THE AUTHOR

Karola was born in Yorkshire to Polish parents who came to the UK after World War II. She has worked in theatre, radio and stand-up comedy. Her passion is making people laugh.

www.twitter.com/karolagajda
www.facebook.com/writingkarola
www.karolagajda.com

ACKNOWLEDGEMENTS

I wish to thank the following people:

My agent Geraldine Cooke, agents Malwina Świerczyńska-Skupień and Lisa Eveleigh, designers David Grogan, Clare Stacey and Tim Peters and my copy editor Janice Brent. Thanks also to Mark Thorpe and to Suzanne Williams, Piotr Kuklinski, Susan Dunigan, Jane Hore and Chris and Beryl Woods for all their help and support.

For my sister

CONTENTS

Chapter 1 · 1
Chapter 2 · 6
Chapter 3 · 23
Chapter 4 · 31
Chapter 5 · 38
Chapter 6 · 47
Chapter 7 · 56
Chapter 8 · 65
Chapter 9 · 75
Chapter 10 · 88
Chapter 11 · 102
Chapter 12 · 115
Chapter 13 · 125
Chapter 14 · 132
Chapter 15 · 145
Chapter 16 · 155
Chapter 17 · 164
Chapter 18 · 176
Chapter 19 · 177
Chapter 20 · 181
Chapter 21 · 196
Chapter 22 · 198
Chapter 23 · 203
Chapter 24 · 206
Chapter 25 · 210

CHAPTER 1
LEAK (*PRZECIEK*)

Today I was found out. I went for breakfast at one of my favourite cafes in Fulham. I love going there because the *pains au chocolat* are massive, about the size of three ordinary ones.

The cafe is full of Polish waitresses, all attentive and hyper-efficient. I hear their rapid Polish but I don't let on I can understand because it raises too many questions: how come I speak Polish, where was I born? For some reason it's intriguing for real Poles to come across fake ones like me – children of Poles who came here after the war. I was born in Doncaster, South Yorkshire, to Polish parents. Not exactly exotic, the Polish Yorkshire mix. Just a bit odd, like chutney is odd. Is it savoury or is it sweet, or is it a bit in-between?

Usually I let them talk and act as if I don't understand. I hear all sorts of secrets – boyfriend problems, money problems – once I became the topic of conversation myself. The red patent leather handbag I'd put on the table – how nice it was, how alluring and shiny.

Today I wasn't so clever. Mama rang me on my mobile. I thought of letting it ring but as she never phones in the morning, I thought I'd better answer. The cafe around me was suddenly hearing my Polish, interspersed with bits of English (Ponglish).

'*Co, pękła rura i potrzebujesz plumera?* (What, a pipe's burst and you need a plumber?)'

Their loo had sprung a leak, a bad one at that, and did I know who to call? Tata – Mama said – was standing in the bathroom with his finger over the leak and flushing the loo every two minutes. Having been in Doncaster for over fifty years their English is good, but in an emergency they still turn to me. I don't know the word for plumber in Polish, and neither, bless them, do they. We just say, 'plu-merr' in a strong Polish accent.

The waitress who has served me so many times looked over, surprised to hear me chirruping away in her mother tongue. I felt as if I'd been outed, as if someone had upturned a stone and there I was, looking out from underneath it, blinking in the light. Ashamed of my deceit, I told Mama I'd get onto it and ring her straight back.

'I didn't know you were Polish,' said the waitress in Polish, amazed.

'Er, *tak*, (yes),' I replied, switching language too. 'Sort of anyway.'

I started an involved online search on my phone to cut off any further conversation. A few minutes later, calls done and plumber found, the waitress came back.

'Your Polish is very good.'

'You've only heard my best words,' I said. 'I don't even know how to say plumber.'

'*Hydraulik*,' she said.

'*Hydraulik*?' I repeated carefully. 'Thanks, I must remember that. I'm leaving London next week – I'm off to Warsaw.'

'For a holiday?'

'No – I'll be teaching English.'

'Fantastic! How long for?'

'I'm not sure.'

'I know some people there if that would help.'

'Thanks, but I'll be staying in my cousin's flat and my aunt's there as well.'

'Well. Have fun.'

She picks up my order slip and I pay by credit card.

'Mikołajczyk,' says the waitress, looking at my surname and pronouncing it perfectly. The times that has happened, I can count on one hand.

Not long now.

Packed:
Warsaw guidebooks (digesting now so don't come across as ignoramus)
Big bar Dairy Milk (for settling-in process)

Pending packs:
Rescue Remedy (for take-off)
Earplugs (for noisy kids on plane)
EU adaptors (so don't electrocute myself or fuse whole block)

Just-about-to-leave packs:
Tweezers (vital)
Coffee (coffee out there awful)
Copy of something by Joseph Conrad (in English) to get me in the mood

Final packs:
Laptop and lead
E-ticket reference, emergency numbers, bank cards, a hundred pounds' worth of złoty
Health insurance (dread Polish hospitals and am a total hypochondriac. I blame Mama for nagging me not to go to bed with damp hair all these years)
Passport (terrible photo, hair like oily pancake)

Things to do at airport:
Have final latte on English soil
Have final leisurely browse of *Hello* in WH Smiths
Top up chocolate stash and buy outsize Toblerone (can carry under arm)

One more email to the school where I'll be working:

Dear Mr Tomaszewski
I am looking forward to starting at Language Zone on July 1 *(hope it's worth jacking in my job for).*
Please can you re-confirm I am starting this Monday at 10am *(and not any earlier as I like a lie-in).*

I understand I will be teaching my beginners' group first thing and will come prepared (must take shed-full of handouts to show have planned).
Kind regards *(tatty-bye)*
Magda Mikołajczyk

Thank God the days of sending telegrams to Poland are over. I remember my mum doing this in the seventies when she had urgent messages to send to relatives about births, deaths and places at University. It was like communicating with someone on another planet and you never knew if the message had got there or not. Now, my message is there at the click of a button.

I wonder what it'll be like, living and working in Warsaw? Maybe I should have written in Polish and got Mama and Tata to check it first? I just couldn't bear the thought of making a mistake. What is the word for 'confirm' in Polish anyway? I have never used the word confirm at home, as there's never been anything to confirm.

Mama and Tata mix Yorkshire into Polish with ease.

'*Zrób dla mnie* cuppa char.'

'*I przynieś* Rich Tea biscuit.'

My vocabulary must now expand. It must become my *nowa obsesja* over and above losing weight, getting a boyfriend and having thicker hair.

Mama and Tata are starting to get really jittery about me going. Mama worries about me excessively; if I'm eating enough (according to her I never am) and about boyfriends (or my lack of a one). She also thinks everyone in Poland's an undercover policeman, a conman or a murderer.

'What if you get killed!?'

'I won't!'

'Or thrown into jail!?'

'Mama, I'm going to your homeland!'

'I know, I left, remember!'

Poles are frequently anti-Polish. Politicians are their first target. They also complain about their jobs, their relatives, their friends, their enemies, the water in the tap, which leads to complaining about the tap itself, the design of the tap, Polish design, Polish manufacturing, until you're back to politicians. On the other hand, Poles defend Poland with pride and its ways to the hilt. It depends on whom they're talking to. And on which way the wind is blowing.

I still haven't finished packing. I won't take my massive dictionary as it weighs a ton. Instead, I've found an online open source one that's quite good, even if some ordinary words have swearwords as translations.

Apparently English is one of the hardest languages to master, but in my opinion, next to Polish it's a doddle. Apart from the proliferation of consonants (Polish is full of z's and s's and c's) and the impossible pronunciation (which Poles love to see you struggle over) Polish grammar's a killer. There are seven cases and nouns change ending depending on the case. Take 'table'. In the nominative case, it's *stół*. In the dative (under the table) it's *pod stołem*. Utter nightmare.

Instrumental's my favourite case. You use it for modes of transport:

'Are you going to Poland by coach (*autobusem*)?'

'Are you kidding? I'm going by plane (*samolotem*).'

When I get into a scrape with a noun or case, which seems to be every other sentence, I vocalize all the possibilities until I hit the one that sounds right.

'*Nie ma deszcza* (There's no rain).' Or is it ... *deszczu*?

I feel like a Polish fraud.

The flat where I'm staying is my cousin Dagmara's old place and it's right in the centre in a huge grey block.

Back to packing. I must take a sane range of shoes and suppress my Imelda Marcos tendencies.

VOCAB CORNER:
Confirm = *potwierdzić*. I have actually heard this before. Must have done more confirming than I thought.
Broadband connection = *połączenie szerokopasmowe*. Hope the connection at Dagmara's is quicker than the time it takes to say it.
My Imelda Marcos tendencies = *moje tendencje Imeldy Markos* (genitive).

CHAPTER 2
LARD, LARD, IT TASTES OF LARD
(*TŁUSZCZ, TŁUSZCZ, SMAKUJE JAK TŁUSZCZ*)

'Lard with bread served on a board.'

Not my first choice for a starter, but it's amazing what Poles salivate over. I'm browsing through a menu in a restaurant, waiting to meet my cousin Dagmara for lunch. *Galareta's* also there, a horrid, cold meat-jelly blob with bits of hoof and eyebrow in it.

'Do you have the menu in English?' I ask a passing waitress. The lard I can translate and the meat jelly I know about, but I don't want a repeat performance of last night's meal. I thought I'd ordered a cheese and sweetcorn fritter but a pancake with slimy yellow mushrooms arrived instead.

'*Tak*,' the waitress replies. She smiles and hands me a menu with a small Union Jack taped neatly on the front. Ah, that's better. Ordering food should be fun, not a test of nationality.

I send Dagmara a text, or SMS as the Poles call them. No kisses either, as Poles don't have the letter 'x'. Dagmara's a dentist, or *stomatolog* which to begin with I thought was some kind of stomach specialist.

Hi Dagmara, Am here. Look forward to seeing you.

Only I'm not. Meeting up with Dagmara is like taking a lemon, cutting it open and squirting it into your eye. But family's family – isn't it?

A minute later she replies.

On tram. There in 15. Been tied up with a root canal.

Lovely.

Never mind, I can compose myself and gaze through the window at the traffic and the trams.

Some people don't understand my move from London to Warsaw. Paris, yes, Rome or Barcelona – but Warsaw?

So why have I come to work here, land of my ancestors? To see how things have changed? To improve my Polish? Or to dig around my roots, which, in spite of my Polish blood, are as wizened as an old man's legs? Mama was deported by Stalin to Siberia during the war, Tata slaved away on a farm in Germany. He hates it when I say I'm not Polish. A frown fills his otherwise potato-smooth face, which normally only happens when Germany thrashes Poland at the World Cup.

'Is an elephant no longer an elephant because it's born in a stable?' he says, as if stating an absolute truth. He retreats to his rocking chair and rocks away his annoyance. When his three wisps of grey hair get going, I don't have the heart to argue.

There have been other, more pressing theories about my move to Poland. Mama's theory is all about husbands. When I went up north to tell them I was moving, and convince Mama that Poland was definitely not a cut-throat Communist den, I heard her on the phone to one of her Polish friends. She sounded thrilled.

'Yes Magda's moving to Warsaw. Maybe she'll find a Polish husband! The best kind, the only kind. She might even have a baby!'

I was washing up as I earwigged, and couldn't help but look at my wedding ring finger – where there is no ring.

The truth is, Mama would hate it if I met someone out there – I'd be too far away for her to badger. Tata, well, I don't think he even thinks of such things anymore. For a while, I think he would have liked me to meet someone who would help me get rid of my Polish surname, as he thinks it's harder to get a job with a foreign name. Also, he's fed up with people mispronouncing it. I remember him watching the TV credits once and saying, 'Look at that, Magda, Fox – that's an easy surname, try to marry someone with a name like that, just one syllable!' He wishes he'd changed his name when he first arrived in England in the fifties. Lots of Poles did that to blend in and to eliminate having their names mispronounced.

Phone call ended, Mama spotted a fatal flaw.

'Wait a minute,' she said, her mind in full throttle. 'Why go to Poland to meet a Pole – you know half of Poland's still over here!'

'Mum, that isn't why I'm going.'

'Of course it is!' she says, ignoring me. 'Anyone can see that. Leave that horrible, dangerous, dirty and expensive London and come back to Doncaster. You'll find someone in no time!'

If I've heard this once, I've heard it a million times. If I could make this rant into a sculpture, it'd be a six-foot wide open marble mouth which I'd christen 'Mama'.

'I could put you—'

'In the Polish Gazette, I know,' I replied.

What a thought, being advertised in the paper. I can see it now.

'Daughter to marry off. 39. Good at most things. *Ma szerokie biodra dobre do rodzenia dzieci.* (Has child-bearing hips.)'

'We all met like that after the war you know – or, why not go to Polish Mass?! Church is simply bursting with them – the Polish priest says he's got a bigger congregation than the English one!'

It's true. In the Polish service it's often standing room only. Poles are still popping up everywhere in England, like mushrooms at dawn. Mama ended with that hopeful look of hers, the one that combines a smile with an expression that asks, 'Where have I gone wrong?'

'What about Lidl?' she continued. 'They all go there.'

'As if I'd go to Lidl to find a husband, Mama, honestly.'

I slapped the rubber gloves, sopping wet, over the sink.

'It's as good a place as any. We found a Polish painter there.'

It's true too. When Mama and Tata needed their kitchen decorating, they went to Lidl. They loitered around, and when they saw someone with a round, serious, moon-like face putting a large jar of gherkins into their basket, they homed in on him in a military-styled pincer movement.

A young couple on a table near me lean over and kiss too intimately. Good grief, I am here too you know. I look the other way. On my other side, a much older couple get on with their meals in amicable silence, exchanging bits of food.

But what if I do meet someone out here? If some eligible (i.e. sane, solvent and non-alcoholic) bachelor with all his teeth throws himself my way, great. I could meet Mr Right now, as I sit with my hot chocolate.

I stare out of the window and look for Dagmara as a tram pulls in and then goes. She's not on it. The last time we met, a few months ago, she had a dyed copper bob which looked totally false, like a perfect wig. The falser the better, it seems in this country, as at least it shows you're trying.

Once I decided to move to Warsaw, other decisions followed, like giving up my job. Until a couple of months ago I worked for an advertising agency in London called Adspeak. I did ads for loo roll and detergent mainly. Mama would proudly tell the neighbours that I worked in 'toilet advertising' and bought any product I worked on in huge quantities.

'It's never going to get me promoted, Mama,' I'd say, watching her stack a dozen bottles of floor cleaner underneath the sink.

'But won't it show them the ad was good, if people go and buy it?'

At first the job was fun, then it became busy, then it became stressful and busy, then boring. Boring and stressful, how could that be? The day I resigned, I caught my reflection in a pane of glass. Me with flat hair, by my computer, tired.

'You're leaving here, to teach English in Warsaw?' asked my boss.

'I saw an ad in the Metro and applied,' I said. It wasn't even a very good ad. Nothing fancy, just plain text in a box. A similar one in England would have looked worrying.

It's great that I'm based in the centre in Dagmara's old flat. She has moved to some suburb, to somewhere bigger and more respectable 'for someone her age' (forty-one). She's single too and in recent years Dagmara's taken to wearing a large sparkling diamond ring on her wedding finger to look respectable. Me, I have a cheap glittery plastic ring on my middle finger to look available. In some ways, Mama is right, I would like to meet someone.

Still no Dagmara. The waitress returns.

'I'm sorry, the person I'm waiting for—'

'Still hasn't arrived,' finishes the waitress. 'No problem.'

I go back to the menu. 'Cheese and beetroot salad' is included in the 'sides'. That's probably a bed of grated beetroot with some squares of processed cheese on top.

Ulica Nowy Świat (New World Street) is very busy now. People on lunch hour. Nowy Świat is one of Warsaw's smartest streets, where many of the sooty buildings have been jet-blasted clean, revealing again the golden stone beneath. The cobbles are immaculate and the shops are full of fur hats and fancy handbags, placed in the windows like lazy squatting reptiles.

For those wanting high street fare, there's TK Maxx and Zara around the back, stuffed with the latest fashions, and Marks & Spencer selling expensive ready meals – a bit of a scandal to home-cooking-minded Poles. Shoppers scurry around with clusters of coloured carrier bags in their hands and there are new wave cafes that do Antipodean-styled flat whites.

Nothing that I see has anything to do with the bleak Poland of the seventies and eighties, when the shops were empty and disgruntled shop assistants seemed to love saying '*nie ma*' (we don't have that) delivered in the flattest tone ever. I remember feeling so unwelcome.

Once, when I was in a major museum, I was told off for daring to change direction and go back one room to revisit a painting I'd taken a liking to. True, I sat down on a fourteenth-century red velvet chair by accident, but it was just plonked in the middle of the room and right in front of the work of art. I felt a firm bony finger poke me on the shoulder.

'Get up! yelled the guide. 'You're sitting on an ancient relic!'

'*Przepraszam*!' I said, leaping straight up. 'I thought it was new!'

'No, it is not new! It's over seven hundred years old – like everything else in this museum!'

I wanted to explain that British galleries have seats for visitors so that they can absorb the works of art – but I thought I'd better leave it before her blood pressure went through the seven hundred-year-old roof.

Now the youngish couple are sharing a knickerbocker glory with two long spoons and feeding one another spoonfuls, giggling. They look so carefree.

That's one of the reasons I've come to Poland now – life's much easier than during the Communist period. One week of queuing for a bottle of malt vinegar and I'd have been on the first flight back to England. Only it would have been far too expensive to fly back then of course, as cheap airlines didn't exist then and Poles couldn't travel – not easily anyway. The options for travel to England were a thirty-hour coach journey or a day on a train and you also needed a visa. When I was in my twenties, I always took the train to Poland, in spite of the intimidating wait at the East German border. The train would be held for hours as soldiers stormed through, yelling in German, turning out all the seats, hunting for smuggled goods or better still, stowaways. Why didn't I go to Benidorm on holiday, like normal people? Poland has always drawn me, like a heart draws blood.

'*Achtung! Reisepässe!*'

The guards were always astonishingly handsome. I'd hand over my precious Western passport and sit bewildered in my Levi jeans, sure of nothing but my status and the emblem on my passport. The Eastern Europeans would wake up to take a look at my little navy hardback book of freedom as it was back then, craning their necks. Then they'd doze off again, blending into their seats like luggage. One night on the train, I took out a banana to eat and the aroma made the man opposite me wake up. You couldn't buy bananas in Poland back then and he was so amazed to see it that I gave it to him instead. I didn't let on that I could speak Polish – I just handed it over in silence. He nodded thank you and ate it slowly, turning it in the moonlight.

I happen upon the dessert page and at last, I see something I want: 'blueberry *pierogi*'. This will be my main course, a large pudding of fruit dumplings. In Poland you can do that with sweet *pierogi*, have them as a main, and no one bats an eyelid. With any luck, there'll be about a dozen of these and they'll be smothered in a blanket of thick sweet cream. What also amazes me is that no one ever seems to get sick of these heavy, crescent-shaped dumplings.

Another text from Dagmara.

There in 2.

Not long now. I brace myself for our lunch together. Crotchety, unique and dear Dagmara. I like her and yet I dislike her.

Unlike me, Dagmara was born in Poland and her late father Szymon was Mama's brother. He was nice, Uncle Szymon. I always wondered how someone so kind and gentle could produce someone as loud as Dagmara. If I had to sum up Dagmara it would be by comparing her to the washing machine in the flat I'm renting off her. Whenever I was visiting and saw Dagmara use it, I remember it always nearly took off her hand. It's like a mechanical alligator with serrated doors and a large flap that bangs down on your knuckles as you fill it with clothes. As it washes it bounces as if having a tantrum, rather like Dagmara herself, and once it's tired, it chugs to a sulky stop. At this point, she had to force open the flap like a stuck-out tongue.

Dagmara's also uncensored and really hates Britain. She says British food is awful and that our tomatoes taste of plastic.

'You know why you're all so pale and insipid-looking?' is one of her all-time favourite questions.

'Why?'

'It's your diet. Full of hormones, chemicals and terrible mutant genes. You should be careful.'

'I am careful.'

'And what a vague and soulless people, all so callous! Never revealing anything, yet always trying to pry. And all those loose morals, Magda! How have you survived? Have you survived?'

All this without ever having been to England. The only reason our thin cobweb of a relationship hasn't blown away is because we each hold a flimsy end with enduring genes of duty. I would never dream of criticising Poland in front of Dagmara. Also, our pasts are so different. When I was little, and all I worried about was if I was going to get a Sindy for Christmas or not, her side of the family would be wringing their hands, waiting for parcels from Mama, usually full of my hand-me-downs. Other goodies would go in too of course: coffee, tea, chocolate, sugar and useful things such as toothpaste, plasters, batteries and matches, things that we could buy whenever we wanted. One summer on a family holiday in Poland, I saw Dagmara in a pair of old trainers that used to be mine. I was just about to say something during dinner when Mama booted me under the table. Boy did it hurt. But probably not as much as Dagmara's fist.

I'll always remember those parcels. Wrapped in brown paper and secured with scratchy string. Mama would scrawl the address on in big, black felt tip letters and it felt as if it were going to some terrible, distant land.

Once we found out that some curtains my Mama had sent over arrived caked in oil and Dagmara's parents wondered why we'd done that. We hadn't of course, they'd been vandalised. I don't understand how they thought we'd send substandard stuff and didn't think they might have been damaged. Maybe because the vandals closed the parcel again? Why vandalise the curtains, but not steal them? Other times things did go missing. Perhaps people at the post office or the Border couldn't resist the temptation, as they knew the parcel, coming from the West, would be full of goodies. Sometimes it would get there, other times not, and if it did it would take weeks. The parcel's condition once it arrived also affected how far away it seemed. If Mama said it had got there battered, it felt as if it had been around the whole world. I would imagine the parcel passing through a thousand arms and in and out of a hundred trains and shudder.

These days, my cousins have 'got' much more than me. Dagmara has her new posh flat downtown; other cousins, dotted around the country, have their spouses, their babies, their booming businesses and their newly built houses. Now that I'm here, I must start to get in touch with all my aunts and uncles in the suburbs – relatives I've neglected over the years in favour of the capital.

I can see Dagmara getting off the tram now, her gestures hurried, her pace determined. I say *'cześć'* a couple of times to myself, under my breath. *'Cześć'* means 'hello' and 'goodbye', a bit like *ciao*. Of course I know this word, I just want to say it nicely for Dagmara. It should be said in a crisp fleeting way but I say it like an out-of-shape ballerina trying to do an arabesque. Polish requires you to be nimble and graceful. For an English person like me (ahem), *cześć* is one of the hardest words to say. If you can rock to and fro between 'ch' and 'sh' with a bit of a 't' thrown in at the front, and do it all rapidly in one syllable, you're there.

'T-ch-e-sh-ch.'

No Brit can say it, ever.

Dagmara arrives, flustered but smiling. She waves at me as she walks past the window and bursts in through the door like a hurricane. The bell above jangles, making people look up. Still copper-bobbed, she's well turned out in a grey pleated skirt, a fitted red jacket and black patent court shoes. Mama would kill for me to dress like Dagmara. Come birthdays and Christmas, whenever I open a present from Mama, it's always something Dagmara-ish, like a cardigan with brass buttons. I immediately fold it away to feed the local moth population. Once, to my horror, I got a briefcase. It was tan and awful. While I held my jaw in my lap, Mama twittered away about how sensational it looked and how it would help me move on in the world. Dagmara has on just a bit too much foundation, thick brown-pencilled eyebrows – always a brave move – and a smear of deep red lipstick.

We greet one another like boxers shaking hands before a match.

'*Cześć kochana!* (Hello darling),' she says, planting kisses on my cheeks. She smells of minty mouthwash and has dazzling whitened teeth.

'*Cześć,*' I reply.

'I'm sorry I'm late. The tram got stuck and for some reason the anaesthetic for this extraction I was doing took ages to kick in.'

'Don't worry.'

'This will be on me,' she says sitting down. 'So, darling – when did you arrive yesterday – morning or evening?'

'Lunchtime.'

'How have your first twenty-four hours been, *straszne?* (awful?)'

'No, not *straszne* at all. The flat's perfect, Auntie Basia's near by and work starts on Monday.'

'What will you be doing again?' she asks, plumping up her hair and checking her make-up in a compact mirror.

'I told you – teaching English.'

'Oh yes. I didn't know you could teach.'

'I did a special course.'

'Oh yes. And how was your flight – that must have been *straszne* surely?'

I think back to the airport where I had a coffee with a triangle of Toblerone sticking out of my cheek.

'No. Rather pleasant, actually.'

'Oh. Right. The food?'

'I didn't buy anything. I'd made a sandwich.'

I briefly wonder what kind of food Polish Airlines would serve. Not full-blown Polish, surely. Fish heads in cream, tripe and trotters – any foreign passengers would stir up an exodus at thirty thousand feet.

'Did anyone try to pickpocket you on the bus to the centre?'

'Well if they tried to, they didn't succeed. And anyway I got the train. Only twenty minutes. Brilliant service.'

'Oh,' she repeats, disappointed. 'Well haven't you been lucky? How about Auntie Basia? I guess it's too early for her to be driving you crazy. But she will. Have you been to see her yet?'

'Only to say hello and let her know I'm here. She's asked me over for dinner tomorrow night.'

'That'll be interesting. Be prepared to get even fatter Magda, living near her.'

'Even fatter?'

'Well, you've never been really slim, have you? Be careful, or you'll end up like a barrel.'

'Thanks. Thanks a lot.'

Aunt Basia, or AB as I like to call her, lives in the flat above me. When Dagmara lived here, she and AB never got on. They were a bit like Hitler and Stalin after things went sour. During every visit I'd be stuck in the middle of their arguments, shuttling messages between the two flats:

Dagmara: (in her flat) Tell AB that if she doesn't muffle that blasted cuckoo clock I'm going to wring its neck!

Me: (at AB's) Er, AB... Dagmara was wondering if you might muffle the *kukułka*? (cuckoo) She can't sleep.

AB: What about her aerobics? Thud thud thud – like an elephant every night – the noise travels up!'

I love AB. She is the classic Polish lady, one with a sturdy edge. When out and about, AB has doors opened for her, seats offered up in the blink of an eye, for this is how the elderly are treated, with reverence and fear. Fear of being hit with a handbag, usually. AB also owns a stout dachshund and it's funny to see it obey 'sit' (*siad*) and 'paw' (*podaj łapę*) in Polish. When I was little, we had a bilingual budgie called GeeGee. As well as simple English we taught it Polish swear words, which was a bit of a problem when the priest came round. How do you explain to your priest why the budgie in your living room just said something obscene? All we could do was say it wasn't us who taught it that, it was the previous owner 'who just so happened to be Polish too'.

AB's dachshund is called Grzybek and they move around the flat as one. Grzybek means 'small mushroom'. It's hard to explain how to pronounce the Polish 'rz' as there's nothing in English that really matches it. The nearest formulation is a gravelly, breathy 'zh', with a bit of a growl thrown in. The easiest way to say it is by trying to create the sound of a Formula 1 car crossed with a bee and you'll be about there. Failing that, smoking ten cigars one after another will definitely do the trick:

'G-zhi-bek.'

'One meal won't make that much difference, surely,' I say to Dagmara. 'I wonder why she winds you up so much?'

'She's just so annoying,' she says.

AB looked after Mama and Mama's brother Uncle Szymon when they made it back from Siberia after the Second World War. They were out there for six years. Their mother died in Siberia and all they knew about their father was that he'd been sent to a gulag in Russia somewhere and was probably dead too. He didn't die though – he made it out with General Anders' army and lived to fight on. In the fifties, the Red Cross tracing service contacted Mama and Uncle Szymon to say their father was alive and well, working in another mine – but this time, in Doncaster.

'AB's waiting for a hip op,' Dagmara adds.

'I didn't know that.'

'You will. It's all she ever talks about – on and on and on. I'm so glad I've moved out. I can still hear her in my head.'

'Stop being mean. I guess that'll explain why she wants me to walk Grzybek,' I reply.

'Oh, she's landing you with that old job is she? I hate that rat.'

'He's not a rat. He's sweet. He gives you his paw and sorts through all the slippers.'

'He should be put down.'

'Why?'

'Because he's old and he smells. His name means mushroom and he is a mushroom, Magda. I can't go round without a can of air-freshener. Pooh!'

'No Dagmara, he's gorgeous. His ears loll back like flowing locks.'

'Pooh! That's so English, to adore animals more than people! Come on, let's order,' she says, catching the waitress's eye. 'The food's excellent here,' she says, leafing through the menu. 'I fancy the *flaczki* (tripe). Do you want *flaczki* too?'

She arches her eyebrows. Dagmara knows full well I don't want tripe. Tripe smells of boiling tights and looks like cut-up mattress.

'Er no,' I reply. 'I think I'll just have the blueberry *pierogi*.

'Blueberry *pierogi*? You can't just have those, I'm paying!'

'But they're all I want. It doesn't have to be a ten-course meal you know.'

'Yes it does. I earn plenty now. There's no need to scrimp.'

'I'm not.'

'You are.'

She says 'you are' in a way that makes me feel like one of her patients, trying to get out of having a filling. When Dagmara says she wants to treat me, she means it. Paying for her British cousin, who knows about the past and those crisis parcels, means a lot.

'I know,' she decides, 'I'll order for us both. You probably don't know half these things anyway.'

'I do! Well, nearly.'

'Just give me an idea of what you fancy. Pork? Fish? Sausage? Anything you like.'

I quickly look through the menu again, knowing she means business. I'd better pick something or she'll go for the tripe.

'Is the lard thing... really just lard?' I ask, fascinated.

'The *smalec*. Yes – it's delicious here. Pork fat with bacon granules.'

'Fat with fat? Right.'

'Why don't we pick that?'

'Maybe,' I fudge, quickly flicking through the pages for more.

For some reason, Poles don't realise lard is a heart attack on a plate. They think that because fat is natural like lettuce is natural, that it's OK. The waitress comes over and Dagmara orders three courses each for us in ten seconds flat. Then, we settle down warily, each in our own corner. I mentally adjust my stance. Dagmara will pull out her upper cut if I don't keep ducking.

'Did you know I went to London for a four-day trip in spring?' she asks, smoothing out her napkin on her lap.

'No. Why didn't you tell me?' I ask, half surprised, half offended. 'We could have met up.'

'Oh no no no no no,' she says. 'It just wasn't possible. I was with a tour, and the schedule was tightly planned. I couldn't have put my big toe out of the coach without wrecking all the arrangements. I'll tell you what though,' she says quietly, leaning over, 'the food was awful. Simply awful!' She screws up her face. 'The fish, Magda. The stinking, stinking fish! That goo you put on it!'

'Batter?'

'And the tomatoes! How can you eat them? As for the bread…'

The Poles hate our bread but I have to say, theirs isn't much better. How I long to tell Dagmara you could wash a car with Polish bread – it's so leathery. On the bread front, I'm definitely 'not Polish'.

'Dagmara, where did you go, a refuse tip?'

'Wild horses wouldn't take me back to London, oh no!'

'Do you think I like to eat bad food?'

'And as for the Olympics…'

'We did very well this time, thank you.'

'Yes, because of all those synthetic preservatives and sugars you eat!'

'What about Poland? All you're good at is the hammer!'

'The hammer is the hardest sport of all, Magda. You try spinning around with a heavy object and throwing it without killing someone. And another thing,' she says, 'why do English women not want children?'

'Where did you hear that?' I ask, incredulous. 'Lots of my friends are having children.'

This is true too. In recent years nearly all of my friends have done nothing but bore me with their scans and photos and forced me to watch them breast-feeding in public.

The lard arrives, a daub of glistening fat on a board. It looks vaguely familiar and then I remember, it looks like the substance that gets squeezed out of arteries on the anti-smoking ads I worked on. Now it's going into mine.

'Here,' Dagmara says, pushing the stuff towards me. I spread the tiniest amount on a piece of bread and pretend that it's pâté. Lard, glorious lard, it tastes of lard. When I taste a bit, it sticks to my palette like salty glue.

'Nice?'

'Hmm,' I lie, nearly gagging. 'Not bad.'

'I'll have to get you a jar then, so you're never without.'

'Dagmara, I don't like it when you say bad things about England.'

'Bad things? When did I ever say anything bad about Anglia?'

'All the time.'

'*Nie nie nie.* You're getting it all wrong. Anglia's a wonderful country! To live in London, to go on the red buses, to have a queen and Big Ben, what could be better? Yes, you don't look after the elderly properly and English women are lazy, but it's one of the most wonderful countries in the world! So free, so polite, so grateful, everyone's always queuing and smiling and saying sorry and thank you – and life is so much cheaper than it is here!'

Oh here we go. Dagmara always says this. No matter how expensive something is in England, it's always more expensive in Poland.

'Only this morning I was telling my patients that I was meeting my English cousin for lunch and they took great interest in hearing how English people are always nice and polite, even if someone murders their helpless little granny.'

'Dagmara, England's my home. I can't help it if I was born there any more than you can help being born here.'

'I'm not saying anything bad about you though, am I? I'm only saying what's true. You're too sensitive, like the English are. You're being true to your colours – red, white and blue.'

'Don't forget the red and white in that, Dagmara – there's Polish colours too.'

'Huh,' she pooh-poohs.

We journey through our main, a large, golden, sizzling potato fritter, flopped in half to encase a hot splodge of stew.

'Honestly Dagmara, I don't know why we're arguing.'

'We're not arguing. We're having a discussion.'

We start our meal and then she passes me a scrap of paper.

'What's this?' I ask, unfolding it. 'Www.PolishMate.com?'

'Your mother rang to say you're looking for a husband, and did I know of any good newspapers. So, I've brought you this.'

'Mama said what?' I ask, inhaling a crumb and coughing so hard that I nearly choke. I drop my fork so that it clatters to my plate and the youngish couple next to us, on coffee now, look over put out, as if we're disturbed their peace (after all that cavorting with their knickerbocker, too).

'Your Mama said she caught you looking wistfully at your wedding ring finger, just before you left. When you were washing up or something and listening in on her calls.'

'I was not!' I reply. Honestly. Yes I was looking at my finger wistfully, but I didn't realise mama had noticed. She doesn't miss a thing. Tata says she's wasted in Yorkshire. She should be working as a mole for the KGB. Before now, she's followed me on dates, rung hairdressers in advance to give them instructions on how they should do my hair and when I was job-hunting, she even rang up some places to complain if I didn't get the job.

'I've signed up,' she says. 'It's great. Why not give it a try?'

'Number one, Dagmara,' I say, picking up an unlarded tuft of bread to mop up my goulash, 'I am not looking for a husband. Number two,' I add, polishing away, 'if I were looking for one, I'd want it to happen organically, not through a website. And number three, I'm not interested in advertising myself like a tin in a shop.'

Dagmara roars with laughter.

'Rubbish! Women are always looking for a husband! Even when they say they're not! And as for organically, as organically as what, as organically as going to the toilet?'

The older couple look over now.

'Dagmara, I mean during everyday life.'

'Magda, it becomes part of everyday life. Anyway, to everyone else, you and I are on the shelf!'

'OK, OK. Speak for yourself. It might be like that here, but not in England. I'm only thirty-nine. People in England fall in love all the time.'

'Up to you,' she shrugs. 'But just remember you're not in Anglia now – where people get married aged a hundred and two.'

There's a lull during which I stare at the piece of paper, written in Dagmara's loopy Polish writing. Why do Poles write in such an illegible way? Polish Mate indeed. I'll have to ring Mama and give her what for.

Pudding arrives and I pop one comforting blueberry *pieróg* after another. Why is nothing in my life ever private, I wonder, as each leathery *pieróg* bursts in my mouth, releasing a burst of intense blueberry flavour.

Dagmara decides she wants to take a photo of me on her phone for posterity, then settles up. Exhausted and stuffed, we take off our sparring gloves and let our stomachs hang out.

'Thank you Dagmara,' I manage, 'that was nice.'

'You're welcome,' she says, picking at her molars with a cocktail stick. 'What are you doing now?'

'Having my hair done,' I sigh, relieved this will be over soon. 'Do you know anywhere good? I was thinking of going to that big modern place on the avenue.'

'Oh don't go there. It'll be ever so expensive. Here,' she says rummaging in her bag, 'this is where I go.'

She hands me a pale pink card with flowery golden writing on it and the silhouette of a female head with an alarmingly long neck.

'Thanks. I might try them. You rate this place, do you?'

She points to her hair as if the answer should be obvious, then snaps her mirror shut and puts it in her bag.

'It's been so nice meeting up. We must do it again – soon. Send my regards to Aunt Basia. She must watch her weight as well as you – no wonder she needs an op. Oh,' she adds, 'is the flat in order? I hope I left it spotless.'

'It is, thank you.'

Don't ask me how or why, but the following words come tumbling out of my mouth.

'Next time Dagmara, why don't you come over? I'll cook you something British that you'll enjoy.'

She looks at me as if I'm suggesting the impossible. I stare at her sullen face that's barked at me for over an hour, realising that I actually want her to say no.

'Well?'

'I like meat,' she replies.

'Then that's what I'll make. And it will be good.'

'All right,' she says unconvinced, getting up and pulling on her coat.

What a cheek. All from a nation that serves lard on a board.

'Ring me, darling. I've got to go. I've got a date off the website.'

'Anyone nice?' I ask.

'What do you think?' she says, walking with a wiggle to the door and giving me a wink. 'Bye Magda. Have fun regulating the boiler at home. Organically.'

She leaves, the ring of the bell signalling the end of our match.

In the distance, a man comes towards her with a bunch of flowers. She flings herself at him and he picks her up, twirling her in the air.

Poor devil.

I pick up the scrap of paper on the table, www.polishmate.com – and stick it in the lard.

CHAPTER 3
WE'LL USE THIS HIGH QUALITY ONE, YES? (*UŻYJEMY TEGO LEPSZEGO, TAK?*)

My mind races as I set off to the hairdresser, weaving through the streets. What Mama and Dagmara both don't know, thank goodness, is that until quite recently, I did have somebody – Matt. Matt worked at Adspeak too, on scripts. He was tall and thin and walked like a wire. He also had irresistible black floppy hair. After months of me liking him, we finally got together at a launch party for a new denture glue that was going to transform pensioners' bedtime routines forever. 'Denture want me baby?' was the strap-line. He thought it all up in the stirring of a cup of tea. The client was delighted. Who would have thought, a campaign that linked dentures to romance? Mama bought two dozen tubes, much to Tata's horror. She doesn't even have false teeth. We had a Human League tribute band at the launch, wonky haircuts and all.

'I'd appreciate it if we just kept this between ourselves,' Matt said, after we kissed in the stationery room.

'Why?' I asked, put out yet devastated. I had a photocopier going ten to the dozen next to me and a laminator poking me in the back.

'People talk, don't they?'

I would have liked to talk, lots.

'OK,' I said, blinded with hope and crunching over a pencil sharpener. I waited for sweet nothing emails, dinner invites, winks and smiles – and got a few to begin with. But then they fizzled out. Quickly, the whole thing became so secret that even I didn't know what was happening. I gradually realised he was more interested in Izzy the receptionist than me. At first I put it down to early relationship paranoia, him talking to her all the time, but I was right. He was constantly hovering around her desk, when he should have been hovering around mine.

What added to Matt's allure was that he did dressage, ballet for horses. He was really good at it apparently, and it went on somewhere in Kent. There was a photo of him that did the rounds once. His horse was mid-pirouette and he was decked out in all his red and gold regalia. I was all set for married life in the country learning to ride (unrealistic as am terrified of horses) and going eventing, or whatever it's called.

Sorry I think u want sthg I just can't give, said a text, sent to me while he was sitting with his back to me just two tables away.

What, like politeness and respect?

Clunk clunk, it ended, like dentures in a glass.

Viv, my closest friend at Adspeak, was livid. She always comes to my rescue.

'What an idiot,' she said when I told her what he'd written. 'Do you want me to say something for you?'

'But what difference would it make? He's ended it, hasn't he?'

'It might make you feel better.'

She could feel my pain. My only relationship in three years had started and ended in record time. I knew she meant business, she had seen me pine.

'Text him from your phone,' I suggested. 'He doesn't have your number. Write you big loser.'

She did. After a few seconds he wrote back, **Sorry, wrong number**. But then she wrote again, **No MATT, that was for you. And by the way, your hair looks like a horse's tail.**

It sent him running to the side office to check his reflection in the glass, the vain thing. How we laughed! Matt did end up going off with clackety-heeled Izzy. Izzy whose nail varnish never chipped, who could wear a white top, eat a curry and not get a blob of korma down it. They mysteriously went on leave at the same time and mysteriously came back at the same time, with the same annoying golden tans that made their teeth glow like luminous plastic skeletons. There was never any gagging order on her. It was 'Matt this' and 'Matt that' – it was all I ever heard about when I walked past her desk. That and the irritating sound of her nail file. No, I never told Mama or Dagmara about that.

I arrive at Dagmara's hairdresser. To my delight, it's retro and quaint with a pleasant family feel. Dom Fryzjera, it says on the pink front in gold flowery letters, just like on the card. A net curtain twitches and a woman with a blond beehive and some brown horn-rimmed glasses looks out, expressionless.

I push the door open. A young man is on his way out. Pleased, he smoothes down his suede head and walks off down the street. Inside, there are four giant egg-shaped dryers, all different colours, with an old lady frying underneath one of them. She looks at me absent-mindedly, as if she doesn't know she's there. I smile and she smiles back.

'Can we help you?' asks beehive woman. Her black charcoal eyebrows are like commas over her eyes. Her lips, a scrunched-up scarlet ribbon, are pinned onto her face in a captivating squiggle.

'Yes, my cousin recommended you – Dagmara?'

'Ah yes, Dagmara!'

I expect her to add something like 'she's lovely' but she leaves her sentence dangling in mid air.

'I've just moved to Warsaw and I'm after a haircut,' I say, to fill in her silence (I'm wheeling out my best Polish and doing rather well).

I go in and sit in front of the mirror. It has a string of dusty fairy lights draped around the frame, set on a slow twinkle with an intermittent rapid flash. She runs her fingers through my hair, her pearly peach nails glimmering through the strands.

'It's fine, isn't it?' she says disappointed. Little does she know this is the worst thing anyone can say to me. It's like a mother telling her daughter that she looks fat but I've had that already off Dagmara. Amazingly,

Mama never says I'm fat as she's very pro obesity. To her being chubby is a sign of health and wealth.

'It is fine,' I say, pleased in a way, that she's pinpointed my problem so quickly. 'I've tried all kinds of things to make it thick – rinses, powders, as a teenager I would even stand on my head to try to make it thicker.'

I laugh at my anecdote but she doesn't laugh back. This doesn't surprise me. I'm not sure if this is due to bone structure, to the cold winters or to all the wars, but at rest, Poles tend to look glum even when they're happy. They certainly aren't in the habit of smiling on photos or at strangers like the British. To the Poles, smiling at someone you don't know is a sign of mental illness.

A pale girl with similar lank hair appears from behind a pink curtain and leans on a broom, listening.

'How about a perm?'

Until this point, beehive-woman's own hair hasn't moved an inch. It's a perfect sugar-spun scaffold; plaited, pinned, folded and lacquered into Soviet submission. Not so much a hairdo as mechanical engineering.

'Oh no,' I say, shocked, 'not a perm. It's not the eighties.'

'I know, but they're in again.'

'Are they?'

'Yes. Just something soft, for *puszystość* (body).' She's said the magic word, body. She lifts my hair and lets it flop to prove her point. 'Hania, get some magazines, and please bring the lady from England some tea.'

We flick through some magazines and she points to a couple of styles she thinks might work.

'They look quite nice,' I say, 'but I'm still not sure.'

'You're new here, right?' she asks.

'I start a new job tomorrow.'

'Then have something different. A whole new you.'

She's right. A whole new me and no fine hair. I'll be working towards a new Matt-free, Mama-free and once my diet has commenced, spare-tyre free me. And won't having more volume on my head immediately make me look more in proportion, head to hips? Plus, it's only fifty złoty, around ten pounds, a bargain. I hesitate, then agree. Before I know it, thin Hania is draping a red-and-white stripy gown around me and leading me to the sink like a servant leads an ass. Well done, I think to myself, as she starts shampooing my hair. You've not gone for the big flash Toni-and-Guy type place, you're supporting a local Polish business, like a true Varsovian. You're weaving yourself into Polish society, so that you belong. Just like Mama and Tata did in Doncaster when they were starting out as immigrants.

The older woman climbs onto a stool and rummages around in a tatty cardboard box. She has thick tights on in this hot weather. What is it with Polish women and tights? They wear them all the time, even with sandals. Poles generally are obsessed with staying warm and particularly hate draughts. Even in utterly boiling weather, they hate opening windows for fear of catching a chill. Go to Poland and see for yourself. A Pole caught in a draught looks disgruntled and upset, like an English person in the rain without a brolly.

Beehive woman fishes out some bottle and shows it to me, smiling.

'We'll use this high quality one – yes?'

'Fine,' I say, enjoying Hania massaging my scalp and not really questioning why she would use anything less. She wheels over a trolley and sorts through lots of hairy curlers.

'Could I have some milk for my tea please?' I ask Hania, pushing the cup towards her.

'*Mleko*?' she says, horrified.

'Yes. That's how we have it in England, All day every day. If I made someone British a cup of tea and didn't add milk, they'd be baffled.'

'*Jejku* (goodness!)' she says, then scuttles behind the curtain.

I look at my reflection. Sitting down in a long striped gown, I look like a head on top of a circus tent.

Beehive woman, though, isn't at all surprised at my milk request. She comes over and pumps my chair with her foot until I'm three feet in the air. The cape falls down around me. Next, she pushes my head around with confidence, like only a true professional does, trimming the ends and winding it around thin rollers. Hania brings my tea.

'You're going to look *seksowna*! (sexy),' she says, while I blush.

I imagine myself bursting into Adspeak with my tousled choppy perm, in a red glittery dress, singing Human League and Matt snapping his pencil in half.

'Right, thank you,' I say.

Ten minutes later, I have three avenues of rollers stacked across my head, front to back, and a dousing of perming lotion. She buzzes off to see to the old lady who emerges from the dryer and is guided to a chair.

'They're so good here,' she whispers to me, in a moment of clarity, and then she's gone again.

I smile with great understanding. I look like a crash victim now but no matter, beauty costs. The old lady's rollers are in three neat rows, similar to mine. Just like mine in fact. They must work with a basic model and use that as a spring-board. I turn my head this way and that. Don't thin rollers give tight curls? The girl starts removing the old lady's curlers and casts them into the sink, like razor shells.

'Usual, Pani Regino?' she asks. The old lady nods.

I love it here, I decide. It's just so real. It will be my regular place over the coming months. I will make friends with Madame, and when I drop by she'll have a slot for me, just because I'm a regular. Correction, friend. I'll casually drop into the conversation that the girl should take some iron because she looks a little drawn, and I might even bring her some, if I'm passing by. Yes, this is what living abroad is about, going beneath the surface. We'll chat cultural quirks as they work magic on my hair. Oh it's all perfect. The orange plastic orchids, so funny and kitsch, the old mottled lino. Good old Dagmara, she's not an ogre after all.

Twenty minutes later, a thousand tiny curls are piled on my head like black baby eels. I am a short-haired Medusa.

'Isn't this too tight?' I ask, shock starting to prickle all over my body.

'Oh no no no no no!' she says. 'It'll drop in a week.'

Drop out more like. The squiggle on her lips matches the frown on my forehead.

'Don't worry, I've not finished yet.'

She plugs an asthmatic hairdryer into a rattling socket and grabs a scruffy hairbrush. 'It's going to look beautiful, just you wait,' she says, glancing at the pale girl who's even paler now.

I've gone from loving the place to hating it in seconds. I glance at the old lady who's looking in the mirror as if reality lies there. Her hair is a perfect dandelion clock of soft grey fluff.

Madame draws out my black hair like strands of squid ink pasta. The hairdryer wheezes. Ten minutes later I have a bouffant hairdo and look like a Caucasian Shirley Bassey. So much for looking irresistible for my new start in life.

'This isn't loose!'

'But it is soft,' she affirms, nearly annoyed. 'You've got to have some curl.'

'But I wanted it ... this way and that way,' I say, not quite knowing the word for tousled.

Thanks Dagmara. I should have known the minute I came in, when I clapped eyes on the place, on the 'bouffant-do,' the old vacant lady and the thin pale girl who doesn't know Brits need milk in their tea.

Madame lacquers me all over. My wispy, fine hair, once as straight as a wire, is now a billowing sculpture that I can tap. I thump my fifty złoty down and leave Dom Fryzjera as I bang the door shut. Frizz is the word. I could have saved the girl from anaemia but now what do I care.

I weave through the streets and stare at my reflection in every shop I pass. No one must ever see this, no one.

Mama rings.

'Hello Mama,' I manage, almost in tears.

'Hello Magda! Are you still alive?'

'Yes I'm still alive. That's why I can answer the phone!' Mama always asks this.

'Where are you? Why haven't you rung?'

'I've just come out of the hairdresser's Mama. It's awful.'

'Why? What's happened? Don't tell me you've gone so short that your head looks like a football?'

She's talking rapidly, probably because she's on her new mobile and she thinks they fry your brain.

'I've had a perm Mama, a horrid cheap perm. I'm a foreigner in my own hair.'

'Oh no! Is it really bad?'

'Yes!'

'Magda – no!'

'Anyway, what have you been saying to Dagmara about husbands – and boyfriends?'

'Darling, I can't hear you,' she says, all of a sudden. 'The line's gone all fuzzy.'

'It hasn't, I can hear you fine,' I reply. 'What have you been saying to Dagmara about newspapers and websites?'

She starts saying something about classifieds and deadlines and then as luck would have it, the line turns fuzzy for me too now so I can't hear either.

'What have you said to her?' I continue, looking at my awful reflection in a shop window.

'... deadline ... put ... .'

'Deadline?'

That's it. I've had enough miscommunication for one day.

'Mama ... let's ... talk ... later ... OK?'

'What?'

'Later!'

'... in then OK? Bye! best ... go ... or ... fry brains ... radioactive pulp!'

She's gone. I stand against a wall with a miserable expression and take a photo of my perm. I text it to Mama, who doesn't reply. It must be bad. I want to go and get an extra big hot chocolate with cream and marshmallows somewhere. Preferably with a hat on.

No one in England (i.e. Matt) must ever see me with hair like this.

I text Viv and Dagmara, though, as they don't count. Viv replies, **Oh no, what are you going to do, buy some hair-straighteners?** Dagmara says, *It looks lovely.*

Later, when I pick up AB's latest shopping list and take Grzybek for his walk, AB's eyes settle above my eyeline. She pauses and asks, 'Have you changed your hair?'

Advantages of new hairdo: none
Disadvantages: look fifty.

VOCAB CORNER:
Tousled = *potargane*
Devastated = *zdewastowana* (feminine)

CHAPTER 4
WHEN IN POLAND, DO AS THE POLES DO (*JEŚLI WSZEDŁEŚ MIĘDZY WRONY, MUSISZ KRAKAĆ JAK I ONE*)

It's noon. I'm outside Strefa Jezyków Obcych (Language Zone) with Polish hair. The smell of ammonia's so strong that if anyone strikes a match near me I might go up in flames. Viv's right, I must buy some hair-straighteners as soon as possible – if they have them in this perm-forsaken city (no idea how to say perm-forsaken in Polish and too traumatised to try to concoct inevitable compound noun). AB says the word for hair-straighteners is *prostownica*. Sounds like a dental implement Dagmara might use.

I gaze at the tatty building. The windows rattle as traffic hurtles past. It's a world away from Adspeak. It's a world away from everything else in the street. An undeveloped relic in a row of modernity. On a positive note, it's close to my flat, whereas in London my tube journey would take over an hour. Today, I simply breezed out of my block, tripped over the big metal step that I always forget is there, took a few lefts and rights and bingo, I was here.

On the way, I took pity on an old man selling raspberries as big as thimbles on the corner. I ended up buying some. I felt sure he hiked up the price when I asked him *ile kosztują* in my British accent, but I didn't really mind. Just as I left, I heard a woman asking how much they were and as I was still within earshot, he quoted her my price. 'Why are they so dear?' she asked, shocked. 'I'm why!' I felt like saying.

Something has changed though since I passed by Language Zone at the weekend. The front door's been painted. Before it was black and peeling, now it's shiny and ladybird red. I'm just about to touch it to see if it's still wet when a builder comes out, opening the door inwards and away from my poised hand. He's thin, short, with a thick black moustache not dissimilar to the paintbrush between his teeth. He's humming and we shuffle past one another sideways like one of those couples that come in and out of a cuckoo clock, me with my bags of books and papers, him with a pot of paint. It seems as if the place might be getting a facelift after all.

I gaze around a hallway completely stripped of paper. 'Up the stairs, chop, chop,' he says. 'Oops – you've got paint on your skirt – only kidding.'

I smile, feigning amusement, check my skirt anyway, then take the stairs up, the only route possible. At the top, I go down a warren of corridors to an enormous, musty office where two older ladies sit working on computers. The machines are running, by the looks of it, on Windows 45. This imposing high office doesn't look as if it's been touched in centuries. It's wall-to-wall files, long dusty velvet curtains that sprawl over the floor, shelves full of jumbled books and rugs criss-crossed over a dark wooden floor.

'Hello,' I say, my nerves aflutter. 'I'm Magda Mikołajczyk from London. I start today?'

'We've been expecting you,' says one of the women in a husky smoker's voice. 'I'm Pani Dąbrowska and this is my sister, Pani Raszewska.'

In their mottled brown Crimplene attire, as much a fire hazard as my hair, they look like a pair of moths that have been fluttering around but are now at rest. I can't help noticing a large suit of armour behind them in the corner. Its arms are akimbo and it holds a collection of scarves and handbags.

'Handsome, isn't he?' says Pani Dąbrowska, seeing me looking. 'You can use him if you like,' she adds, bending his arm out towards me. She goes over and kicks at a chain that has him attached to the radiator by the ankle and straightens him up with the slack she's loosened. 'He belonged to our great-great-great-grandfather. They fought the Cossacks in the seventeenth century.'

'How interesting,' I reply as I fumble through my bag for my certificates.

'We're having a spot of work done,' she adds after a pause. 'Tomorrow they're starting in here.'

'Well I'm glad I saw the place before it changes,' I add, mid-rummage.

The talk of having work done makes the other one, Pani Raszewska, rush over to a host of objects on the mantelpiece and, somewhat panicked, stuff them into a cardboard box. A black statuette of a topless mermaid in all her naked glory goes in first, beside which gasp several small male busts, erstwhile kings of Poland.

I scan the office from left to right. Against the drabness, the most colourful things are the scarves on the knight and these ladies' billowing hairdos, which to be honest, are more like mature and mastered versions of my own.

Above the fireplace hangs a framed Polish flag, a white stripe above a red stripe.

'My teaching certificates,' I pant, triumphantly pulling out some slightly dog-eared papers and slapping them on the Berlin-Wall-like counter. Pani Dąbrowska looks at them uninterestedly, slides them to one side and then opens an old-fashioned register, the yellowish paper cracking.

'Here are your students,' she says, showing me a sheet filled with passport-sized photos. 'Intermediates – twenty-five of them – and a small group of beginners. You'll just have the beginners today.'

The intermediates are much younger than the beginners. They must be polishing their English before going away to work. I warm to the older group, probably because I've been surrounded by Polish pensioners in England all my life. In a way, I see them as part of the one big flock that's been scattered all over the world. There are just six beginners in this motley collection and I wonder why on earth they want to learn English at this stage in their lives. Thinning hair, dyed hair, the odd gold tooth and a big moustache, all with deep, piercing Polish eyes. Older people, looking out for answers.

Pani Raszewska finishes her bout of packing and drifts over to look at what I'm wearing. The neutrality of her face is betrayed by a roving eye. She won't be able to fault me, not today. I've put on some of the presents Mama has given me over the years and that I dug out from my wardrobe in Doncaster for moments like this. Mothballs have preserved these garments perfectly, like a corpse in formaldehyde. A black skirt with a single pleat (awful but practical) a red-and-white polka-dot blouse (which although patriotic makes me feel as if I have measles), flesh-coloured tights and something that is nearly a court shoe – luckily sans ugly buckle. I don't know why I packed them. Mama must have smuggled them into my subconscious. No doubt it'll be downhill all the way after this. As the days go by it'll be some old trainers here, a casual T-shirt there, until I'm in torn jeans, flip-flops and a vest top. The only thing I feel Pani Raszewska doesn't examine is my crazy permed hair (obviously so frumpy that she thinks it's perfect).

'Our nephew, Pan Tomaszewski will be sitting in on your first class, but don't worry,' she adds, my blood pressure hitting the roof, 'he does that with every new teacher. He only wants to see how well you communicate the unpredictable world of English grammar to a wave of new students.'

Only? I nod and gulp, trying to gain courage from all the advertisers I've presented to: 'Kleen Loo' and 'Magi-mould' – the pinnacle of my career thus far. I'm asked to stand in front of an ancient camera on a tripod, ordered 'not to smile' and am blinded with a flash that leaves a silhouette image of Pani Dąbrowska and her hairdo on my retina.

I'm packed off with a register and directions to my classroom. As I walk down the corridor, I start to feel ever so slightly sick; the boss of the school is going to be watching my first lesson!

When I open the door, the painter I met earlier is revealed, tearing up the old carpet with surprising strength. He's throwing it around like a pastry chef throws dough.

'Shan't be a minute,' he says in Polish. 'I know you're in here next.' His arms are thin and sinewy, without a scrap of fat on them. His frame seems tiny in his big and baggy, paint-splashed overalls.

'No problem.' I put down my bags and try to take in the space, full of dust and paint fumes. It's a high-ceilinged room, draughty and cold. Old chairs with flip-up desks are in an untidy stack at the side and at the front, there's a six-foot long blackboard with smudged layers of chalky writing.

'Jacek,' he says when he's finished, wiping his working-man's hand and offering it to me. 'I was only joking earlier.'

'Sorry?'

'About having paint on your skirt.'

'I know,' I reply. 'I'm Magda.'

'Did you find the office? You must have,' he says, pointing to my register. 'Where are you from – Germany? You look a bit German.'

I catch my terrible perm reflected in the glass door. If I were German I'd be thoroughly insulted.

'No. I'm British.'

'Ah yes, I can hear your accent now.'

'My parents are Polish. I was living in London until last week.'

I explain my family background which over the years I've honed to about two phrases flat. Mama and Tata came to England when the war ended, met, got married and had little old me.

'If only I could speak English like you speak Polish,' he says, wistfully.

'Why not do a class?' I suggest, sorting my papers.

'Prices have shot up since their nephew arrived. They've got to pay for all this somehow, haven't they?' he says gesturing to the debris that he's clearing up. He pauses and ponders something.

'I'm going to London to work soon. For a week. Do you mind me asking why you left?'

'No not at all. It's a good question. Why does anyone do anything? I guess I'm on a journey.'

'A journey. Oh.' He says this rather blankly. They do this, the Poles, get to the nub of something in two minutes flat then leave you filled with doubt. 'Well, good luck for your first lesson. I'll leave you to it. If you need anything, just shout – I'll make sure I'm nowhere near to help.'

'Sorry?'

'If you need something, just ask, OK?'

'OK. Thanks.'

He takes the roll of carpet, puts it under his arm and carries it out of the classroom in a three-point turn. As he leaves, an old lady shuffles past him examining a daub of red on her glove, tutting. Then the rest of my pupils stream in, followed by the nephew boss probably, a man in a shiny suit with Brylcreemed hair and a jotter.

'Hello,' I begin, switching to English and writing my name on the blackboard in capitals. At least they'll pronounce that correctly, if nothing else.

I'm going to give a good class if it kills me.

And it nearly does. One hour later, I'm frazzled.

I try to teach them something, but it's like pulling teeth. All they want to know about is me. Where am I from, how come I can speak Polish, am I married, why aren't I married? When will people stop asking me this – when I finally tie the knot, or when it becomes too embarrassing to ask? Mama and Tata are also subjects of great interest: their stories, their survival.

Pani Teresa, the old lady who arrived first, saves me when she whips out some food cans that she wants translating into Polish. She's had them for decades. Whiskas and some Knorr mushroom soup. I dread to think what's inside them now. Her daughter's joined the class too – her name's Ewelina.

There's also a white-haired Catholic priest called Father Marek, two middle-aged Polish ladies who are friends and Pan Piotr (Peter), a gift-shop owner who also owns the gold tooth and handlebar moustache. They're all so different.

After going through the tin cans, I whip through the verbs 'to be' and 'to have' as a sort of finishing flourish.

Afterwards, Pan Tomaszeski, the boss, says I've done *nie źle* (quite well). So much for dazzling him. He asks me to call him Pan Tadek, Pan meaning 'mister' and Tadek being his first name. Using Pan (Mr) or Pani (Miss/Mrs) plus a first name is much less formal than using someone's surname and if someone asks you to switch to this, it's generally a good sign. Pan Tadek says his background is in real estate.

'My job is to help my aunts catch up with the rest of Warsaw and migrate into the twenty-first century,' he says with a smile.

His mobile rings and he goes, leaving me to tidy up. I don't think I've done too badly and I'm on a bit of a high. I connected with them all, dodged Pan Piotr's roving eyes and dealt with Pani Teresa's old tin cans. Phew.

I rub out the board. My name's in the centre, with random words dotted around. They reflect the phase of rapid changes in my life, meeting new people and constantly explaining: 'I am... you are?'

As I rub them out, Jacek pops his head around the door again with another bloke.

'How did it go?' asks Jacek.

'OK, I think.'

'This is Miles from Canada.'

Miles stares at my hair, as if deeply disturbed, flashes me an ultra-white smile and greets me in Polish with the tiniest of accents. Jealousy flashes through me. Why-oh-why were Mama and Tata not stricter when we spoke Polish at home, instead of mixing it with English all the time? Miles is good-looking in a male-model sort of way.

'I was wondering,' says Jacek as Miles saunters off. 'You know I'm going to London?'

'Yes.'

'Could you help me before I go? Maybe an hour one lunch-time? Some basic phrases. I don't know anything. I can pay.'

'I can help,' I reply. 'For free.' On some level, Jacek reminds me of Tata arriving in England in the fifties with hardly any English. He only had scraps of words that he'd gleaned along the way. 'Danger,' 'Keep out' and 'No entry' – words he'd seen here and there as he went from being a displaced person in Germany to an immigrant abroad.

'Then I owe you a favour. Thanks.'

We arrange to meet the next day. If I can't help him with something so small, who can I help? As I leave the classroom, I bang the door shut and think I hear plaster falling.

CHAPTER 5
PASSING ON THE BATON
(*PRZEKAZANIE PAŁECZKI*)

My first day at Language Zone is in the can. On my way home, I smile at the raspberry man who diddled me earlier, walking past with a skip in my step.

I must be proactive about my hairdo. Mama has been texting, **Done anything yet?** every few hours, which is really weird, and Viv has asked too. I'd better start looking for a *prostownica* straightaway. When I run my hand through my hair it feels as if I'm patting a poodle.

I go into the biggest shop I can find and come across about four different makes of hair-straightener – all of them over fifty pounds (the price of a normal perm, basically). I can't pay that much. Being half Polish and half Yorkshire means I'm simply not programmed to spend that much on a small piece of metal that heats up. I leave disgusted, bristling with indignation.

I know. I've time before AB's. I'll try online. They'll be cheaper there.

At home, I fling open the balcony doors to air my baking hot flat, switch my computer on and type 'hair-straighteners Warsaw' straight into Google. A list of links comes up, and quite a few English-sounding ones at that. I didn't know so many people were looking for the things. I click at random on a link, 'Hairtodaygonetomorrow.' Depilatory, I don't want that. I want to have straight hair, not be bald. The next link's better 'Hairqueen4U.' This site's all pink and jolly with lots of testimonies about how brilliant it is. Hair-straighteners...here we are. They look like the ones I saw in the shop and they're only fifteen dollars, plus ten dollars p&p. Based in China, but what isn't these days?

I sign up to the site, encouraged by photos of Chinese women with straighter than straight hair smiling out at me, and click 'Buy'. Flown out within forty-eight hours, amazing. Still, everything is flown or shipped these days. The whole planet must be covered with stuff in orbit. A receipt awaits in my inbox saying they'll be with me within three days, among a whole load of other stuff written in Chinese. That's good. I know it's not ideal looking like a microphone for the next few days, but it's not that long. I update Viv and Mama.

I shed my work clothes and leave them on the floor in a big frumpy heap. On come jeans and a cool floaty top thing in their place.

I wrap up AB's gifts. I bought them from Harrods, her favourite shop. A tea caddy in the shape of a red phone box and a green-and-gold lead for Grzybek. Dear AB. Now there's a simple life if ever I saw one. AB doesn't go out, so nothing bad happens. Although nothing particularly good happens either. She just spends her day watching TV, eating, doing Word Search puzzles and studying her barometer. Poles are obsessed with air pressure. It's the evil behind of all kinds of misfortune such as dodgy knees, persistent headaches and marital snoring.

Before Dagmara moved, she did AB's shopping – but now it's me. In preparation for tonight's dinner, AB sent me to Hala Mirowska, a big old market hall with outdoor stalls too and where Margaret Thatcher bought a pound of tomatoes in the eighties. Among other things, I had to buy a fresh carp, and by that I mean pick one from the tank and have it slaughtered on the spot. Call me soppy, I just couldn't do it. I asked the fishmonger to choose one and picked it up later, all wrapped and safely dead.

Time for some make-up. Polish women take care of their appearance and now I'm here, I'm going to join the club. A bit of eye-liner, on it goes. They're all so feline, these women, with their endless broad faces and their piercing almond eyes. I don't know why I missed out on the cat gene. I'm more Slavic cuddly toy, like Mama and Tata. When you're a Pole you fall into one of two camps, the angular kind, or the doughy kind like me.

I put so much mascara on that my eyelids feel heavy and could glue together. Next, lipstick. As a 'first day at my new job' treat, I bought myself a pink lip gloss on my way out of the store. The tube makes a pleasing crack as I twist it open, and I squeeze some onto my lips.

Mmmm, the smells wafting up from AB's are amazing. Onions, dill and sizzling butter. AB's clock cuckoos seven from above: the cuckoo's a scrappy feathery thing that shoots out on a spring and suffers whiplash when it retreats. I'd better get moving. Just as I'm about to slip into my sandals and leave, I notice a small wet puddle in the bathroom by the washing machine. I look around, then pat the wall. Bits of paint flake off revealing plaster, moist and uneven like crumbling cheese. Drat, there's a bit of a leak. Not so bad I need to act right away, but there nonetheless. I put down a towel, hoping I don't return to a deluge, and bound up one floor to AB's.

'It's me!' I shout, waving at the tiny peephole.

AB opens the door and I'm drawn in with tentacles of pensioner-strength central heating even though it's July. The light's vivid tungsten yellow and the TV burbles on in the background.

'Come in child,' she says, guiding me in with her broth-covered ladle.

As soon as I'm in, Grzybek starts yapping at my heels. I pass his basket, where over time, layers of blankets have been fashioned into a sort of a static woollen whirlpool to form a cosy nest around his body. Next to the basket there's a mountain of shoes and *kapcie* – slippers, an abundance of which is a must in every Polish household – and a hat stand where every prong is taken. Next to that, there are piles of letters, papers, books and trunks.

AB disappears and reappears, bringing me lemon tea in a glass in a special metal cradle, a classic among pensioners.

'It's not like you to wear so much make-up,' she says peering at my face. I inevitably come close to hers, which, make-up free, reveals burst blood vessels on her cheeks and two wiry eyebrows. Strands of dark and grey hair coil around her ears and her glasses are mid-brown plastic with flecks of ochre mustard. Poles age in an interesting way, I decide. It's happened with my parents, with the registrars at school and looking at AB, I can see what the future holds. As they age Poles start to look like potatoes. The word 'Poles' means people of the fields and this is what they literally become. Everything falls into a sack-like round thing, and there you see them, potatoes on the tram, potatoes in the park, potatoes in the square, until they finally disappear back into the ground.

'I thought I'd make an effort,' I reply, looking in a mirror in the hall. 'It is my "welcome to Poland" dinner, isn't it?'

'It most certainly is.'

I go into the lounge where the table's laid with enough food for six. Mama's like this too. Once, years ago, when we were watching TV together, Lech Wałęsa was meeting President Clinton off a plane, and his feet had barely touched the ground when she yelled at the TV, 'Offer him some food, you idiot!' Mama and AB also forget the meaning of 'that's enough' when it comes to shovelling more food onto your plate (must be a wartime thing).

Salads, hams and cheeses arrive, plus the poor old carp I bought dressed with dill mayonnaise and surrounded by a moat of boiled eggs. All spread out on a vast white lace tablecloth, which matches the lace on the armchairs, sofa and sideboards. AB's lace mats are so abundant, it's as if she's got a giant, lace-spinning spider somewhere resident which comes out now and again to spin a new doily.

I sit down on a chair while she insists she can manage in the kitchen on her own. She then begins to serve up, dear old bean. Hmm, my stomach is rumbling. I can hear what she's doing. A lid off here, a bubbling there, a stabbing of some potatoes to see if they're done.

AB asks me about my day and brings out a dish of potatoes smothered in butter, beetroot soup – sloshing around a large white bowl, more fish, fried mushrooms and a plate of rye bread.

'One second,' she says, vanishing again. Aha. This must be the source of the mystery meaty smell, the dish of the night, the *pièce de résistance*. Perhaps she's done a roasted rack of ribs? They were on my shopping list. When I wheeled them back in AB's tartan shopping trolley, they stuck out of the top like a prehistoric xylophone.

Imagine my horror when she waltzes in beaming, with a huge *galareta* on a plate – the dreaded meat jelly I saw on the menu when I met Dagmara!

Interestingly, now that AB's parading the disgusting stuff, her hobble has miraculously gone, as if the joy of serving it up has healed her. The wobbling thing's placed on the table like an innocent strawberry jelly.

I sit and stare.

'Like you put it yourself, this is to celebrate your move to Poland. I made it myself, especially for you – so I don't want any refusal.'

She must be telepathic – as old Polish women normally are.

I shake out my napkin like a flag of surrender.

'Go on,' she says, egging me on.

I appear to be gazing at a giant veiny eyeball.

'It's beautiful,' I lie. Exasperated by my delay, she scoops out a spoonful with a squelching noise and plops it on my plate, then shovels some onto her own.

'Eat up!'

'*Tak, tak.*'

I put the tiniest amount of the stuff on a slice of bread and cover it with ham. In it goes. Ugh, ugh, it's like eating dog food. I'm sure there is some cartilage in there somewhere. I add more things to my plate to take up all the room but it's the jelly she's obsessed with.

'That was a small, English mouthful,' she says piling on some more. 'All English people have weak constitutions. But you are not one of them!'

A huge quivering mound of the stuff arrives on my plate on top of everything else. It's no good – I can't avoid it, it's almost an initiation of sorts.

'Are the mushrooms your own?' I ask, coming across a large rubbery thing.

'No, all mine are gone – these are from the shop. It's much less trouble to buy them than pick your own.'

My parents do this – talk about nice things as being trouble. Day trips, going out for lunch, baking a nice cake, it's all trouble. Every year till now, AB has gone mushroom-picking and dried them on strings of cotton all around the flat.

She pops out and comes back with a small sharp knife and starts to slice a coil of sausage. Several slices arrive on my plate.

'Perhaps we could go mushroom-picking one day, when your hip's better? Dagmara told me.'

Her eyes light up for a moment but then go dim again.

'No, no. I'm afraid those days have gone.'

She opens her gifts, flipping the caddy open.

'Ah, wonderful, the smell of London!'

The smell of India more like.

'Is it true Mohammed Al Fayed wears his tie on elastic so no one can strangle him?'

'I think so. I'm not sure.'

While AB puts the kettle on, I stagger to the sofa, drunk with food. It's a good vantage point for the flat. I can look at all AB's photos on her shelves. Pictures of people frozen in time. There's a black and white photo of her parents. Another is of AB in her twenties with a rosary wound around her fingers. My favourite one, though, is of AB with Mama when Mama was fourteen. Mama and her brother had made it back from Siberia and spent five or so years in a convent orphanage. Then when Szymon joined the army, Mama was taken in by AB. In the photo, Mama's sitting next to AB, in a straw hat that looks totally incongruous, with a thin ribbon around the rim. AB's looking at her as if to say, 'Don't move or this photo will be ruined.'

I can't imagine Mama being fourteen, let alone with AB as adoptive young mother, and a single one at that. I've never seen them together. Just as I'm about to ask what Mama was like back then, a crash and a yell break out in the kitchen. I run in and find AB on the floor, with a long greasy skid mark next to her and some broken crockery.

'Ah!' she says, wincing and clutching at her side. 'My hip!'

'Oh no – your bad one?'

'Yes!' she gasps. She scrambles around, trying to lift herself up.

'I'm such a fool!' she says. 'I knew I should have wiped that up.'

I try to help her get up, but she's too heavy.

'Wait!' she pants.

She grasps a handle on the cupboard below the sink and the lip of the sink is the final lever up.

'Goodness. Goodness.'

'Is it bad?'

'Yes… no… yes,' she says, trying it out. 'It hurts all the time anyway, child.'

She leans on the side as I clean up the mess.

'How many more weeks to your op?' I ask.

'Sixteen. It's in early November,' she says, rubbing her hip and motioning with her head to a calendar of the late Polish Pope, John Paul II. It has red felt tip crosses over every day until today – days she's crossing off until her operation. AB's had a calendar of the Pope ever since I've known her. Even though he's passed away, calendars starring John Paul are still very popular. In this particular one, every month sees him in a different set of robes and in a different pose – kneeling in prayer, holding up his mitre or having tea with Mother Teresa.

I don't leave AB until she's sitting on her bed and we agree that if there's a problem she's to knock on the floor with her stick and I'll come up. We leave in a flurry of mutual fussing. She also insists on giving me the left-over *galareta* which I will either force down the sink or throw into the bin as soon as I get in.

I click the door shut behind me. I stand for a minute and listen, my ear to the wood. All I hear are some springs creaking as AB gets changed. When I left, I gave her a kiss and a hug which felt like pressing into a slightly deflated, large, warm balloon.

Downstairs, I collapse onto my bed. My warts-and-all stay in Poland has really started. The hairdresser, the school and AB have all given me the baton.

Too full to lie down I get back up and go out onto the balcony to tune into life around. Above, AB's clock cuckoos eleven. Below, a baby bawls. Over to the left, pots and pans are clanked and washed. Then there's the hum of the building itself.

Up here on the tenth floor, the lights of Warsaw twinkle before me down its wide, straight, endless avenues. Advertisers take advantage of these sweeping vistas by displaying huge tarpaulin ads down the sides of scrapers. The result is you can see some Hollywood celebrity advertising a watch for miles and miles. Sometimes, the ads are fixed in such a way that they cover people's windows, but residents remedy this by snipping out an oblong.

I can also see the Palace of Culture, Stalin's 'sorry' present to Poland after the War. It's a gigantic monolith that looks as if it's been uprooted from Moscow and plonked by crane in the middle of the city. Down below I can hear trams rumbling past and see people gliding around like moving dots.

Still, I'm glad it's a warts-and-all experience. Happy it's light and shade. I'm also glad I moved here in July when it's hot. I can stand barefoot on the concrete at night and it's warm to the touch.

Before I left, someone at Adspeak asked me if it's always cold in Poland. 'No,' I said. 'And they don't just live on sauerkraut and sausage either.' Although actually, I think they do.

No, as for the weather, the seasons in Poland are still pretty distinct. None of this wishy-washy eternal grey damp you get in England. In Poland, summer's summer and winter's winter. Summer sees frogs leaping, monster poppies unfurling and geese beating their wings as they skim across lakes. In winter, it's beautiful in a different way. It often snows heavily and can be freezing – minus twenty is not uncommon. Ice-skaters appear on ponds, padded out with coats and thick sheepskin mittens. Big fur hats never leave people's heads and for months they look taller than they are.

It's all quiet on the AB front.

I turn in, pulling the windows to. In the bathroom, there's a tiny shallow puddle. I'll have to ask Dagmara about a *hydraulik*.

I think about Mama and Tata who haven't been to Poland for over thirty years. They'd like the boiling summers and hate the freezing winters – but I bet they'd feel like foreigners in their own land. England can be freezing too though. Once, when I was little and it was a bad English winter, the three of us were shivering away in front of *Three Two One* with Ted Rogers. As a couple were about to win a car or Dusty Bin, Mama asked me to fetch her the green and brown blanket from upstairs.

I fetched it, a very scratchy thing it is too, the brown and the green primitive and vivid, the pattern a violent zigzag, and she slung it over our knees on the sofa.

'Do you know where this is from?' she said, getting comfortable. I shook my head. I didn't. It had just always been around. 'From my childhood' would have been the most accurate answer. To be honest, I never liked it because it was so rough to the touch.

'Your grandmother wove it. It's been everywhere... Poland, Siberia - where it kept us alive – and now, here.'

I was dumbfounded. This strange old thing had been in our house for so long, yet I hadn't known its significance.

'Oh no, they've got Dusty Bin!' she shouted, pounding the blanket, now precious in my eyes, with her fist. 'To think – they could have got the Ford Fiesta, but instead they've got a bin!'

My mind was far away. The blanket didn't keep her mother and her sister alive. They died out there, in vast, snowy Siberia. Her father was somewhere out there too, in a gulag.

'Look, special deals to Majorca, Magda,' Mama said hopefully, pointing at an ad during the commercial break. 'Why not go there instead of Poland all the time? It'll be warm.'

But I wasn't thinking about Majorca or even Poland. I was thinking about Mama and her family. Her mother and her sister died within months of arriving, leaving behind Mama, aged four and Szymon, aged eight, all alone, to be brought up in their huts by whoever was left. The snowy earth reached out its hand and pulled them silently away.

CHAPTER 6
FLOWERS AND A MILK-BAR
(KWIATY I BAR MLECZNY)

The next day, I leave a message for Dagmara about a plumber. When I pick up Grzybek for his morning walk, AB's hip's too stiff for her to dress. Instead she's shuffling around in a quilted dressing gown and she hasn't put her teeth in.

'You shouldn't be here, bothering yourself with me,' she mutters. Deep down, I think she's glad I'm there as she makes me tea and toast. 'Did you put the *galareta* in the fridge last night?'

'Yes,' I reply guiltily, spreading honey on my toast and knocking back a gulp of tea. What she doesn't know is that only half's in the fridge. The other half is in a Tupperware container in my bag and will be heading Grzybek's way when we go out around the block and he'll get the rest tomorrow. From the way he's dancing around me, I think he can smell it.

'Your Mama also rang.'

'Oh?'

'We had a good catch-up. She wanted to know how you were.'

'Oh. OK. We only spoke the other day.'

'I didn't tell her about my hip – as she'd only fret. I said all was well.'

'Good. *Chodź* Grzybek,' I say, going, clipping on his lead. We take the lift down. 'Who's in for a treat?'

We amble around the flower beds for a token few minutes and then I open the Tupperware and dollop the contents out onto the pavement. It comes out in one big wobbly piece and Grzybek goes berserk. Just as he's wolfing it down and as three other dogs shoot towards us from all different directions, AB appears from around the corner in her dressing gown, all buttoned-up, holding up a poop scoop and plastic bag (have no idea what poop scoop is in Polish).

'AB! What are you doing here?'

'And what are you doing with my *galareta*, Magda?'

Oh no, I've been caught red-handed by an ailing pensioner, greasy Tupperware undeniably in my hand. Not wanting me to be caught unprepared, she must have hobbled to the lift and made it downstairs.

'The *galareta* – you're giving it to Grzybek! Didn't you like it?'

Time to backtrack, and quickly.

'It's not that I didn't like it AB—'

'You didn't!'

In the awkward beat of silence that follows she thrusts the poop scoop and bags into my hands and goes. I'm left with the sound of dogs gnashing jelly.

Ten minutes later, dogs gone and poop scoop and bag in hand, I call Grzybek and we go back in.

'I am sure Grzybek enjoyed my beautiful, gourmet *galareta*,' says AB upstairs. 'It's funny how times change. When I was in the war, we only had weeds to eat. How we longed for meat, how we cried for a slither of ham, or the tiniest scrap of fat! Today, you buy your choice cut off the fattest beast going, spend all day preparing it with the best herbs, and it gets thrown away by your guest to a dog. Didn't your Mama teach you about what we went through?'

'Not really,' I reply. 'Although her stories of starvation were her primary blackmail weapon to get me to eat my greens.'

AB's changed into a dress now which she must have found easier to get on than trousers. She's on the sofa with a sandwich, poorly hip up, watching TV.

'I'm sorry,' I add, then she huffs a bit and softens.

'Go on then,' she says. 'You'll be late for work.'

Pleased we're friends again, I slip back downstairs to have breakfast on the balcony. In a way, it's good this has happened. It's been a strange kind of ice-breaker. As if my mess-up means we're family now, and not just guest and host. Drama over, I stand outside with my coffee, reassured by the noise of the TV coming from AB's, and looking at the boulevard below in constant motion.

I balance my coffee on the rail which I shouldn't do really, being ten floors up and with people walking below. I also like looking at the balconies opposite and inside the flats. It's like watching rows and rows of TVs. I can channel-hop by moving floor or flat and stare at what's happening. Usually not much, it has to be said, but even that has its own micro-fascination. Northwest of where I am, some pink plastic clogs air on a balcony, changing position every day. In the flat below that one, a broom comes out in the morning, dances over the balcony floor with its owner and is twirled back indoors at night. People having dinner are harder to stare at because they start to stare back. Right opposite, at about four o'clock every day, a woman in a flowery house-coat takes food to her husband who sits at the table. One flat has dogs poking their heads out of the balcony railings.

And way up above all this, clouds like white chalky scribbles float on a backdrop of pale blue. I can also see distant logos up here, stuck on the top of blocks advertising Sanyo or Fuji. Funny how they get you, even up here.

As I'm relaxing on this flowerless balcony – which Dagmara has never filled but which with time I will – the intercom buzzes.

'Halo?' I answer.

'Parcel!' yells the concierge right into my ear. I say concierge, but it's really Pani Zosia, the woman on the kiosk in the lobby. Pani Zosia has worked on this indoor kiosk for decades and I've seen her and the kiosk go through various phases. In the eighties, this six-foot by six-foot structure was tragic and drab. Every day Pani Zosia's moribund face told you there was nothing to buy and probably never would be. She'd spend all day rearranging her paltry supply of depressing grey toilet rolls in a zany geometric pattern to try to make things look more plentiful.

The kiosk began to change as Communism started to crumble. It began to blossom and then flower. Gradually, the tiny stall metamorphosed into a bonsai hypermarket. Every time I visited there was something new – a range of washing powders, more western European chocolate bars and an expanding array of glossy magazines. This prosperity and rebirth was matched rather movingly by Pani Zosia, married for years but hitherto childless, suddenly becoming pregnant.

Today, Pani Zosia is at least two stone overweight, has three boisterous kids and her stall heaves with produce of every kind. When she isn't polishing the floor with a cloth underfoot or reorientating a lost visitor, Pani Zosia's busy either stocktaking or eating. There are no more ghastly grey loo rolls either. These days they're all multicoloured and triple ply.

'Don't leave it too long before you come down,' she says. 'Or it'll wilt.'

'Wilt?'

I take the lift downstairs.

'Boyfriend missing you already?' she asks, handing me a long red rose in a thin cone of cellophane. She rustles her crisp bags and plumps them up, bursting with curiosity.

'Er, no,' I mumble, thinking for a moment of Matt and Izzy, their thin bendy-doll arms inseparable with happiness. 'I don't have a boyfriend.'

'You don't?' she asks, stopping mid-rustle. 'Who's it from then?'

'Maybe it's for Dagmara. She must be still getting post.'

'*Nie, nie Magda, patrz,* (look),' she says, showing me the label. 'It says Magda.'

She's right.

'*Dla Magdy, od M.* (To Magda, from M).'

'Did you see who brought it?'

'No. It was delivered by a florist.'

She thumps a half-dozen vacuum pack of loo detergent on the kiosk front as if that might knock some information out of me and props her elbows on it.

'There must be another Magda in the block,' I say.

'*Nie* again. You, Magda, are the only one.'

Leaving her immersed in mystery, I trundle back up in the lift, the strip light flickering as I turn the rose in my hands. I rest my nose on the petals, which smell of cellophane. What is going on? I don't know anyone whose name begins with M, apart from Miles the Canadian male model teacher and Matt. It would never be Matt. He's far too interested in himself, his hair, his horses and Izzy to send a rose to me in Warsaw. It's nice to think he might come grovelling back on one level, fantasy on another. What about Miles? I only met him for a minute and he seemed about as interested in me as being poked in the eye.

I drop in on AB, who's intrigued and excited.

'Maybe someone saw you when you arrived? It's definitely someone who knows where you live, isn't it?'

Perhaps it's someone in the flats opposite, I think, jabbing myself on a thorn. There I've been, playing James Stewart in *Rear Window* – or Kieślowski in *The Dekalog* – but maybe someone has turned the tables on me?

'Was there anyone on the airport bus?'

'I don't know. They would have to have followed me all the way here.'

'Anyone at the door, or at school? That hairdresser's, maybe?'

'No, AB.'

I set off for work, baffled yet flattered. A rose is still a rose. I've never received one before, not even on Valentine's Day when closet admirers are meant to come out of the woodwork to show you how they feel. Actually, I tell a lie. I once got a rose when I was eighteen and had a Saturday job on a butcher's stall (my most vivid memory is of being clunked on the head by a frozen ox heart one day as I entered the walk-in fridge. It was hanging up on a hook and was about the size of a human head). A young butcher on another stall who had a ruddy face and wore a bloodied apron bought the rose for me but I wasn't interested. Who on earth could it be?

When I arrive at Language Zone, the place is crawling with workmen. There's a smallish orange bulldozer in the yard clearing up rubble.

Next to all of this, Pani Dąbrowska and Pani Raszewska stand huddled together, their fingers hooked through the wire fence, like prisoners in reverse. Pani Dąbrowska has a satisfied glow about her, but when some piece of old furniture comes hurtling out of their office window, her sister claps her hands around her face and looks like Edvard Munch's *The Scream*.

One worker starts hacking at a piece of wall that hasn't quite come down. One particular part of it, maybe where the brick is poor, creates a hollow, tinkling sound as he hits it, like a rotten nut, or like the disappointing sound a Christmas bauble makes when it's broken by accident.

Jacek's there too. I join the registrars, spluttering in the dust.

'Classes are cancelled today, Magda,' says Pani Dąbrowska, turning towards me, blinking through the debris. 'We'll let you know where you're teaching as and when.' She flicks away a speck of rubble that's landed on her sleeve as if it were a fly.

I nod, observing her sister who is looking on, anxiously fingering the pearls around her neck.

Pani Dąbrowska says something to her sister which sounds a bit terse, but Polish can sound like that – highly emotional when nothing much is wrong. I take out a piece of gum and slip it in my mouth.

Miles arrives, also chewing gum, and my heart starts beating so loudly I can hear it in my head. He looks like the rose-sending type, but how would he know where I live? His brilliant white teeth are like a set of toy falsies on brand new batteries. I decide to interrogate him gently and more crucially, I decide I rather like him. I can do model-types, if push comes to shove.

'Hi. It's Miles, isn't it?'

'Yes. Hi. Sorry, I know we only met yesterday but I've forgotten your name.'

'Magda.'

'Oh yeah,' he says, glazed over.

He puts his headphones back on and chews as he views the demolition spectacle. He's either doing an excellent job at hiding he likes me or it's definitely not him.

'Can you still do two o'clock?' yells Jacek, spotting me.

'Sure!'

'I know a place just around the corner. The *bar mleczny* (milk-bar), you can't miss it. We could work there!'

I know the place he means from previous visits. A now-rare Polish equivalent of the greasy spoon. Milk-bars used to be much more numerous and were created by the state in the fifties for workers whose factories or offices didn't have canteens. Today, the only milk-bars that remain are one-off vintage gems like this one and they're privately owned.

Miles drifts off on his cloud of designer masculinity, and I walk off too, crunching over rubble. I go inside to see what's happening.

Lessons may be off today, but the sister registrars have left the door slightly ajar. Inside, the place is empty and quiet. A milky cloud of plaster hangs in the air and the stairs are carpetless. All that's left are bent nails with bits of red carpet on them, stuck around the heads in small telltale tufts. Upstairs, some skirting has been removed, revealing ancient wires.

'Hallo?'

No one answers. In the staffroom, a Hispanic-looking guy with a mass of long black curls sits poring over grammar books with headphones on his ears.

I head for the office around the corner and go straight in. It was crammed full yesterday but now it's empty with just a few bits of broken china on the carpet. The room has been stripped of all its files, pictures and framed certificates. The messy paperwork, the old computers and the ancient stationery have gone too.

One thing has survived though – the knight in the corner. He stands slightly skew-whiff, a posture that belies his status, and he is rather sadly pitted against a tall grey cabinet. The chain around his ankle has been his salvation. The cloth Polish flag lies beside him, crumpled.

Female footsteps approach, rapid stiletto heels.

'Magda!' says Pani Dąbrowska, bursting in with a kettle in her hand and a bunch of cups in the other. 'Doesn't it look marvellous?' Her sister follows, wan.

'It's definitely – empty,' I reply, not knowing what tack to take, given they're on opposing ends of the excitement spectrum.

As the new kettle goes on with an excited click, Pani Raszewska goes and stands in the centre, full of regret, like a tearful Edith Piaf. Pani Dąbrowska picks up bits of china, tutting at the builders' carelessness. Today her blond hair looks like a child's ice-cream with the top licked off.

'It's awful,' says her sister. 'They must have stormed through like Panzers.'

'I couldn't have stood it as it was for a minute longer.'

Today, Pani Raszewska has two knitting needles criss-crossed through her bun and a stressed haze of stray hairs. As she wanders to the knight and takes his creaking hand, I decide to leave them to it.

The milk-bar's a bittersweet place. Austere but lively, old but fully functioning.

Before I go in, I study the socialist carvings on the walls outside – victorious workers holding sickles aloft.

Inside, it's a stark, light blue dining room with worn, mottled grey Formica tables.

In the service area, a row of steel food cabinets verge on the surgical, although someone has tempered the overall starkness by sticking big yellow paper flowers in large pot vases along the sills.

I take a seat and as I absorb the atmosphere, Jacek wanders in like a regular and waves hello. He greets a big-hipped, big-bosomed woman at the counter who calls him by his first name and asks us for our order.

The menu is huge. The board has those white snap-on letters that cafes in Soho use to look cool and retro. Meat with this, and meat with that. Pale, grey *pierogi* sit steaming in bowls, ready to go. I choose *szczawiowa* – sorrel soup (green sludge with half a boiled egg floating around in it). It feels like the healthiest option.

We wait for our food to shoot out of a two-foot by two-foot waist-high hatch where only midriffs and plump, dimpled arms are visible.

Within minutes, our order appears from out of the hatch – colour-drained yet homely-looking food piled onto semi-translucent white crockery. My soup is spirulina green, and Jacek's got what I can only assume is a pork knuckle with mashed potato and some raw white grated cabbage. The Poles are obsessed with these coleslaw-esque side salads or *surówki*.

Jacek stops and takes a large bunch of keys out of his trouser pocket, depositing it on the table before starting his meal. His key ring is a cut-out enamel 'M'. Not another occurrence of this mystery letter.

'Why is that an 'M'? I ask, sipping at my soup.

'It stands for Marzena. My late wife.'

'Oh. I'm sorry.'

He looks rather thoughtful and drums his fingers on the table.

'Shall we get to work?' I say, switching into teacher-mode.

When I get back in and walk past the kiosk, Pani-doesn't-miss-a-jot-Zosia calls me over. The way she says 'Magda' has the same strange effect on me as a shepherd's crook does around a sheep's neck.

'These have just arrived, Magda,' she says significantly, passing me some multicoloured tulips. This time the card says 'Andrzej', not 'M' and there is a phone number.

'Someone's popular,' she says, desperate to know what's going on.

'It must be a mistake, or some kind of joke.'

'But who would do that to you Magda?'

'I don't know.'

I leave, feeling Pani Zosia's gamma-ray eyes burning into my back as I step into the lift. The doors close, and cradling the flowers, I trundle back up.

But, tulips bobbing around my face, I know exactly who's behind this. Not Miles or Matt, or some oddball across the street. The mist is clearing and I've begun to smell a rat. A Polish Yorkshire rat. The penny has dropped. Mama has gone and stuck me in the classifieds.

CHAPTER 7
BEAUTIFULMAGDAUK (*PIĘKNA MAGDA, UK*)

'Mama! Pick up! I know you're there!' Nothing. 'I know what you've done!' Big significant pause. 'Come on. Answer the phone. I'm getting flowers left, right and centre!'

She picks up the receiver with a clatter. I knew that would get her.

'You can't be, it's only out tomorrow.'

'Tomorrow? I've been receiving bouquets every two minutes.'

'What?'

'I've just got a big bunch of tulips!'

'Oh... Right. I see. She must have... done it then. Well that was quick.'

'What was?' Awkward silence.

'I, we...'

'What? Who?'

'*I've* put you in the *Polish Daily*. Dagmara's put you on that site she told you about.'

'Without me knowing? Without asking?'

'I tried to ask you. The day you rang – when you came out of the hairdresser's.'

'But I couldn't hear you! The line was bad!'

'You said it wasn't!'

'It was – on and off!'

'Magda – is your hair really that bad?'
'It's terrible!'
'Do you think it will put people off?'
'You mean men?'
'Yes.'
'It'll do that all right.'

With no Chinese *prostownica* yet, I can barely look at myself in the mirror. But back to my trans-European row. Who'd have thought a bad hairdo could be my greatest weapon?

'Mama, this is not on!'

'Don't say that,' she says all calm, trying to act as if I'm the one that's crazy. 'You always said London was big and how hard it was to meet somebody.'

'I'm not in London, I'm in Warsaw!'

'Yes, another big capital,' she says, sounding remarkably rational. She can do this Mama, be preposterous, but throw in logic.

'I'm thirty-nine! *Nie rób tego* (don't do this) ever again!' I say in high volume top-notch Ponglish. 'I thought I had a stalker!'

'A what?'

'A stalker! Someone who follows you incessantly and tries to convince you that you love them.'

'That sounds perfect, just what you want.'

'No it isn't! Mama, ring up and cancel it – now!'

'I can't. It's gone to print, or to press, or whatever the phrase is!'

'Oh great. Thanks. Thanks very much. You've not put down the flat number, have you? Please tell me you haven't.' I'm trying to sound super calm now as only the livid do.

'Of course I've not put down the number. I'm not stupid. I just put down the block – they have to have something!'

'Mama, the concierge thinks I'm some kind of – hussy!'

'You are not!'

'It's a total *wstyd*! (disgrace),' I yell, '*wstyd*' being Poland's number one word for expressing moral outrage.

Conveniently, her front door bell goes.

'Mama, don't go. I haven't finished yet.'

'Yeeuu-huu!' she shouts off into the distance, Ponglish for 'yoo-hoo'. 'I've got to go, Magda, there's someone at the door. Don't worry. By the way, if you do meet someone, maybe tell me where you are, in case they're a murderer?'

She bangs the phone down and I look at my handset. 'Call ended, Mama,' it says. If only it were that simple. As I go to my computer and search for Polishmate.com the buzzer goes again.

'Flowers from Bogdan and a helium balloon from Krzysztof13,' says Pani Zosia over the phone.

'Did you see who brought them?'

'The florist brought the *orchidee*, and a postman the balloon. Magda, it's as if you're on one of these dating sites.'

'That's exactly what I'm on. Dagmara's put me on one.'

'Dagmara?'

'Yes, and my Mama has put me in the paper.'

Downstairs, Pani Zosia passes me a pot of orchids. I could set up a florist at this rate and my Polish floral vocab is positively burgeoning.

'Flowers are more classically romantic, but this,' she says, untying a red heart helium balloon with 'Magda' written on it, 'it shows someone fun, don't you think?'

'All this will end soon,' I say, looking around for a child to give it to. 'You can keep the orchids, if you like. I don't want them.'

'You can't give them away – they're a gift! What's the name of this site you're on? My sister wants to join one and yours seems really good.'

'Polishmate.com,' I mutter, watching her write it straight into a text. I try to give the balloon to a little girl with her mother, but she isn't going for it as her name isn't Magda.

'How generous of Dagmara to sign you up,' says Pani Zosia, hitting Send. 'I always thought there was another side to her.'

'Anything from China for me while I'm here?'

'Er no. 'fraid not. You're not getting interest from there too?'

'No. I'm expecting something else.'

Back upstairs, I resume my search. Polishmate.com, got it. A ticker-tape of pink flashing hearts sails across the top – I try to find myself – nothing.

On one side there's a long list of Polish men, photographed beside their cars, mainly, and on the other side, an equally long list of Polish women in too much blue mascara.

Dagmara rings. Mama must have filled her in.

'Take me down now, Dagmara!'

'Oh don't be like that. I thought you'd love it!'

'I don't! It's tacky!'

'Tacky? It's high-class and expensive! Do you think I'd be on it if it were tacky? Thousands of people are on it. Look up BeautifulMagdaUK.'

'Is that what you've called me?' I type. 'The password, Dagmara, now. Then I can shut it down myself.'

'Er – we'll come to that.'

'You are going to give it to me. Don't think you're not!'

'Or what, Magda?'

Good point.

'I'll... I'll... disown you as my cousin!'

'Oh big deal!'

Just at that moment, my profile sails into sight on the screen. It's me in the restaurant, with straight hair, wolfing down *pierogi*.

That's why she wanted to take my photo!

Instead of screaming like I did with Mama, I get up and sway in my sandals, wounded. There I am online, for all the world to see. Is there no limit to what Mama and Dagmara can do?

'I'm amazed you've got all these flowers. Maybe it's because you're foreign and exotic?'

'I am not exotic. I'm from Doncaster with Polish parents. That's like crossing a *kabanos* sausage with a pork pie.'

'A what?'

'Forget it.'

I read my profile summary, created by Dagmara.

'"Highly intelligent, attractive, British Pole, former advertising executive, now working in Warsaw. Enjoys cooking, cleaning and... ironing"? Dagmara, since when did I like ironing? "Would like children as soon as possible"? DAGMARA!'

'OK, OK, I'll take that bit down! Although I find it's good to put them in the picture as soon as possible!'

'How could you?'

The ticker-tape at the top suddenly changes to include a string of people's faces – including me with the *pierogi*.

'No wonder I'm getting all this interest, I'm on the ticker-tape too!'

'Oh yes. I paid extra for that. Good, isn't it?'

'No,' I reply, seeing if a deeply disappointed, offended tone will work instead of hysteria. 'It isn't good at all. You've really done it this time. This beats all the other things you've done, Dagmara, every last thing.'

'Like what?'

'You really want to know?'

'Yes! Tell me, what exactly have I done to make my English cousin's life a misery?'

'Where can I start? How about the time when I was little and you put salt in my jelly, and telling me your Wendy house was haunted so I'd be too scared to go in and you wouldn't have to share it' (she laughs at this point), and all the times you've laughed at me when I tried to do your stupid and impossible Polish tongue-twisters!'

'Oh they were funny, Magda. Do the one about *Król Karol*...'

'No!'

'Magda, do you know how much this site has cost me?'

'I don't care, I don't want to be on it.'

'Just click on the other photos – they're brilliant!'

I do and find more photos of me – one of me aged six on a swing with my pink knickers showing and one of me at my Holy Communion. How did she get these? Of course, Mama's parcels in the eighties, they contained photos – these photos! Dagmara must have scanned them. She could blackmail me forever.

'Anyway, *kochana*. There's something I want to ask. You know that dinner you promised? Can Stefan come too? We're back together.'

'What – you and Stefan? You're kidding?'

This is dreadful news, big enough to divert me from my current rampage and from the cheek of her asking about dinner after what she's done. This is typical Dagmara. She dumps on me and then expects dinner for her and Stefan. Stefan has been Dagmara's on-off boyfriend for years and is a total nightmare.

'I know what you're thinking – but this time it's going to be different.'

'How?'

'He begged me, basically. Look at me, pussycat12, will you? You're attracting a better class of male than me and I want to know why.'

'I am not looking you up. And what about Stefan, if you're back with him?'

'Oh I'm not going to do anything. I just want your advice. And anyway, I've been too busy managing your account. I bet the place looks lovely, filled with flowers. Stefan's only ever got me plastic ones – he says they last forever.'

'You shouldn't have gone back to him, Dagmara.'

'No one's perfect. Oh look, Magda, Bogdan's asking if you got the orchids. Can you see?'

'No, because I don't have access to my own inbox, do I?'

'Oh yes. But you got them, yes?'

'Yes.'

'Yes thank you, they were lovely,' she says, typing.

'Are you answering on my behalf?'

'Well someone's got to say thank you. Oh Magda, he's so nice. Look him up – Bogdan67 – you can do that without a login. Blue eyes, blond hair – and he doesn't look like an alcoholic.'

'Dagmara, dinner is not happening while this is up. Never mind Stefan. If you don't take me down, I'm going to, I'm going to – write in and complain!'

'Pah! That's what you British do – write in and complain!'

'No we don't! We started a war for you, remember?'

'What's the war got to do with Polishmate.com?'

'Everything!'

I hang up. That's the only bad thing about mobiles – you can't bang them down like before, you can only press a button and stare.

A text arrives from Mama.

Tried to call but you're on the phone. It's in today's Polish Daily online, but the printed edition is out tomorrow. Also, there's a little mistake. Which actually is rather big. It says you're 89, not 39.

Small victories like these are not to be dismissed.

The next morning, I'm still on the site. I feel really homesick.

THINGS I MISS ABOUT ENGLAND:
1. Speaking English. I know it's been barely ten days but it feels like a lifetime since I've been here. Everyone speaks Polish, everything's in Polish, everyone is Polish. I'm going to have to start talking to myself in English like a mad woman as I roam the streets.
2. Normal chocolate. The Toblerone's long gone and the Dairy Milk demolished. The chocolate here is not creamy enough.
3. News bulletins I can understand. The newsreaders talk so fast, the only words I understand are *'i'* which means 'and' and *tak* and *nie*. And maybe the odd country like *Afryka* and *Ameryka*.
4. I miss baked beans and sliced cheap white bread. Not that I ever had them in London, but now I'm here they're all I want. And doughnuts too – the spherical soft ones rolled in sugar, mmmm, (not hard Polish ones you could smash a pane of glass with).
5. The English sense of humour.
6. A decent cup of tea.
7. Good coffee (Polish coffee tastes like bitter, burnt mud).
8. Fray Bentos pies. Again never bought them, but really want one.
9. And finally, and oddly, Mama's Polish cooking. I know I'm mad with her, and I'm also in Poland, surrounded by Polish food – but I really miss her Polish pickled beetroot. I can see one now on the end of a fork – a golfball-sized, wine-red round thing – delicious.

For penance, I'm going to tell Mama to send me one of her emergency parcels, but this time, to make it à la twenty-first century. Luxury items, not bare essentials (although right now, they feel pretty essential to me). She can easily get a couple of Fray Bentos tinned pies and some baked beans. And knowing her, there are probably jars of pickled beetroot in the pantry. She can get one of those and wedge everything safely between some loaves of white bread for cushioning. I'll ask her to throw in some bars of Cadbury's and Green & Black's chocolate for good measure. The one with butterscotch bits in them are like crack cocaine (not that I know what crack cocaine is like).

At Language Zone, Jacek stops me in the corridor after class with the *Polish Daily*. Mama's ad is in it. Figuring there can't be many former advertising execs from London called Magda, he asks if it's me.

'Yes, it's me. Magda from London, who likes ironing – not.'

'Hey Magda – you managed to say that without moving a single muscle in your face. Is that a British thing?'

'It must be.'

'You'd better let them know that they've got your age wrong. Look, it says you're eighty-nine. You're not eighty-nine. You could get a free week for an error like that.'

'I don't want a free week. It's my mother, not me.'

'Your mother?'

'She put me in there.'

'Why?'

'Good question. She's put me in there without me knowing. Welcome to my *świat* (world) Jacek. Send my love to London when you get there. I wish I was coming too.'

I feel better when I get back to my quiet, safe flat. Free of balloons, classified ads and well-meaning plumbers and relatives. On my way in, I spotted an elderly gentleman standing against the wall outside the block with a rose in his hands. Probably waiting for eighty-nine-year-old me, poor soul.

I fling open the balcony doors and look at the deep pink sky. Warsaw simmers, its sprawling blocks throbbing in the heat. Time to relax with some Balcony TV. I cut my helium balloon free, and enjoy watching it diminish into the sky.

If I'm going to complain to Polishmate this evening, I'd better get my dictionaries out and start writing an email. I brew a jasmine tea, and prod at the big clumps of dried flowers rehydrating in my cup.

I have another look at the site. Turns out I'm still on it.

No matter, I think, as I get my dictionaries off the shelf. It'll be over soon. I'll explain and it will all be fine – any reasonable person will see in an instant and take me down. I shouldn't doubt Polish customer service anymore – the days of steely-faced shop assistants giving you accusing looks are gone. Who knows, they might even have procedures in place for meddling relatives? I can't be the first, surely.

I can't resist having a peek at Dagmara, pussycat12. She has lots of red lip gloss on and is poignantly holding a daffodil.

I decide to ring AB.

When I ask her about her hip she says she's got a big purple bruise down her side in the shape of Germany.

VOCAB CORNER:

Immediate cancellation of internet dating site = *natychmiastowe anulowanie matrymonialnej strony internetowej* (cue nervous breakdown).

CHAPTER 8
ROCK–PAPER–SCISSORS
(KAMIEŃ, PAPIER, NOŻYCZKI)

Dagmara and I have always had a paper to scissors, paper to rock relationship.

One of the first times I had a run-in with Dagmara was when I visited her family home in Barlinek one summer all on my own. Mama and Tata thought it would do me good to spend a longer period of time in Poland and there was even talk of there being a regular exchange if things went well.

I got plonked on a plane (very expensive in 1988) aged twelve, with Father Wiśniewski, our Polish parish priest. Father Wiśniewski always spent his summers in Poland and said he'd accompany me to Dagmara's door, so Mama and Tata wouldn't have to worry about a thing.

The journey was super exciting and super confusing, as Father Wiśniewski looked just like Fred Astaire. The glamour of a flight made me think my suspicions were right – he really was Fred Astaire and being a priest in Doncaster was just a cover-up and a way of dealing with fame while his next film was planned.

So off to Dagmara's we went and I arrived, suitcase on step, one very hot day where the brightness in Poland seemed turned up to full. Father Astaire then departed, tap dancing (it seemed to me, he was very nimble) saying he was straight off to the post office to send a telegram home saying I was safe and in situ. In situ I was, safe I wasn't.

From day one, I was Dagmara's plaything. Her cousin from England whom she loved to show off to her friends yet boss around as well.

Back then, Dagmara was keen on Polish national dancing, as were lots of girls her age (and some boys too, it quickly transpired). It was a relatively cheap thing to do I suppose – you only needed a place in which to dance, some other dancers, a tape cassette machine and a teacher.

Dagmara was really rather good at it, so letters read out loud by Mama said, and this year, she was practising every waking hour for a big dance competition. Having won two years running, her group had got through to the final in Gdansk again and it was quite a big deal.

A few days after I arrived, we got some bad news. Dagmara's partner Adam had fallen out of a tree and had broken his leg in two places. Disaster! He'd have to have it in plaster for at least six weeks. All I can remember is Dagmara crying for hours – not so much over Adam's poor leg but because she would not get to dance in the show (Polish national dancing relies heavily on partners).

'Who on earth could be pulled in at the last minute?' everyone was asking.

There were no other boys in the village – none that wanted to learn a complicated dance anyway. Who was there who would be able to spend lots of time with Dagmara, drilling all the moves and the lifts?

As I sat twizzling the Rubik's cube that I had brought over for company (and I realised, as a potential defence weapon against Dagmara) I had the distinct impression that all eyes were starting to land on me.

'Oh no,' I thought, as I stared at my two finished sides, the rest of the cube still fully jumbled up. I was even considering peeling off the stickers.

Dagmara's ploy came out, like a golden goose egg.

'YOU will be my partner!' Dagmara proclaimed over dinner that night, pointing her knife, which was covered in mashed potato, at me.

'Me? But I'm a girl. How will it be possible?' I asked, startled, in a Virgin-Mary-talking-to-the-Angel-Gabriel kind of way.

The fact that I wasn't a boy didn't seem to matter but what can't have helped my case was that, at the time, I looked like a boy, my long thin wispy hair having been hacked off by Mama before the trip so that it would be short and 'easy to keep'.

I didn't mind in a way, as the prospect of playing with my Rubik's cube all summer and moseying around the cabbage patch in the garden with Dagmara when she wasn't rehearsing, wasn't exactly thrilling. With school over for summer, all we did was play ball in the concrete square outside, ironically called Freedom Square, then sit around looking to see who else was around until we were called in for dinner. My strongest memory of Dagmara's mother, Auntie Katarzyna, back then is of her reusing a match (sent by Mama) about six times as they were so scarce.

'Let's start rehearsing now!' said Dagmara straight after dinner.

'Not yet,' said her mother, much to my relief. 'You'll get a stitch if you jump around too soon.'

From that night onwards, we had the rehearsal regime of a Soviet Olympic gymnast team. (I'm not sure how strict the Polish team are but the Russians are bound to be a hundred times stricter.)

'What, you mean I've got to lift you?' I asked her one day, as we were rehearsing in the hallway.

'Well I can't lift you,' Dagmara said. 'Your stomach's saying hello and your bottom's saying goodbye!'

I looked at my waistline, felt ashamed, and proceeded to try to lift Dagmara.

'You're going to have to lose weight and strengthen up! No more pudding for you!'

'What?'

'Maybe you could do some weights?' she said, going into the kitchen and finding two jars of sauerkraut. 'Start lifting these, and once an hour, you can try to lift me.'

And so it continued. I attended all Dagmara's official dance classes for the next five weeks and we worked at home too. I enjoyed it really and didn't even mind her bossing me around too much, as when it came to Polish dancing, she did know more than me. I'd only done a bit in Doncaster, as part of Polish school, which all Polish-British kids went to every Saturday morning. I really hated Polish school at the time, but now I regret not making the most of it. Mama taught our little class Polish grammar but I was always bored. We also had to recite poems at do's and put on plays. I once had to dress up as a toadstool in a show all about fungi (something else the Poles are obsessed with).

Eventually, I did end up being able to lift Dagmara, just for one second, as she jumped and twirled through the air.

And as long as Dagmara had the upper hand, was the scissors to my paper and the rock to my scissors, things were all right.

The date of the final arrived. About a week before, Adam thought he might be able to get his plaster cast off early and dance after all. I was gutted. By now, I'd got into the competition as much as Dagmara and I was very excited about going to Gdansk – I'd never been before. I also had a gorgeous new Polish national costume – a girl's one not a boy's one – which I absolutely loved. The prospect of it all being snatched away now was terrible. While Dagmara waited for a verdict – hoping that Adam would be dancing and not me – I sat there wondering what was going to happen.

But it was a false alarm. Adam's plaster was staying put – and I was still understudy.

Understudy extraordinaire.

When the big day arrived, we got the coach to Gdansk – a dance troupe of twenty-four young teenagers, plus parents, Adam and his plaster cast and cases of costumes.

'You're going to Gdansk thanks to me!' said Dagmara, plonking herself next to me. 'Who said you could have the window seat?'

'I got here first,' I replied, annoyed.

She stuck out her tongue and looked the other way.

When we arrived at the venue – a theatre in the centre – we were bundled off into some changing room with the other participating dance schools.

Several technicians were rigging and adjusting the lights and rushing around with coils of cable. Every group needed something different: a glitter-ball here, a spotlight there. They looked like grown men, these special stagehands, but were probably only a little older than us.

A group of ladies with baskets of flowers arrived to do our *wianki* – floral headpieces that make you look like you're sprouting flowers. They were the crowning glory to our flowery skirts, embroidered blouses and sequined bodice jackets.

The boys' costumes consisted of baggy blue-and-white-striped trousers, billowing white shirts, red velvet waistcoats and caps with long pheasant feathers in them that poked you in the eye if your positioning was wrong.

Unlike me (with short dark hair), Dagmara had long blond hair back then, and that day she had it in two long plaits that were coiled around her ears like Princess Leia off *Star Wars*.

We were told the running order – we were on fifth in the show – a very good spot. Not so early that the audience would be cold, and not too late so that our nerves would have peaked.

'Remember, the place will be heaving,' said Dagmara, mopping her brow like a robot melting down. It was boiling under the lights as we stood waiting for our spots to be fixed. She liked giving me these pep talks. 'You won't hear the audience because of the music, but you'll feel that they're there. Don't let their gawping send you off track. Let them skewer you to what you're doing...' Frankly I was beginning to wish someone would skewer her.

There were two big dressing rooms for the groups, one for the boys and one for the girls. Each *zespół* (group) kept to itself, but of course we were all stealing glances at one another's costumes, sizing them up. Every sequin in Poland was probably in this room right now, along with the highest concentration of red boots, red ribbons and embroidered blouses ever brought together. Our changing room sounded like seagulls chattering – Polish girls and women talking in high-pitched voices, incredibly fast. There was also a black and white TV monitor so we could see the stage and hear what was going on. I had never seen anything like it in my whole sheltered life.

At around seven o'clock, technical rehearsal and dress rehearsal complete, the volume began to rise in the auditorium. We knew the place was filling up. The adrenaline in the changing-room started to rise too, along with the amount of hairspray being sprayed and make-up being applied.

Finally, kick-off.

A crackling tannoy summoned the first group – I remember there was a frisson around them as they were our staunch rivals from Kraków. I couldn't watch them on the monitor; Dagmara watched through open fingers, her hands over her face.

'They're really, really, really good,' she said, sounding hollow.

'Really?' I asked.

'No, I'm joking. They're terrible! They're not even keeping time, Magda. If they're all like this, then we're laughing.'

I looked at the screen. The timing looked perfect to me.

'Have you seen those costumes over there?' she whispered, looking at a troupe in the corner. 'They look like scarecrows!'

'Don't be mean. They've still made an effort.'

'I'm not being mean, I'm just in a winning mindset, that's all,' she piped, flicking back the long twists of coloured ribbons that were pinned to her plaits.

'You're what?' I asked.

'In a winning-mindset. You know. Or do you? We've got to win, Magda. That's why we're here.'

'I know. I'm not stupid.'

I think Dagmara was nervous too as she finally shut up. The fourth group was on and then it would be us. I felt faint with nerves and the pins holding the flowers to my head were creating some weird acupuncture effect that made me feel sick.

Why am I doing this? I wondered, thinking of Mama and Tata in Doncaster and wishing I was with them, or they were with me. 'These flowers are killing me,' I said to Dagmara, who was transfixed to the monitor. I fiddled with them and shook my head.

'Leave them alone,' she hissed. 'Come on, we're on!'

'*Numer pięć* (number five),' said the MC.

I remember it so clearly. My head felt totally disconnected from my body, my left foot felt as if it was over here and my right one over there. How on earth was I going to walk, let alone dance?

Looking back on it, what made the whole process bearable was our fabulous dance teacher, Pani Anna. As a professional seamstress, it was also she who had come up with my gorgeous costume (it was nicer than Dagmara's as it had more sequins on it – a thank you, I think, for stepping in for Adam).

Pani Anna was amazing. When she said jump, you jumped, usually literally. But most of all she loved us, treated us well and she was good at what she did. Each class felt important and she always wore an immaculate white leotard and tights that looked brand new every time – they sort of raised her status to that of mythic perfect goddess.

I tried to regain composure as we walked down a long corridor to the stage. I checked Dagmara's laces and ribbons and she checked mine. We had no idea how many people were out there, but we knew it was lots as we'd seen the number of seats during rehearsal, and there was a tremendous amount of whooping and clapping. Dagmara's parents, Uncle Szymon and Auntie Katarzyna, would be out there somewhere, and if Mama and Tata had got our telegram, they'd be thinking of me now.

Suddenly we joined up with the boys. The girls found their partners, but as I was Dagmara's partner, we stayed together, nervously joining hands.

All of a sudden the music for our first number started and we were off. We entered the stage, where we were plunged into strong, hot lights. Dagmara grabbed me by the arm and pulled me into the opening steps of our group's first routine. Having won the last two years, our welcome on stage as current champions was electric.

I didn't attempt to look at the sea of people before us and besides we were moving too fast, Polish dancing's like that. I concentrated on looping my arm into Dagmara's as we jigged around and for a split second, I caught her eye. Catching someone's eye that you don't really like when they're decorated with flowers is hilarious anyway, never mind when they're mid-jig and have too much blusher on their cheeks. I remember I wanted to laugh but she gave me such a glare that my giggles were extinguished in half a second flat.

Then, to my horror, I felt my *wianek* shift slightly during a turn. Oh no, I thought, it's coming off!

Why had I adjusted one of the iron-grip pins in the changing room before we came on? I must have loosened the wretched thing and now I had a rogue flower wandering down my cheek. There was a bar of violent jumps coming up, what would happen then? I looked at Dagmara, who, by her horrified expression, had noticed too.

All my hoping was in vain, as when 'jump jump jump' finally came round, my vision was suddenly impaired by two white dahlias descending over my brows like a pair of ping-pong balls. I couldn't see a thing. 'I'm going to have to whip it off,' I thought, 'I'm going to have to whip the stupid thing off and get rid of it, otherwise I'll grind us to a halt.'

We were jigging around and just as we were about to launch into a whole sequence of twirls I yanked the wretched *wianek* off my head and flung it as hard as I could into the audience like a flowery flying saucer. I also heard clumps of my hair being torn out at the same time, but there's something about being on stage, you just don't feel pain like you do in real life. A peal of cheers and laughter rang out – the audience must have seen it.

Yes, I might have bald patches on my head, but *wianek* gone, I was worry-free again. I was relieved and Dagmara looked relieved too, sort of.

Next, it was time for the piece, where I had to lift Dagmara. I was wrong before when I said I had to lift her for just a second, that was during training. In actual fact I had to lift her for about ten seconds, her waist right in my face. I got goose-bumps as our group's lifts cascaded perfectly along with the music. All those drills, all those counts, all that nagging and prodding from Dagmara were finally paying off.

Some of the flowers from my lost headpiece were getting thrown back on to the stage whenever Dagmara and I came to the front. Cheers and yelps and 'bravo' came from the audience.

I looked into the wings at Pani Anna our teacher, dressed for the group's finale as a giant swan. She looked beautiful and majestic. How much one could still think about while doing a complicated routine in front of so many people bewildered me.

'Focus you great nana,' I could see Dagmara's face was saying.

'I'm focusing, I'm focusing,' I tried to say back.

Next, time for Dagmara to lift me – a move we'd added only just last week. She lifted me in such a way that I don't even remembered being lifted. Never would she be able call me 'podgy dumpling' again. I was much more svelte and twice as strong. At the end, a massive, massive cheer – and that's when I think I saw Dagmara's parents not far from the front, and Adam with his plaster-cast leg, sticking out of one of the rows.

We bowed. It had been a huge success and we skipped to the back of the stage to watch our dance teacher and her partner's big finale.

Two golden spotlights came on and Pani Anna appeared looking like Concorde covered in a thousand white feathers. She had only worn her headpiece and wings in the dress rehearsal, but now she was fully covered. It was electrifying.

The audience 'shushed' itself to silence to watch her and her partner.

What can I say? They looked like two warhorses jousting with one another. Strong yet graceful, precise yet free. Our teacher stood with her arms on her hips as her partner – the group's best male dancer – did a bizarre Polish stunt where he picked up his foot and jumped over it back and forth with the other – forty-three jumps he managed. Then there was our teacher's spectacular lift at the end – and we were done.

We bowed once more and ran off stage, ecstatic, waving the boys goodbye as they went the other way. We followed Pani Anna, who'd strictly told us not to get hysterical in front of the other groups, back to the changing room. Dagmara turned to me, clearly annoyed with me for my *wianek* falling off.

'What happened?' she asked. 'I nearly went flying because of you!'

'Sorry, I didn't know what else to do. I think I've pulled some hair out, can you see?'

'I'll give you pulled-out hair,' she said, going for me.

'Agh!' I yelled as she grabbed my hair.

'Stop it now, Dagmara!' said Pani Anna stepping in, feather costume and all, but with her visor up. 'What's going on?'

'Nothing,' I lied, as Dagmara let go.

'She tripped me up!' said Dagmara.

'I didn't.'

'Dagmara – that's enough.'

'But I slipped because of her!'

I would have happily taken the blame for the event, been the paper to her scissors. But something changed our course.

'Dagmara,' said Pani Anna, pointing her finger (her wing really) to halt the protestation. 'Can't you see that without your cousin – you wouldn't be here? We did very well. Magda, I'll get the lady to pin it again for you.'

Perhaps to appear more approachable, or perhaps more normal, she took off her visor-like headpiece and chucked us both under the chin.

'If we win, we'll have to go out again, won't we, girls? So make up and be done. Tonight, Magda, you really proved that you are a Polish rose, not just an English one. Dagmara – what's that ugly pout for?'

While the judges made their minds up at the end, around a thousand human fingernails started being chewed in the dressing room, and around five hundred ribbons were fiddled with. Dagmara decided she'd forgiven me as she came to sit next to me, twizzling the sequins on my waistcoat. We huddled up together, hoping and expecting to hear our group's name being read out next.

Result aside, all I could focus on was how lucky I was to be part of the whole thing – and all because Adam had fallen out of a tree.

Pani Anna, expectant, and in her full swan costume, looked as if she might lay an egg.

'Finally, in first place, this year's winners are...'

The changing room was totally silent as we all held our breath and looked around.

'For their very entertaining performance, and for a third year running' (at this point we were yelping), 'Barlinek's *"Polskie Róże"* (Polish Roses).'

Jubilant, we ran back out and danced our pieces once more. I had a new sprig of flowers practically nailed to my head and Dagmara her first place.

We'd won, and for those few moments, it was wonderful.

While Dagmara acted as if she'd forgiven me, I wonder if she had, deep down. All I know is, those regular summer exchanges never did take off.

CHAPTER 9
BIRDS HAVE GOT EARS TOO YOU KNOW
(PTAKI TEŻ MAJĄ USZY, WIESZ?)

Nearly thirty years later and I'm still trying to get one over on Dagmara. Why do I always feel that with Dagmara, I lose?

My attempts to get myself off Polishmate have failed. I've emailed them several times, called them, had a few limp replies – I've even considered going round to their offices, only they're not in Warsaw. I must say that my ability to complain in Polish has advanced considerably. I know all the fancy words.

'This is a breach of privacy!'

'I will appeal!'

This is what they have sent:

Dear Ms Mikołajczyk
Thank you for contacting Polishmate.com. We have examined your account and considered your circumstances. Unfortunately, only the subscriber can cancel the contract and we do not offer refunds. Yu have stated that you do not use or wish to use the site, however we can see you have used it every day since it was opened *(that was Dagmara, not me!)*

We suggest you contact the account holder to resolve the matter *(I have. But you try dealing with Dagmara, matey)*
Yours faithfully *(go away)*
Polishmate.com
Helping You Find Your Perfect Polishmate *(pah).*

On a positive note, Mama's emergency luxury parcel's arrived, minus pickled beetroots as she said they were bound to break or leak. Everything else I requested is there, Fray Bentos pie and baked beans with a mountain of chocolate.

Still no *prostownica* though, and it's been a few weeks now. I've even been down to the Chinese takeaway with a printout of my emails from them. (Felt had to get sweet-and-sour chicken to be polite, was rather nice). Out of stock, it turns out. How can hair-straighteners be out of stock? I wonder if I can claim some kind of compensation? Aren't there laws about this kind of thing? I think there are in England, but what about the rest of the world?

Why-oh-why didn't I ask Mama to get me a cheapish pair somewhere and put them in the parcel too? Even Viv? Jacek's also back from London. I could have asked him too. Basically, I could have asked about a hundred different people to get a pair for me – but where do I turn to instead? China.

My current daily routine involves washing my hair with heaps of conditioner, combing it for ages (before, a comb would sail through it effortlessly), then I have to blow-dry it for at least fifteen minutes using special anti-frizz lotion you can only find in African shops (there's about one in Poland, never mind Warsaw, and I've found it).

Just when I can't take any more online dating stress or hair disappointment, I'm woken up one morning at five o'clock. It's AB.

'What is it?' I ask, worried that she's fallen again.

She sounds bright and breezy.

'You know you said you wanted to go *na grzyby* (mushroom-picking) – well, today's the day!' She's talking so loudly I can hear her through the ceiling. 'We should go right now. With the rain and the warmth... the forest should be bursting with them.'

'But what about your hip?'
'What about it? Do you want to go, or not?'
'Well, yes.'
'Good. Put on some proper shoes and I'll see you in five minutes.'
'Wait, AB. How are we going to get there?'
'In the car of course.'
'Car?'
'Hurry up!'

The phone goes dead. Forest? What forest? Where? And what's all this about a car? I didn't know AB could drive, let alone have a car – even after all my visits over the years.

I pull on some clothes in an early-morning blur, grabbing my phone and Tata's pocket mushroom book that I've brought to remind me of him. All the common ones have photos, but the rare ones have been drawn by hand, like never-seen extinct creatures.

Still half asleep, I'm out of the flat, fiddling with the door. Locking up seems all the more dramatic at five, with my half a dozen keys rattling around in the quiet of the corridors. It feels as if I'm escaping and locking someone in all at the same time. A thin wash of light graces the bare hard floor. Sharp shadows, broken momentarily by my movements, snap back into place as I move away. I love the fact that there are no coats of magnolia here, just bare concrete. This block has been made to last, come Communism or Capitalism.

Not trusting the lifts at this hour, I gallop up the stairs two by two.

AB's door is ajar and Grzybek's ecstatic. It's obvious we're going somewhere and with AB holding his lead and ball he knows he's coming too. She has one of those contraptions that help you pick up and throw a saliva-sodden ball – a long plastic stick with a circular bit on the end.

'How's your bruise, *Ciocia*?'
'*Ciociu*.' She corrects my Polish at 5.15 a.m. 'Long gone. I'm not too bad.'

Surprisingly AB isn't in her usual skirt and stockings. She's donned tweed-like trousers and some ancient-looking moccasins. They look hand-made, faded and turned up at the toes, slightly fungal even.

'What are you looking at?'

'Your shoes, AB.'

'You're not normal. Come on.'

She grabs her painkillers, her keys and a neckerchief. AB also has on a dappled gold and black satin blouse, with a light jacket on top, all of which clash. Around her neck are glasses hanging on a chain and a pair of binoculars. A couple of carrier bags with food, a map and some water surround her feet in a semicircle, and to complete the sculpture, her varnished wooden walking stick is propped up by the radiator like a straightened out pretzel.

'Where are we going exactly?'

'To Kampinos, outside Warsaw'.

'Kampinos? I've never heard of it.'

'What did you learn at Polish School?'

'All kinds of stuff.'

'Not geography?'

'Not much.'

'Kampinos, child, is vast. It's north-west of Warsaw. It's where all our rivers converge.'

'All of them?'

'Yes. We'll probably see storks,' she says, putting on a wide-brimmed hat. 'That will be fun, won't it?' She knows I love storks, quite a strong Polish trait. Poles take great pride in knowing that one in four of the world's stork population nests in Poland – there's even a Stork Association. One of my other cousins has a stork nesting in his back garden, a sign of luck. Maybe it doesn't count though, as he bought land with the stork's nest in it on purpose. The stork didn't fly past and think, that's a nice spot, I'll nest there. No, the stork got a house of people in its patch, and not vice versa. In fact my cousin also had the stork's nest, or rather the pole the nest sat on, moved, so it would definitely be in his garden. He had to bring in expert nest-movers, or expert pole-movers at the very least, so that the stork (away in Africa at the time), wouldn't notice.

As AB takes the lift, I take Grzybek down the flights of stairs. By the time I arrive on the ground floor, AB's pulled her gherkin of a car out of the long line of garages at the back and has driven round to the front. A tiny old Fiat Panda, light green, going phut-phut-phut at the kerb.

I wonder how long it is since AB, in her late eighties, has been behind the wheel? Once we're on our way I realise from the orchestra of car horns around us that it's probably been 'quite some time'. AB relies on me for news of upcoming traffic and road signs and in a way, we drive the car together.

'*Ciociu* – we're swerving.'

'It's the roads, child! Terrible workmanship!'

She's hunched behind the wheel like a capital 'C,' her face scrunched with concentration.

There's nothing else for it, I start to pray. A tiny card of Jesus with 'Trust in me' written at the bottom swings violently beneath the mirror.

We must be doing over seventy. I steal a sidelong glance at AB, who clearly sees the car as a catapult taking us from A to Z, the driving in between as purely incidental. It's true what they say. Polish drivers make the Italians look mild.

I look the other way at the landscape racing past. It must be that obsessive mushroom-picking gene kicking in. In autumn you see people (usually the elderly) on street corners selling mushrooms in punnets. Passers-by haggle and try to find out where they were picked. On a visit a few years back I asked a man where he'd picked his. 'You can tell me, I'm a tourist,' I said, but he wouldn't.

A driver we pass scowls at us and shakes his fist.

'What is the speed limit in Poland?' I ask AB.

She doesn't answer.

'We'll have breakfast when we arrive,' she pants, staring at the road.

'Dear Jesus,' I pray to myself. 'Please stop swinging so violently.'

Three-quarters of an hour later, we're still on the road.

'Do you go to this forest often?'

'In memory of my parents.'

'What happened to them?'

'They were killed in the Warsaw Uprising.'

'Oh,' I say, taken aback. 'I never knew.'

'I don't talk about it often. As I don't know where Mother and Father are buried, I liked to go there to remember them. There's the insurgents' cemetery in Wola of course, but I like to go to the forest too – it's beautiful and unspoiled.'

'Are there lots of graves there?'

'Cemeteries and monuments, yes. But not just that. We're nearly there now, you'll soon see.'

It's after seven when we arrive. We drive through the park for at least another fifteen minutes, startling a deer along the way, and finally stop, rolling into a clearing.

'Wonderful,' she chuckles. 'Wonderful you've come.'

There are no other cars, only us. It feels like it does when you're camping and you first wake up to check what insects might have slept with you and may have nested in your hair. You adjust to the light and to nature being all around, and to the fact that you're not near anything such as a kettle or a loo.

We eat in the car, and I'm glad of the ham-and-tomato sandwich start to the day. AB has also brought her salt cellar in her pocket and proceeds to salt the contents of her sandwich. She lifts the salt up high and lets a stream pour down.

'We're not going to go too far, but we'll go far enough.'

The forest is stunning. Raw, virgin beauty. Pine trees stretch before us as far as the eye can see and fern sprawls out like a quilt. AB walks from one tree to another, moving back the ferns with her cane.

'Aren't we following a path?' I ask. We've lost sight of the car and it's gone very quiet.

'Don't worry, I know this area like the back of my hand.'

She stops and whips out a penknife to pluck a mushroom out of the earth. It's about five inches high with a broad, pale brown and shaggy mottled cap. How did she spot that, old eagle eyes?

AB's a mushroom expert and knows which ones to avoid, a bit like Tata.

'These are *kanie*,' says AB, slowly straightening up.

I, the novice, watch her work. Our catch grows quickly, and consists of different kinds of mushroom. I happen upon two, their pale hats visible against the dark soil.

'Are you having fun?' she asks.

'Yes. It's just the—'

'— sort of thing that you came out here to do, I know. Now,' she says, delving into the undergrowth again.

While AB forages, I go on the lookout for storks and any other forms of life. I cast my gaze upwards. It's so quiet and vast. Perhaps I would feel more at ease with a ranger, someone who knows the forest – and has a gun. But here I am with a frail old lady on painkillers and a sausage dog as backup.

Grzybek's hardly visible – I hear him rustle and scamper through the undergrowth, occasionally reappearing to check where we are.

Suddenly, there's a flurry from the canopy above, a large bird. There's a shrill, plaintive cry, a bird of prey perhaps. Elsewhere, a woodpecker drums.

A clearing materialises and we come out by the banks of a river, swampy and still. Lo and behold there's a stork's nest as big as a sofa high up in the trees with a black stork standing in it on one leg, his long beak pointing out.

'He's here every year,' says AB, sitting down on a stump. 'At least I think it's him.'

'He's gorgeous.'

AB smiles and nods.

An email arrives, the 'ping' of which makes the stork fly off.

It's a message from Polishmate.com. Another 'fan', probably. I can't resist having a look.

'Birds have got ears too you know,' says AB, as he flaps across the sky. 'But he'll be back.'

Dear Magda *(in bright pink italics)*
You've been favourited! *(not again)*
Click here to read all about Łukasz and message him back *(can't as still don't have password and don't want to message him anyway).*
Happy dating,
Polishmate.com
Helping You Find The Perfect Polishmate

'Something wrong?' asks AB, sensing my displeasure.

'No,' I sigh. I put my phone back in my pocket. 'Is this where you came with your parents, AB?'

'Roughly this area, yes – but we'd go everywhere. Some time after the war, I started to come to this spot once a year on August 1st. On my own.'

'Why that date?'

'It's the anniversary – of the start of the Uprising – don't you know?'

'Not really.'

'Magda,' she huffs, 'you really need to know about these things. It's what you're made up of.'

'I know. I need to know more history. More of everything generally.'

'I haven't been here for the last two years though – because of this nonsense.' She gestures to her hip. 'I'd always say a prayer right here, pick some mushrooms, like I did with mother and father. Then I'd go.'

I leave AB to have some time alone and wander to the tree with the stork's nest. I feel bad I haven't asked her about her family before. I turn to look at her, expecting to find her poised on the stump, absorbed in history. But she's carefully peeling a hard-boiled egg over a paper bag.

'Do you want some?' she calls.

'No thanks.'

'That's why you're so pale and can't get up in the morning.'

I pause, pondering her statement. It's a bit like being dowsed with essence of AB.

'Have you always lived in Warsaw?' I ask, when I go back to join her.

'For most of my adult life. I was a medical secretary after the war you know.'

'But before all of that. You said your parents died in the Uprising. What happened to them, and what did you do?'

'You mean how did I survive?'

'Yes.'

AB adjusts herself, brushing away the crumbs on her skirt.

'The Warsaw Uprising,' she says, taking herself back to that time, 'August 1st, 1944. What can I tell you? Where do I begin? The Armia Krajowa (Home Army) rose up against the Nazis who wanted to have Warsaw as a defensive centre. Sixty-three days we fought them. We thought it would only be for a few days and that the Russians, who were close, would soon come to save us. But they watched us from the other side of the river. Ten thousand fighters and over two hundred thousand civilians died – there were makeshift graves all over the city. Some of the Polish Forces under Soviet High Command made it across – Berling's Army – but they had no reinforcements. Terrible things happened Magda, terrible. We rose up, but so did the Nazis. The Nazis weren't very strong then, but they still had more equipment than we did. They swarmed through the streets, too fast for us to act, burning, killing, destroying. When the Home Army lost, the Soviets came and occupied what little there was left of Warsaw. You should read about it Magda. I mean it.'

I listen, not saying a word.

'The day they took my parents, we were all at home, in the district of Wola, my mother, my father and I. The soldiers came in, and I was upstairs, doing some schoolwork. Suddenly I heard them shouting and slamming things, so what was I to do? I hid – under the bed, stuffing my bag, my books and shoes away too, so it didn't look as if I was there. I heard my mother and father shouting terribly, telling them over and over again there was no one else in the house. If you were over fourteen, which I was, they took you to go and work – slave labour you see – but they could also kill you. I wanted to run down to them, but I was paralysed with fear. Of course, one soldier came upstairs to look around. He came into my room. I saw his big boots stop and turn this way and that way; I could have reached out and touched them. I even heard him breathing, he was so close. My heart was beating so loudly I thought he would hear it. I can see those boots right now – I was sure he was going to look under the bed and pull me out – but he didn't. After what felt like an age, I saw his feet turn and walk away. I heard them go, taking my parents with them. Mother was hysterical. She wasn't calling out my name, she was just crying. I'll never forget her cry. The house fell silent but I was so scared I stayed there for hours, until it was dark.'

Tears fill my eyes. You don't have to talk to someone elderly for long in Poland before you hear dreadful tales about the war. Deep down somewhere, I know I'm also crying over what happened to Mama and Tata. In 1944 Mama would have still been in Siberia not knowing what was happening. Tata meanwhile, would have been doing forced labour as AB had said, in his case working on a German farm.

'Under Communism, child, we weren't allowed to mention the Uprising.'

'Really?'

'Not for decades. Why they didn't burn our house down I don't know. They burned so many homes. When I was sure I was alone, I ran to a neighbour's, a woman we knew. She hadn't been taken either. I stayed the night there – no longer as it wasn't safe. My parents didn't return. With this lady's help I managed to get to my aunt's near Poznań and I stayed with her. I was seventeen, so not a child anymore. But I never saw my parents again.'

We sit on the bench in silence.

'I hope you never experience anything like what happened then,' she says, beginning to pluck at some long blades of grass. 'It was hell on earth. Around a quarter of a million died and many were expelled. And it's odd – when you don't find someone, the mourning goes on. You have times when you're sure they're alive, and then they pass. Yes child, it's true. But,' she rounds off, 'the Polish spirit is to fight on.'

AB starts to lead the way back to the car, with Grzybek at her heels. She's hobbling more now than when we first arrived. We walk in silence, hearing nothing but our breath and our footsteps through the grass.

'Did you ever find out who sent you that rose?' she asks, changing subject.

'Dagmara.'

'Dagmara?'

'Yes. She's put me on an online dating site and it was someone off there.'

'What do you mean?'

'A dating site, AB. It's a way of meeting people. On the internet.'

She listens baffled.

'The things they think of.'

'And not just that. Mama's put me in the *Polish Daily*, but the ad said eighty-nine, not thirty-nine. If you went wandering around the quad AB, you'd probably end up meeting someone.'

AB laughs.

'Why have they done that?'

'To help me meet someone. I'm getting flowers, chocolates, cards. I didn't know anything about it. It's their big mission.'

'That's a bit cheeky.'

We start to climb a little incline and AB slows down.

'Why did you never marry AB? Did you not want to?'

'I did. Of course I did. Come this way, let's walk along here. The path is clearer, and flatter. I did have someone, once. We were engaged.'

'I didn't know that.'

'No one does. Not even your Mother. Or Dagmara.'

'Oh,' I reply, amazed at being party to this private piece of news. 'Who was he?'

She stops for a minute and we find ourselves in a clearing of big beech trees, tall and spread out, like dancers ready for the off.

'You're hearing it all today, aren't you Magda? Are you sure you want to know?'

'Yes of course I do.'

'Well. He was called Władek. I loved him so much. But one day... I couldn't find him anywhere. No one knew where he was.'

'What happened?'

'Now this was before the soldiers came and took my parents. He disappeared, and I kept waiting by his house, leaving him notes. He only lived a street away you see. I waited and waited but neither he nor his family were there.'

'Where had they gone?'

She stops in her tracks.

'Oh child – how can I explain it to you? The time was so chaotic, so full of fear, people were disappearing; everything was being destroyed. You think it was as easy as it is today – like with this site of yours? With all these tricks and clever little gadgets? We were like leaves, blown everywhere. One leaf gets caught here, another gets blown there and that's it. Separated forever.'

We move off again, leaving the path and taking a winding, fern-lined track. I offer AB my arm so she doesn't lose her footing.

'It was so unsafe. And then you see, after my parents were taken, I ended up at my aunt's outside Warsaw. I only came back in 1951, seven years later. I looked for him of course. I went to church, all the places we knew… but everything was bombed – destroyed. And then one day in spring 1956…'

'You saw him?' I ask, my heart filling with hope.

She nods, but her expression isn't happy.

'I did. I remember it so clearly. I was walking along – like we are now – and I saw him from afar, near where the Old Town is. He looked exactly the same. He was walking with a woman who had a baby in a pram. He'd found someone else.'

'Did he see you?'

'Yes. He looked shocked – as if he'd seen a ghost. I looked at him and lifted my hand. To say goodbye.'

'What do you think happened?'

'I met someone who knew us both, months later. Władek married because he thought I'd died in the war. While I was looking for him, they must have escaped and gone somewhere to shelter. And when they returned, I wasn't there. Do you see?'

'Yes, I do.' I pause and we walk on through the ferns. 'That's the saddest thing I've ever heard. Is he still alive?'

AB stops and takes a deep breath.

'Probably. The truth is, I don't know, and that is sad. But he really was my sweetheart.'

My eyes fill with tears.

'And you didn't find anyone else?' I ask. I'm trying to find a happy ending in all of this. AB had been so beautiful.

'No, I didn't. There were fewer men you see. Life was hard.'

I take her puffy red hand but it's she who comforts me.

'Don't cry child,' she says. 'It was a long time ago.'

'It wasn't AB. It wasn't.'

'Many terrible things happened back then. And not just to me. Look at me, I'm all right now aren't I? It was just the way it was.'

We're both subdued during the drive back. I sit back and let the fields sail by and as the city grows closer, blocks repopulate the landscape. How I wish I could turn the clock back for AB – but I can't. Not for her, or for

Mama, whose terrible suffering in the war is never far from my mind. What she and others went through is not long ago – not really. And the effects trickle down the generations.

When we arrive back in central Warsaw, we sit for five minutes in the car in a perfect pocket of forest air, admiring the mushrooms on my lap, earthy and uprooted.

AB becomes upbeat again as she heaves herself out of the car, chatting about how good our pick is and how much she's enjoyed it.

'OK?' she says chucking my chin.

'OK, AB.'

'Don't think about what I said too much,' she says as we walk towards the lifts. 'Now as for this site, child, and Dagmara and your Mama. Either forget it and move on, or why not give it a try? In my day, we would have been glad to have something like this. But we... Magda, we just had our lives.'

We ascend in silence, listening to the sound of the cables running through the shaft.

CHAPTER 10

POKING AT THE RIPPLING LINO

(SZTURCHAĆ LINOLEUM)

'**G**ood hello. I am Raban, a Polish Hungary mix man. Are you interest be my cooker-wife?'

A chat-up line in pidgin English.

My outing with AB and hearing about Władek has made me have a change of heart about the site.

I've been oversensitive!

Had the wrong perspective!

I've not realised that I could be clicks away from the love of my life!

And I mean a few clicks. A few days and weeks of exploring the site and I'm a total convert. It's brilliant! Let's have a closer look at Raban. Raban looks as if his photo has been taken in the mountains somewhere. A dusty face, weathered skin.

'Hobbies: play cards, the drink, woman.'

Goodbye Raban, you're not for me!

It takes time, surfing for men. It's like having a second job.

My reluctance with Polishmate was all to do with Dagmara and Mama cooking it up behind my back. Before I left London, Viv said she was going to join one, so they can't be that bad. I also know quite a few people who have ended up getting married.

I've been on quite a few dates so far. None of them have gone anywhere, but no matter, at least I'm trying.

First I had a date with Wolfgang the German. We met in a dingy basement bar, painted black with fake cobwebs on the ceiling (at least I think they were fake). The bar played heavy metal so loudly that all I could do all night was shout, 'Pardon?' very loudly. Wolfgang also had a spike through his nose and a thin long goatee that looked like a piece of string. It was horrific, and while I didn't want to look at it, I couldn't really avoid it, being where it was, on his face. He also had to move it out of the way when he drank his beer, and couldn't help fiddling with it. He didn't look like that on his photo, that's for sure.

Next there was Marek the graphic designer. I was quite keen on him at first and I even saw him twice. Once for breakfast in Wedel in Szpitalna Street (an olde-worlde cafe miraculously not damaged in the war and now a discreet yet major chain). I adore Wedel and had one of their mammoth breakfasts involving about ten different pastries (mistake: when will I learn that having ten pastries, even two, makes you look greedy) plus one of their luscious thick hot chocolates you can stand a spoon in (I asked them for the recipe once. I fully expected they would give it to me so I could rustle it up at home with a whisk but it's a thousand-year-old, secret family recipe). The second time was in a bar with lots of mirrors and such big leather sofas that I couldn't help but slide down them (mistake: strange position I found myself in got reflected to infinity). When I got fed up of straining to understand Marek's rapid Polish and wondered if I should take a *badanie słuchu* (hearing test) after all the loud techno, I collapsed into a heap and said, 'Sorry Marek, my Polish isn't very good.' He turned to me and said, 'No, it isn't.'

Then there was Piotr, who I met in a cafe-bar that was so dimly lit, I could hardly see his face. I wondered for a moment if I should book in for a *badanie oczu* (eye test) too. Perhaps it was just as well it was dim as we ordered *bigos* – the Polish equivalent of going on a date in England and ordering spaghetti bolognese. *Bigos* is a sloppy, cabbagey mush with bits of sausage and bacon in it. Not something you'd want stuck in your beard if you have one, and Piotr did.

After Piotr there was photoless Michał, who sent me some nice messages. I didn't end up meeting him because when I asked him for a photo, he didn't write back. Who joins a dating website and doesn't put up a photo? Come on!

Next there was Krzysztof, who had an experimental theatre company. I rather liked his Polish intensity, even when talking about fancying a bag of crisps. He had just spent a week locked away in a hut with no food or light in order to get in touch with his 'raw self' on stage. By the looks of his crazed stare, I think he was still in touch with it.

Last as well as least, there was chancer Gregor, a craggy old hack who worked on a suburban newspaper. Either Gregor was about twenty years older than his profile photo or he sent his dad along instead.

I glance at my laptop clock. Crumbs, it's gone six. I'd better stop browsing. Dagmara and Stefan are over for dinner tonight and because of all this surfing, I'm running late. I need to prepare all the vegetables and stuff a joint of lamb the size of a traffic cone with a dozen cloves of garlic. It wasn't easy finding the lamb. I've had it deboned, yet stuck the bone back in for flavour, so Dagmara can't wag her finger and say it's bland, which she will do if it is.

There's also another reason why I'm running late. My hair-straighteners from China have finally arrived. Only five weeks late. The only trouble is, they've not sent hair-straighteners but some grooming device for dogs. When I opened up the box, it was some kind of electric comb for the 'pooch with curly hair'. I've had to package it all back up again and send it back with a letter of complaint. Meanwhile I have a centimetre of straight regrowth to deal with too.

Lamb stuffed with garlic cloves.

Ten more minutes while the oven heats up. The perfect amount of time for another quick mini-surf. To think I can be really productive on the romantic front without leaving my flat, and cook dinner. I love Polishmate. There's a whole world of men out there and they've not all got handlebar moustaches.

Dagmara's delighted that I've changed my mind. At first, she refused to give me the password. But then, when she got so tired and jealous of dealing with all my messages, which she could do nothing with anyway, she yielded.

'The password is the same as the username,' she rang to say.

'You're kidding? And there was I thinking it would be something impossible to guess.'

'You think I'm more cunning than I actually am. I can't believe all the interest you've had.'

'Don't sound so surprised.'

'I only ever had the dregs of society coming after me. At least I've got Stefan now. So is dinner back on?'

'It is.'

Which brings us to today. To deter Dagmara and Stefan from arguing in front of me, I've invited Jacek, who's back from London and is, I've realised, one of these people with an eternal 'feed me' look. It also means he and Dagmara can hopefully sort out the leak, which is fast becoming an interior water feature. She didn't have a plumber of her own and Stefan's pretty useless.

Oh. Oh... Who do we have here? Suddenly, someone rather interesting catches my eye. A Polish professor of history – Paweł is his name – and he works at Warsaw University. Age forty-two (perfect), glasses (understandable) and mad bird's-nest hair (a bit of a turn-off, but I can talk, with my perm). Perhaps I'm subconsciously going for men with bad hair? Mama would be delighted if this one came off. She must never find out.

Time's really getting on, so I'll send him a quick wink. Who'd have thought it could be this much fun? Dagmara was right – why wait until I'm a hundred and two?

Lamb sprinkled with dried rosemary (could not find any fresh anywhere) and in the oven it goes, gas mark something.

I fling open the balcony doors and go outside for some fresh air. On the balcony opposite, a woman who's now familiar to me is hanging out her washing again with a mouthful of plastic coloured pegs. I give her a wave to try to be neighbourly, and do a wide toothy smile across the street so she can definitely see. She looks over, squints, then goes back in.

I feel a bit nervous (terrified actually) cooking for Dagmara. Besides being fussy, she's a stickler for order, so I must tidy up the place or face the music. Cushions. I beat them into submission and create two improbable symmetrical towers on both sides of the sofa. I stand poised, wondering what to tackle next, when I feel my computer beckoning.

Another surf won't hurt and then I'll start the veg.

No reply from Paweł the Prof but it's only been minutes. The knickers-on-the-swing photo and the one of my First Holy Communion are no more. But the straight hair's still there. Is that OK, or is it dishonest? I activate my phone camera and point it at myself. No. I can't.

AB is also pleased that I've taken the plunge.

'Very good news,' she said. 'Good to see you're using your head and taking some action.'

When I told AB that Dagmara was bringing Stefan along for dinner, though, she put her teacup on her saucer in silence and froze. She doesn't like him either.

'Don't bring him up here,' she said. 'I can't bear the sight of him.'

Cutlery out. Forks, knives and spoons for pudding.

By the time I finish circling the table I'm conveniently back at my laptop, and hit refresh.

The Prof has replied! A wink not a message but I can soon remedy that.

Hi Paweł,' I bash out. 'How are you?'

Oh no – the intercom – it must be them and all I've done is put the meat in the oven. I quickly press Send and leap into action.

Dagmara has a key so she and Stefan will be here any minute. They'll have breezed in downstairs and only rung the bell to be polite.

One final tidy, which involves a scan of the flat and a leap into action. Slippers into cupboard (Dagmara hates stray footwear), dirty cups in sink (she despises western laziness) and just as I hear their footsteps approaching, I turn the fruit bowl around so the fresh stuff's at the front.

'*Cze-ść!*' she shouts in a singsong way. I don't know anyone else who can sing while shouting. Dagmara thuds against the door for some reason, like a bull about to break in. I put on my calmest hostess face and open up.

'Darling, it's so kind of you to invite us!' she says, waltzing through the door. Her clothes, my goodness. White ribbed tights, big dark sunglasses and a pink baby-doll outfit with leg-of-lamb sleeves. How apt that she matches dinner.

'Hi Dagmara. Hi Stefan.'

I can't help it, but I sound really unwelcoming.

'Let me have a look at this deluge in the bathroom. Oh no, Magda, it's terrible! I think it's coming from AB's!' she says, off. 'She has to get me, even when I'm no longer here!'

'*Cześć*,' clips Stefan. His voice is deep and gravelly and he looks thinner than before. He steps into the lounge in a pair of pointed shoes with the ends curled up and plants three kisses on my cheeks, doing the whole Warsaw criss-cross thing.

'Not too many of those,' says Dagmara, coming back in. 'I'm counting! Darling, it's so hot in here – phooh!'

'Sorry, it's the oven. I've just opened the doors. Let me get you some drinks.'

I pass her and Stefan a Żywiec beer while she wafts her blouse up and down. Once I made an embarrassing mistake with a Żywiec beer. I went into a restaurant and ordered one, thinking it was a bowl of *żurek* (soup). Five minutes later, a tall, cold foaming glass of beer arrived instead.

'We've brought you your favourite drink,' says Dagmara.

She takes a bottle of Żubrówka out of her handbag and plonks it on the table. This is a yellowy, bison vodka with a blade of special grass in it (I assume it's special and not a couple of blades matured in bison urine).

'Be an angel and pop it in the freezer?'

I jam the vodka between two bags of peas and stand in front of the freezer compartment, enjoying the cold.

'You haven't changed things much,' says Dagmara, looking around the place.

'I didn't bring much over.'

She peers in through the glass oven door.

'What's in here? It looks very interesting.'

'Lamb,' I reply, closing the freezer.

Sheep?' she says with disbelief. 'Stefan,' she yells, even though he's only about three metres away, smoking on the balcony, 'we're having a sheep! No one eats lamb in Poland Magda, it's too tough! Why didn't you ask me? You could have made a simple salad, or some nice, cold soup!'

'You said you wanted meat. I thought a roast would be special.'

I look at her with big, wounded, hostess eyes.

'Oh all right,' she says. 'To be honest, I'm amazed you even found some. It must have been the size of a pony to have a leg that big.'

Stefan muffles a titter. She can be funny, Dagmara.

I start to chop the cabbage on a chopping board I've bought.

'Where's my chopping board?' she asks, clocking the new purchase.

'I bought one of my own.'

'I can see that. Why aren't you using mine?'

'You don't like yours being chopped on, do you?'

When I used Dagmara's chopping board once before, she told me to press the knife through the onion and slow down towards the end so that it wouldn't hack the wood. I was at it for half an hour.

'Don't be silly. That's what it's for,' she says.

'I know. Mine is hacked. Yours is un-hacked.'

'Magda, you're being ridiculous. Use my chopping board!'

'No.'

'I said, use my chopping board!'

'No!'

'Magda, you're making me out to be some kind of crazy person who's obsessive about their possessions!'

'You are!' I say, regretting it immediately.

Stefan looks in, baffled at how quickly voices have been raised, even by our standards, and all over a chopping board. I know it's ridiculous but this is what we're like when we're together. Stefan remains where he is on the balcony. He has a drag on his cigarette and flicks his ash over the edge.

Annoyed, Dagmara picks up a magazine and starts to fan herself. I'm still on my chopping board and am even too scared to chop on that now.

'OK. Use your own board. See if I care.'

'Thank you, I will. Jacek will be here soon,' I add, changing subject. 'So that's good, isn't it?'

'Oh yes, your plumber-painter-builder bloke. I'm glad you mentioned him. Is he any good?'

'Well he does everything at Language Zone, so he must know something.'

'Hang on,' she says, looking at the cabbage which is starting to spill over the worktop. 'Who's all this for? The vegetarian five thousand?'

'Cabbage shrinks when it's boiled. At least it does in England.'

'Well it doesn't over here. Where did you get it? *Towarzystwo warzyw genetycznie modyfikowanych?* (The Society of Genetically Modified Vegetables?)'

Stefan squints at us in the sun and laughs again. Dagmara picks up one of the bigger, outer cabbage leaves that I've discarded and starts to fan herself with that instead.

I should involve Stefan but I honestly can't be bothered. He seems happiest when he's being ignored anyway. He exhales a thin cone of smoke and wipes his nose. Besides, Dagmara requires all my effort.

The computer pings twice.

Perhaps it's the Prof sending two messages in rapid succession?

'I'd better have a look at that,' I say, trying to sound as if it's work. 'Shan't be a sec.'

Dagmara joins Stefan outside while I look at the site: first, a whole row of kisses and a smiley-con from Raban – and second, a message from Paweł.

'What are you doing?' says Dagmara, peering in.

'Nothing.'

'Liar. I can see your reflection on the glass door. You're on Polishmate!'

'Dagmara, you've been trying to get me on it for weeks, now I'm on it, can't you just leave me alone for two minutes?'

I tilt the top of my laptop and angle it so she can't see. Honestly. If Dagmara were a spice she'd be cardamon. You think it makes a difference but deep down, you want to spit it out.

Back to the Prof. I don't care what Raban's put.

'I'm very well,' says Paweł. 'What are you up to? It would be nice to chat.'

'Yes,' I type. 'I'm about to have dinner at home with my cousin and her boyfriend.' (This actually sounds much nicer than it is). 'Perhaps later, if you're about?'

'Can I have a look?' says Dagmara, unable to resist wandering in. 'Is it one of mine I was nurturing for you or is it someone new?'

'None of your business,' I reply, hitting Send.

'Spoilsport. Your Mama will be delighted.'

I snap the laptop shut and glare. I haven't told Mama yet. And never will.

'I'm just going to change. Don't even think of touching my computer. Stefan – watch her.'

I'm not normally this bossy with Dagmara but, sometimes, needs must. She complies, surprisingly, and plonks herself on the black leather sofa in-between the teetering cushion towers which threaten to fall inwards.

In the bathroom, I start to freshen up. My hot face looks like a punchbag and my hair is frizzing up like the matted bit of a corn on the cob, but no matter.

I change my top to one that's loose (spare tyre diminished), put on some powder, some lippy and a spray of perfume. There, done. If only Paweł could see me now. I feel so excited. More excited than I have for ages.

'That's a nice blouse,' says Dagmara as I come out. 'Big and baggy suits you.'

I throw her a dirty look which she doesn't seem to register. She returns to Stefan on the balcony and they intertwine arms like plants that haven't the stalks to stand up on their own.

I crack open more beer and Stefan comes in briefly to put on some terrible Polish music. The CD cover's a combination of women's legs and snakes, woven together into a swirling wreath.

Jacek arrives. I greet him in a pair of thick oven gloves that make my hands look like lobster claws. I'm so glad he's here to normalise the evening.

A quick check on the lamb – it's still pink so I turn the oven up.

'Did you weigh it?' asks Dagmara, seeing me study the tray.

'No. It was just handed to me in a plastic bag. I never weigh lamb. I just stick it in.'

'Oh,' she says, looking worried.

I have to say, it's not looking good. As well as the lamb looking like a bloody rubber stump, the potatoes are pale too. If I dropped one over the balcony, ten floors up, I could probably kill someone. While Jacek and Dagmara pop into the bathroom to poke at the rippling lino, I revive my laptop.

It's Paweł again. Oh I can't deny it, I rather like him, mad hair or not. 'Dinner with your cousin sounds fun,' he says. 'I hope it goes well. Yes let's talk later, or maybe meet up? I'm free tomorrow if you'd like to have dinner. How about a pizza?'

'That would be great,' I reply in a frenzy, hoping I don't sound too keen. 'When and where?'

'Just as I suspected!' says Dagmara, bursting back in. 'Jacek says it's seeping down from AB's too, so it's official! We'll have to go up after dinner to sort it out. How about we crack open that vodka, Magda?'

'Crack away,' I reply, staring at my message and wondering if I should be displaying a little more restraint.

'Oh look – she's at it again.'

'At what?' asks Jacek.

'Looking at that online dating site,' quips Dagmara, pouring out some shots.

'I am not.'

I am, though, and quickly hit Send (stuff being forward).

Jacek looks interested and tries to have a look at my screen without appearing nosey.

'Is that the one you mentioned the other day?'

'Yes,' I reply.

'It's the best,' say Dagmara. 'Polishmate.com. Not that I need it now of course,' she says quickly, chucking a suddenly surly Stefan under his unevenly bristly chin. 'Magda's seen the light. She's ditching British men, isn't she Tiger? She's going to steal one of ours instead!'

'Dagmara,' I say, trying to stay calm. 'Please could you serve Jacek a drink while I check the meat?'

'Sure. I can do that. I can do that as easily as you could have weighed the lamb on those weighing scales just there.'

She chinks out some icecubes while I check the lamb again.

Oh no, it still looks raw.

I look at the clock. It's half past eight already.

Alternatives, it's time for alternatives.

It's never going to cook now, not unless there's a nuclear setting.

I try to act calm while going through the fridge.

To cap it all, AB rings. Can Stefan stop smoking on the balcony, the smoke is wafting up into her lounge.

If tonight comes off it'll be a miracle.

Dinner is a slaughterhouse. By the time we eat, it's nearly ten o'clock and Dagmara and Stefan have had far too much to drink while waiting.

I give Dagmara the end bits, which are slightly more done, and some of the better-looking potatoes. The cabbage is cold and watery, the carrots like boiled wood. As for the gravy, it's come out dark and lumpy. I had to thicken it at the end and now it looks as if it's got a colony of tadpoles in it. I pile Stefan and Jacek's plates high – just a morsel on mine as my appetite has gone.

'There,' I say, passing them their plates. 'Sorry the spuds are like goose eggs.'

'Thanks,' says Stefan, staring at his plate.

'Thank you,' says Jacek picking up his fork. 'It looks much better than anything I could ever make. My first English roast.'

'And probably your last,' says Dagmara.

The dinner that has taken me over four hours to prepare is over in minutes. There's something really rather tragic about the sound of plates being stacked after a disappointing meal. Sort of clattering and irregular.

'*Dobrze,*' says Dagmara when she's done. Not so much a compliment as a statement that it's over. Stefan burps and yawns.

The conversation moves on to Jacek's London trip. Dagmara manages to crowbar in her hatred of baked beans, how the English care more for dogs than human beings and how they take hours to say goodbye after dinner.

'They say goodbye on the sofa, they say goodbye in the kitchen. Then, as if that's not enough, they say goodbye on the doorstep, in the garden and as they're climbing into their cars. Then, when they get home, they send an SMS – to say guess what – thank you and goodbye – all over again!'

I look over at Jacek who is either surprisingly interested or is doing a great job at lying.

He explains he didn't have time to see any sights as he was on a twelve-hour shift every day. He shared a flat in Seven Sisters which he called Seven Poles, as there were seven of them there. I laugh at his joke but Dagmara and Stefan look on blankly.

Why oh why has tonight not worked? I always imagine dinner parties going so effortlessly and smoothly. Perfect guests, smiling and laughing away, flowing conversation, a warm glow on everyone. But this? I'd rather be with the Prof somewhere.

Before pudding, Dagmara and Jacek go upstairs to AB's to 'discuss' the leak, leaving me and Stefan together.

Deflated but persevering, I make a start on the lemon sponge. As I put the bowl in the microwave, Stefan gets up and shuffles over.

'You're making it in that thing there?' he asks, getting up close.

'It'll only take five minutes. Not like the lamb.'

'Only five minutes? Amazing.'

I'm about to expound on the wonders of microwave puddings when a big hot hand arrives on my bum. For a moment I think it's my own but it can't be – both my hands are right in front of me and are busy holding cutlery.

'Ooo! Stefan! What do you think you're doing?'

'What do you think?' He smiles and leans towards me, beery-breathed, angling for a kiss. Upstairs, I can hear voices and chairs and things being moved around. 'Come on,' he leers. 'You don't need that stupid site. Just put on a short skirt and you'll find a fella in no time!'

'Stefan!'

'Come on. You don't like Dagmara anyway.'

'What's liking got to do with it?'

His face comes towards mine, but being much more sober I'm off in a flash. Within seconds I'm dialling AB's number, my body like jelly.

'Are you done?'

'What?' she yells. 'I can't hear you.'

I can hear lots of banging.

'AB. Tell them to come down – now!'

'What?'

'Tell them to come down!'

'There's no need to shout!'

Stefan pads off to the bathroom while I switch the microwave on and stare at the turning plate behind the smoky-brown glass door.

I don't care if he's drunk or not – it's not on.

Dagmara's in haggling mode when she comes back down. She seems even more drunk now as her hair is everywhere and she staggers around. I dread to think what AB must have thought. The vodka must have hit her. Unusual, as while Poles might be known for drinking a lot, they pride themselves on knowing how to drink, i.e. properly paced and with a meal. I guess it's because we ate far too late.

She happens upon the remainders of the lamb. 'Poor little sheep!' she sings, 'poor little sheep! Where's Stefan?'

'In the bathroom.'

As if on cue, Stefan comes out and the two of them head for the sofa where they collapse in a heap and fall asleep.

The microwave pings. Dagmara and Stefan are too far gone for the yellow gloopy sponge that I start to serve up. It's just me and Jacek and we go out onto the balcony, our pudding vaguely luminous underneath the stars.

'It's good you've struck a deal with her,' I say, swallowing the delightfully sweet hot sponge.

'Yes,' he says. 'Mmm, this is really good.'

'Thanks.'

'I don't think it will be too hard a job. I just need to order some parts.'

'I'm sorry about the raw dinner and those two,' I say, glancing over my shoulder, then staring at the city lights against the bluish nightlight. Below, the traffic's petering out and only the trams can be heard as they pull in to a stop.

'It's no problem,' he replies, looking in at them. 'They're not going anywhere tonight, are they?'

I turn round to see Dagmara and Stefan deeply exhaling and inhaling in unison, fast asleep. I never thought of that but Jacek's right. Dagmara and Stefan are out for the count. I'm going to have to sleep with him just next door. Poor Dagmara. Poor me too. What on earth am I going to do?

As Jacek leaves, he sees a photo of Mama and Tata in a frame on a shelf. They're at Robin Hood airport, near Doncaster. They have their backs to the camera as they're looking at the runway.

'That's a nice photo,' he says, slipping on his jacket.

'It's my parents.'

'Where were they going?'

'Nowhere. They've never flown. They just like to watch the planes. Bye Jacek. Thanks for coming. Goodnight.'

'*Cześć*,' he says.

I wave him off as he walks down the harshly lit corridor. And were I not so preoccupied with Stefan and Dagmara, and writing to Paweł on my laptop, I might have thought more about his lingering look as he turned and said goodnight.

CHAPTER 11

MOISTURISER ... THEN FOUNDATION – NOT TOO MUCH (KREM NAWILŻAJĄCY ... POTEM PODKŁAD – ALE NIE ZA DUŻO)

The refurb at Language Zone is nearly complete. Old is making way for new in every nook and cranny: new carpets, new chairs and a suite of new computers and listening booths. Best of all, the wiring's been done. I no longer live in fear of flicking on a light and bursting into flames.

That said, when I went into the office for my register at lunchtime, I thought for a moment that Pan Tadek may have taken the modernisation a step too far. I found two twenty-something-year-olds typing away in place of Pani Dąbrowska and Pani Raszewska. Thankfully, they haven't been replaced permanently, they've just gone on holiday to Lithuania.

I headed down the corridor to take my beginners' class, springing along the thick new carpet. I hoped that throwing myself into the teaching would be a good way of:

a) not thinking about my date with the Prof later and

b) stopping thinking about Stefan too.

He is the cloud to my otherwise silver lining.

Should I tell Dagmara, or not? The thought of saying anything to her makes my mind tie itself into a horrible knot.

Advantages of telling her:
1. She will know what a rat he is and end it with him for ever
2. Justice would be done, whatever justice is

Disadvantages of telling her:
She will probably
1. blame me
2. not believe me
3. kill me

Taking class didn't help that much. Half way through, Pani Teresa tugged at my sleeve. The headphones I had clasped around my head weren't plugged in she said. I thanked her and said I was having 'a little think'.

It's half past five. One and a half hours before meeting the Prof and I'm beside myself with nerves. Aren't dates meant to be fun?

I've eaten the last of my chocolate from Mama – now I just feel sick and on a massive sugar high. I've got just over an hour to do my hair and somehow get myself looking fantastic.

I've bought a big fat roller brush and some Afro hair-calming lotion from an ethnic stall in the market.

Back to getting dressed. What am I going to wear? I start to play mix and match with the items in my rather sparse wardrobe – nothing really goes. My floaty orange and red top's a no-no as there's a grease stain down it. Something nice but not over the top.

Jacek's started work at AB's. I can hear AB firing out instructions amid bursts of hammering and floorboards being taken up. I'm glad he's up there keeping her company and sorting things out. It means I can stress out in peace.

HAIR GRAPH: Implements and time spent wrestling with them

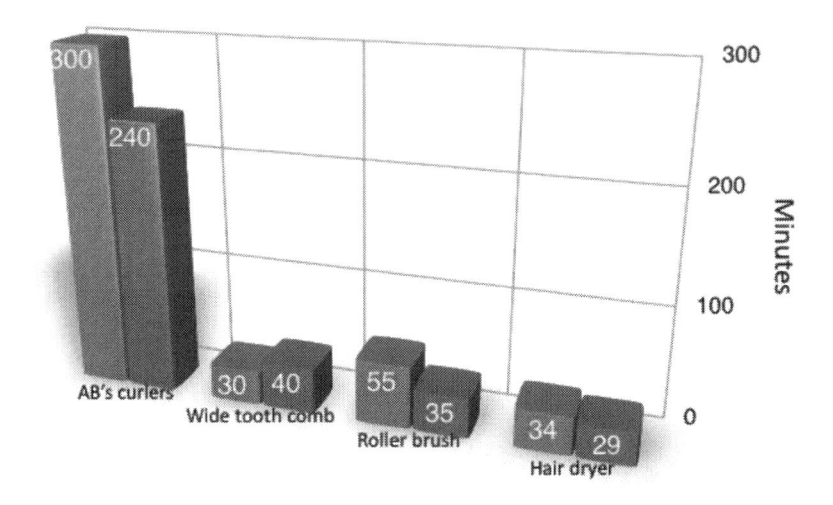

■ Yesterday ■ Today

- AB's curlers: 300 / 240
- Wide tooth comb: 30 / 40
- Roller brush: 55 / 35
- Hair dryer: 34 / 29

(Minutes)

I make some tea, dunk a tasteless Polish biscuit in it, then put the whole thing in my mouth so that it dissolves into a goo. I've also got an oat bran face pack smeared on my cheeks to try to reverse the merciless call of gravity. I find I'm needing more and more of these. My face is falling like a soufflé when you open the oven door too early. How is one meant to carry out these procedures with a boyfriend or spouse looking on?

I told AB I had a date with someone really rather nice. She's ecstatic.

While my face pack hardens, I Google the Prof – Paweł N. Borkowski. Goodness, why didn't I do this earlier? He has five pages of entries all to do with history or law! He must have started reading when he was a baby. He's written heaps of books, given countless lectures and he's the head of the law department and about a dozen societies.

There's also a book I recognise: *The Companion to European History*. It's on Dagmara's shelf. I've frequently looked at this book and marvelled at its thickness but never read it. I have a quick flick through. Golly. It turns out he's written the foreword and a very long chapter on the Katyń Massacre of World War II. Even his footnotes have footnotes. There are several black and white grainy photos of this dreadful crime, when over twenty thousand Poles – soldiers, police officers, landowners, lawyers, officials and priests – were murdered by the Soviet secret police in 1940. Stalin blamed the Nazis and the truth only came out in around 1990. Some of the pictures are of ordinary men – possibly the victims – some are of generals and some are of huge pits. If you didn't know the chapter these photos were in, they would look like archaeological excavation sites, not mass graves. I snap the book shut.

Next, I Google myself, as he's bound to have Googled me. Quite a few entries, all of them as an exec for Adspeak with the different ads I've worked on, i.e. toilet detergent products. Great.

My face is starting to crack, so I wash off the face pack and rinse away the ensuing porridge. My faces re-emerges taut but soft, clean yet perfumed.

Moisturiser... then foundation – not too much.

The truth is, I know so little about Polish history. I only know the Katyń stuff because of an Andrzej Wajda film I saw. Paweł and I will be on opposite ends of the scale. All those dates and treaties.

Blusher... lipstick... mascara.

He's bound to want to know about my Mama and Tata. And then there's Grandad who was in Persia, Egypt and who fought at Monte Cassino in when was it again? 1944 – and it opened up the Allies' road to Rome. (Best check up on facts for that in case he tests me.)

There. Curlers out, lotion on. I roll out a sausage of cotton wool and tuck it in around my hairline over my ears so it doesn't run into my eyes. As I sit with the hairdryer on, and enjoy the warm air blowing out onto my head, I put my cup of tea on Paweł's big thick book and wonder what will happen.

After a dash through a freak summer downpour, which dampens my blow-dried Marie-Antoinette curls and reactivates my frizz, I reach the pizzeria and peer in through the window. I can't see a man with bird's-nest hair inside, but then again, I'm early.

I'm led to a table by the window and try to look calm. It's a nice place actually, cosy and authentically fake at the same time. Plastic lobsters and starfish have been nailed to the walls and there are paintings of Tuscan vineyards and villas across the back. I'm glad I'm early. I can compose myself and adjust my mask of calmness until it's perfectly in place.

It's pleasantly busy, with couples chinking their cutlery as they work through their pizzas. I nibble on a complimentary olive. What will he be like?

Raindrops blur the windows and fuzzy-edged passers-by hurry past. Green gingham curtains have been painted on the windows for a quaint peasant look and each table has a candle in a bottle caked in years of dusty wax. Classical music tinkles from a piano at the back and every time the kitchen door opens, aromas of garlic, tomato and artificial air-freshener pulse out in waves.

Seven o'clock comes. And goes. This must be a *znak* (sign). That's what Mama would say, and AB and Dagmara.

At seven fifteen I receive a text.

Ten minutes, am in a taxi. Sorry.

It's OK, I tap back, unimpressed. **I'm sitting by the window.**

He'd better have a really good excuse because it's a cardinal sin to be late for a first date.

I ask for some more olives and peruse the menu. Pizza with cheese, pizza with minced pork – pizza with sauerkraut?

I practise some poses for when he arrives. Ones that say poise, confidence and glamour, ideally. Hand under chin, legs demurely crossed – hang on a minute though, I think I'm getting cramp. I think I can see him coming!

The revolving doors spin around rapidly, whirling in a man with very wild hair. It's him! Excitement pushes all annoyance out of the way.

A waiter greets him warmly and whisks away his coat. Paweł looks around, turning his head this way and that, looking, for some reason, everywhere but my way.

I uncoil myself from my sophisticated pose and stand up, snapping back to shape like an unscrunched silicone mould.

'Paweł! Hello!' I shout, hoping my teeth are olive-free.

Heart rate while waiting for the Prof

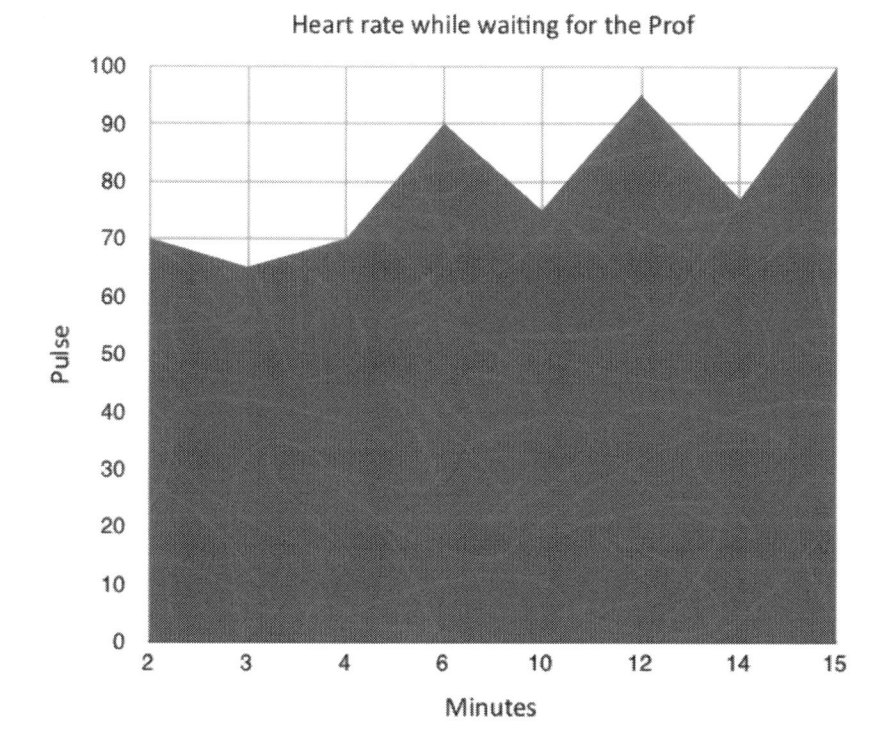

(Chart: Pulse vs Minutes. X-axis: 2, 3, 4, 6, 10, 12, 14, 15. Y-axis: 0 to 100. Values approximately: 70, 65, 70, 90, 75, 95, 75, 98.)

'I'm so sorry I'm late,' he says, coming over. 'It's unforgivable. I had an interview that ran late.'

He calls the same waiter who produces a wine list in a plastic jacket to protect it from splashes of tomato and oil.

'Oh it's fine,' I reply sitting back down.

'No, it's not.'

'I know myself that students turn up with questions at all kinds of hours.'

'It wasn't a student,' he replies. 'It was an interview for the 7.30 p.m. news.'

'The news on TVP1?'

'Yes.'

He clears his throat and flicks through the menu while I bite on an olive, forgetting it has a stone in it. AB watches the 7.30 news every day, so she will have seen him. She makes her supper by it, shouts and tuts at it, as does most of Poland!

'It was nothing,' he says sensing my surprise. 'They always want you at the last minute and they take longer than they say they will. It's very rude. I should have said no.'

'No, no. It's fine.'

Thank God Mama doesn't know who I'm with right now as she'd be telling all the neighbours and cartwheeling down the street.

'Magda's seeing a Professor! From Warsaw University!'

Paweł crunches on a breadstick while I steal a glance at his face. I can't see it properly because of all his hair.

My initial excitement has sort of sunk to the floor somewhere and I can't muster it up again. I can't deny it, I don't think he's my type.

Or, could he be?

While I try not to pick at the wax on the bottle, Paweł orders some wine and when it arrives, he invites me to taste it. I have a sip. It's reassuringly lukewarm and slightly acidic, not bad for Poland, where bars often advertise the fact that they serve the 'cheapest wine in Warsaw' as if it's a good thing. I say it's nice and the waiter tops me up.

While Paweł delves into his menu and I look again at mine, I try to examine his mountain of dark hair which, wrapped around his head, looks like a sort of turban.

'Forgive me for saying this,' he says, blushing yet forthright, 'there's something different about you.'

'Really?' I ask, knowing full well what he means.

'It's your hair. It's curly. On your picture, it's straight.'

'Oh that,' I reply, blushing with a half laugh. 'It's only temporary. I was trying something new – for this evening.'

'It's nice,' he says, the right thing to say. 'Now, this will be my treat. Would you like pizza or pasta?'

We both choose pizza, and after we order, I return to the topic of his interview.

'So what was it about?'

'Some war criminal on trial in the Hague. It'll drag on and on like it always does. More wine?'

'Please. It sounds very interesting.'

'Not as interesting as working in advertising. What sort of ads were they?'

I'm not going to talk about 'Kleen Loo' or Magi-mould' with Paweł now or ever.

'Some household products you wouldn't know about.'

'Oh go on.'

'No.'

'Really?'

'Yes. It's confidential I'm afraid,' I lie, 'I had to sign a special contract – in case of competitors.'

Our meals arrive. Never have I been so relieved to see a twelve-inch Pizza ai Fungi.

I'm not remotely hungry, having stuffed myself on chocolate, macaroons, olives and breadsticks. Nevertheless, I start on my rim so as to save the big splodge of yellow cheese in the centre till last. Fancy cheese hasn't hit Poland yet – but melted cheese has. As for Paweł, he starts in the middle of his pizza and works his way out. Wonder what that means?

It's odd, but as we talk, the way I see Paweł and his hair seems to metamorphose. It's the interview that's done it. It's gone from hairdo of a vagrant to hairdo of a genius.

I mention that I browsed through his book before I left. It's probably having a tea ring printed on it as we speak. I find myself telling him about my family's experiences during the war well before he asks me. I start to trot off my spiel; Tata doing forced labour in Germany and my Grandad (on Mama's side) being in a Russian gulag. I'm finding this emotive, a bit like telling a doctor about your symptoms can sometimes be emotive. 'It sounds like your grandfather ended up with Anders?'

'Yes.'

'The army of seventy thousand formed from the original one and a half million deportees, no less?'

(Uh-oh. The history exam's started.)

'Yes. The Second Corps I think.'

I know this from his gravestone in Newark where several hundred Polish Airmen are buried.

'Amazing he survived. Did he know Wojtek the Soldier Bear?' he says, thankfully lightening the tone. 'He was with the Second Corps. You must know all about it – wonderful story.'

Actually, I do know quite a bit about this bear cub Polish soldiers found in the Persian outback. He was an orphan cub and they adopted him as a mascot.

'Yes, yes,' I nod.

Wojtek, as he was called, went on to be raised by the soldiers and he even learned to smoke and drink beer like the soldiers. It sounds like a joke but it isn't. There's old black and white footage of him loading shot into a cannon and when it came to crossing the waters to get to Monte Cassino, the soldiers hid him and added him to their passenger list, making out he was one of them.

Next, Mama. I only have to say Siberia and Paweł nods. The times that's happened in England, well. Never.

He dabs his lips with his napkin.

'I know some people who were deported to Siberia, although they're dying out now. Where exactly was she?'

'Oh, er, wait a minute – it's gone straight out of my head.'

I know this sounds odd, but even Mama gets mixed up. Some days she says Kazakhstan, other days Siberia, as sometimes, northern Kazakhstan gets rolled into Siberia. 'She mentions Kokchetav,' I add.

'Ah, Kokshetau, formerly Kokchetav,' says Paweł, steepling his hands. 'Have you ever been?'

'No,' I reply. 'I'd like to, one day.'

'You must.'

To be honest, I've always thought I'd like to visit, but where would I go? Would I land in Kokshetau and head for the outback? Or would I close my eyes and put a pin on a map?

'Kokshetau's the administrative capital of the Akmola region now – and it would probably be very interesting to you,' he says, unaware that I've already been there and back in my head in the past few seconds, and discounted the idea as pointless. He passes me some garlic bread, cut on the diagonal and smeared with melted butter. 'It would be a memorable journey, if you ever went. Very different to the journey your mother would have done, of course.'

'Indeed,' I reply, hurtling cattle trains filled with terrified people flashing through my mind. She was only three when she was sent there in 1940 and she returned in 1946 with her brother, Dagmara's late dad.

'She often says she can't remember anything about it.'

'You mean she doesn't want to. If she was nine or ten when she left... she'll remember lots, surely?'

'I suppose that could be true.'

'Must, not could.'

He pours some more wine. I dwell on his words. Mum always says she can't remember, but is it a lie? A way of shutting the door on the too painful past? I feel as if I've always been rattling at this door, trying to force it open – but all this noise between Mama and me – it gets in the way. Or maybe noise is precisely what she wants?

'It's common to not want to talk about it. Few people do,' he adds in a reassuring tone.

'I think I'd want to talk about it all the time.'

'You say that. But would you?'

I look through the painted mock-curtains out onto the streets, grey and wet.

'Shall we change the subject?' he suggests over the chatter and clatter of cutlery on plates. 'Talking about this is hard for you, isn't it?'

'No no,' I reply surprised, 'it's fine. It's not hard. My mother mentions howling wolves the most. And being cold and hungry. She lost her mother and sister to TB.'

'It was a terrible episode in Poland's history,' he says gently. 'A forgotten odyssey.'

We turn to the dessert menu, which seems to vanish from my eyes as my attention wanders.

Trifle, or ice-cream?

Siberia, or Kazakhstan?

I remember when I was around eight, Mama would draw the curtains in my room every night. Occasionally, she would throw out a morsel about the war.

She might say how when they went to sleep, there was often no night because of the light on the snow. I'd never grow tired of hearing this – it always fired a match in my imagination.

Oh how I wished that I could have seen this snowy, light-filled night in that wasteland of pain. Perhaps because I wanted to take her pain away. Or perhaps because I wanted to own this tale of survival myself.

I'd imagine a vast land covered in snow, existing only in different tones of black and white. I'd imagine blizzards, wolves howling in the distance and people clothed in rags, freezing and desperate.

Most of my knowledge about the period comes from reading about it or from Dagmara, who can talk about the subject obsessively.

February 10th, 1940.

It was what they dreaded: three loud knocks in the middle of the night – armed Russian officers at the door.

The men were taken first – they were taken to the gulags in deepest Russia. A few nights later, the soldiers came back for the rest of the families. Mama and her family were given just fifteen minutes to pack at gunpoint. The terror they must have felt. What would they take? Food and clothes? Or precious items too?

They were herded onto cattle trains along with many other families.

No seats. No toilets. People just standing, all cramped together.

It was minus forty degrees, so cold that people's tears froze on their faces. Even some of their captors cried, knowing the people's fate.

They were left on the trains over night and the next day, the frozen dead were dragged out. After that, the journey began. Weeks and weeks to Siberia – huddled crying in those trains, being fed watery soup and hard black bread, not knowing how long the journey would last.

Over one and a half million Poles were sent east to die in four waves of deportation.

'Where are we going?' I imagine Mama asking, aged three, wrapped in her green and brown blanket. 'Where are we going?'

'Would you like to meet again?' he asks at the end of the evening as he walks me home. 'I've really enjoyed your company. You don't have to say now, if you're not sure.'

His eyes are a-twinkle as he flags down a taxi. I wave and watch his car disappear down a side street.

It's late, but when I turn and see that, eleven floors up, AB's light is still on, I can't resist calling on her.

'I didn't know it was Paweł Borkowski you were meeting!' says AB amazed, as I take my coat off in a haze.

'Neither did I!'

She throws the kettle on.

'He was on the news just a few hours ago! Talking about some Bosnian Serb trial!'

'Yes, that's why he was late, AB!'

She shoves some biscuits onto a plate and motions me into the lounge while she makes tea. 'I want to hear all about it!'

I sink into the cushions on AB's prized armchair. Now I'm here, I'm not sure I should have stopped by. I'm – I don't know what – rather overwhelmed. By Paweł, by what to do about Stefan... and by Mama and Siberia.

'Sorry, AB,' I say, getting up to go. 'I wanted to pop round – but I'll tell you all about it tomorrow. Promise.'

'Oh,' she says, disappointed. 'Didn't it go well?'

'It did...'

'But?'

'I mean he's very nice and everything...'

'But?'

'Oh. I may as well tell you now. I don't know, AB. He's just not—'

'Your type? How do you know what your type is Magda?'

'I don't know. I think that in a way, I'd feel as if I was in a trial of my own all the time. About Poland and Polish history.'

'Don't be silly.'

'No, AB.'

'I think he would have quite liked the fact you didn't know who he was. It would have given him a clean slate. Don't write him off just yet. He sounds nice. And it's not every day you get to meet someone like that.'

She gives me a funny look that says she's going to Oh-Magda me about something else.

'What's that in your hair?' she asks instead. 'It looks like oats.'

'Oats?'

I take a look in the hall mirror. I've got face pack in my hair. Heaven knows what Paweł must have thought. She picks it out, hoping, I think, for more information.

'Your Mama rang.'

'Right.'

'Don't worry. I didn't say a thing.'

'Thanks.'

'Jacek's made a wonderful start on the bathroom – have a look.'

'Nice,' I say peering in at the excavation by the boiler.

'Off to bed then, young lady. You need your beauty sleep. For the next one you meet!'

I wonder about telling her about Stefan and the other night but think better of it. She'll have me on the phone to Dagmara immediately.

I bid her goodnight and leave, clicking the door shut before Grzybek runs out, and amble down the grey stairs with a slight swagger. I feel quite pleased because even if I don't see the Prof again, I've done it, I've been out on a date and it's not been a disaster. I feel quite excited. Brave. And it's completely different from my life in London.

Maybe I will see him after all.

Advantages of being Paweł's girlfriend:
1. My Polish will be perfect in no time
2. We can talk about Siberia from dawn till dusk
3. I'll have had an interesting life going to soirées with all his brainy friends

Disadvantages:
1. I'm not sure I fancy him.

I go out onto the balcony and look up. No chance of it not being night out here. A sharp crescent moon hangs poised in the sky.

I lean back so that the horizon is no more and all I can see are thousands of stars. I could be in any country now – England... Poland... Siberia... any country.

CHAPTER 12
MAMA ON A PLANE
(MAMA W SAMOLOCIE)

I'm in a bakery, waiting to be served. I'm waiting patiently and politely behind a middle-aged couple who are debating how much cake to buy for some special occasion – in Poland, cake's often bought by weight. They're talking about a *sękacz*, a golden-yellow, regional cake that's made with hundreds of egg yolks and is baked over a spit so that it comes out spiky (weird, I know). The spiky bits are formed as the batter, applied bit by bit, oozes down as the cake turns.

As I wait, two more customers sail in and barge in front of me. Now I know that Poles can't queue and that I should be more used to it by now, but I still find it annoying.

Both customers are standing further along the counter and I don't know what to do. Do I move and try to recreate the queue over by there, or is this the 'real queue' and if I move I'll lose my place? They don't look bothered. The other thing that's racking up the tension is that there is only one loaf left and by rights it's mine. There's only one thing to do, that thing where you stand with your mouth open, ready to speak as soon as is physically possible and then get in there as quickly as you can. Just as my turn approaches, AB rings. I can't ignore AB's calls in case it's something serious, so I answer, hoping it doesn't undermine my place in the queue.

'Hello AB?'

'Magda!' She sounds bright and cheery so it can't be an emergency.

'AB, I'm just about to be served in the bakery. Do you need anything? As I'm next.'

'Magda, guess what, your Mama's here! Can you buy some nice cakes for us all to enjoy when you get back?'

'Mama? Mama? Are you joking?'

I must be hearing things, or maybe AB's hallucinating because of a change in her medication. Mama can't be here, it's not possible. She'd never leave Tata, the house, her pots and pans and the blackbirds in the garden that can't survive without her. Also, she's terrified of flying.

'Dagmara's here too. She just popped by to check on your plumber friend's work so far. We've had such a wonderful reunion! I wouldn't have been more surprised if my own parents had turned up at the door!'

'So you weren't expecting her either?'

'No.'

'How long's she here for?'

'Just the weekend.'

Thank God.

Sękacz couple pay and go, and the other two customers swoop in like vultures before me, ignoring me completely as I stand there, phone to ear and mouth wide open. My loaf goes to the first woman, who leaves, and the second woman takes whatever rolls are left, and cakes.

'Hello Magda!' Mama yells in the background.

'Hello... Mama?'

'Is the bakery far?' she says, off.

'No. It's just around the corner,' Dagmara chips in.

'What cakes would you like, Bolesława? Tell me, Magda's about to be served.'

'*Proszę*! (Can I help you?)' says bakery woman to me. I point to the handset.

'She can get me anything!' says Mama. 'A doughnut? We'll be having dinner later, won't we?'

'Of course, *Ciociu*,' says Dagmara in the background.

What is Mama doing here? Can't I get away from her anywhere? This is my new nest and she's crashed into it, like a big cuckoo. I know what this is. She's doing a spot check, that's what, an impromptu spot check – on where I live, my job, AB, everything.

'We'll have doughnuts if they've got them,' says AB, coming back. 'Can you believe your Mother has already done a three-hour bus tour, been to the Old Town and been shopping?'

'I can believe it, AB. Mama's capable of anything.'

Scuttling back home, my world upside down, I wonder where Mama will be staying. Not with me, surely? There isn't room, but Mama doesn't do hotels, they're for royalty only. And how is Tata going to manage? He doesn't know how to use a tin-opener, never mind cook a meal. Mama has never left him for more than a couple of hours. Seeing Mama must have been a shock for AB too. They haven't seen one another for how long? Over fifty years!

Deep breath as I knock and enter. Inside, Mama is sitting on AB's sofa in a flowery dress (M&S label hanging out, she must have just bought it) and a pair of large-framed sunglasses on her forehead (must be from the seventies). By the looks of all the tissues and their teary eyes, they've had a good cry, and by the amount of crockery on the table, they've had several pots of tea and a round of sandwiches.

'Mama. You're... you're...'

'Here!' chips in Dagmara. 'Isn't it amazing?'

'Why have you come?' I ask, ignoring Dagmara. 'What about Tata? And the house?'

'They'll survive without me. I just thought I'd surprise you.'

'How did you get to the airport?'

'Tata took me. We had quite an emotional departure actually. I think because he knew I was going a long way, not just to the supermarket. Anyway, Magda, I thought you'd be pleased.'

'I am. I think.'

'Magda, your hair.' (Oh dear, I forgot about that.) 'It's... it's...'

'A disaster?' says Dagmara.

'You look as if you've tried to use the gas-ring at close range and set yourself on fire.'

'It'll grow out, Mama.'

'In a year.'

'You've lost weight too,' she adds. I know exactly what this means and it's not about weight. She thinks I'm not coping without her cooking.

'Lost weight?' asks Dagmara. 'No, '*Ciociu*! Magda looks...healthy.'

'Magda, why didn't you tell me Poland is normal? I've been in culture shock all day. Cars, buses – people in clothes! I've been to that shopping centre – the one with the fancy glass roof...there's every shop you can think of!' (She points to her new dress.) 'Have you been there yet?'

'Yes. Once. I keep telling you that everything here is different.'

'Oo – listen to you, your Polish is better than mine, now.'

'Where are you staying?' I ask, glancing at her worryingly large suitcase.

'Here,' says AB, patting the sofa. Thank God.

'Before you worry, I'm only here for the weekend.'

'Good. I mean, how nice. Fantastic. Great.'

'I'd like to have stayed longer, but when all is said and done, I do have to think of Tata. I've got the neighbours looking in on him and meals marked up in the fridge. '*Ciociu*,' Mama adds, turning to AB, 'are you sure it's all right me staying, with all this work in the bathroom? I could always stay with Magda. That would be all right, wouldn't it Magda?'

AB must sense me nearly faint on the spot because she jumps straight in.

'After over fifty years of not seeing you, *kochana*, it doesn't matter what's happening here! Of course it's fine. How we've both aged,' she laughs. 'We're both old women now! You in your seventies, me nearly ninety!'

'I only thought I was going to England for a fortnight,' continues Mama. 'To see Father. And then when I fell ill, everything changed.'

'I know,' says AB. 'I was so worried. So worried. No one told me anything,' she says, turning towards me, 'but how could they? We had no phones back then, no internet, no mobiles, nothing.'

They take one another's aged hands and hug. Perched on the sofa, they look like a pair of plump, ragged birds. I glance over at Dagmara, who for once looks moved. I guess it is moving, really. When all is said and done, this is a momentous, emotional reunion for Mama and AB.

I know what Mama's referring to when she mentions falling ill and going to see her father. She's referring to her trip to England – the trip that would bring her to Yorkshire for the rest of her life. It was 1957 and the Red Cross contacted Mama through their international tracing service to say her father was alive, not dead, and working in a mine in Doncaster (the irony, he went from a gulag to north of England). Grandad ended up in Doncaster along with a whole community of Poles, displaced after the war. One of my most vivid memories of him, a man who'd fought in battle after battle and walked thousands of kilometres across the Soviet Union to join Anders' army, is of him making me baked beans on toast as I watched *Play School* on TV.

Mama, around twenty by then, was only meant to stay in England for a month, but while she was out there, something major happened. She grew very ill, too ill to travel, and almost died from a rare kidney condition which had been triggered, apparently, by being exposed to TB in Siberia. The doctors didn't know what was wrong at the time – they couldn't agree on what she had – and to make things worse, Mama couldn't speak English and explain what might be happening. She was slipping away, hour by hour. Thanks to one persistent young doctor, they diagnosed the disease just in time to save Mama's life, but too late to save her from permanent damage to her legs. She would never walk properly ever again and they also said she would never have children. Of course, I am living proof that that wasn't true!

During her time in hospital, she met and fell in love with Tata. He knew my Grandad and accompanied him on visits, as his English was better than Grandad's and he could talk to the doctors. Weeks turned into months and months into years – and before she knew it, Mama was in England for good. Mama learned English from children's books, the neighbours, the television and little old me. Tata honed his English through poring over his dictionary, making lists of new words which he'd chalk up in his shed.

'It was a miracle that you went when you did. '*Bolesława, kochana*, I've often thought that you wouldn't have survived your illness if you'd have stayed here. Yes, you have slightly poorly legs but at least you're alive. And you have Magda now, too!'

'*Ciociu Bolesławo*,' Dagmara says, an alarmingly difficult grammatical formulation rolling off her tongue (the very pesky vocative case which has me fumbling every time), 'Magda likes the site now – don't you Magda?' Oh dear, I was wondering when she'd get onto that.

'Kind of,' I reply, suddenly taking great interest in fiddling with the teabags in the teapot.

'Did you meet that guy you were obsessively emailing on the site?'

'Obsessively emailing?' says Mama.

'Er, yes.'

'Who was he?' asks Dagmara. 'Don't tell me, a supposedly normal person who turned out to be a head case?'

'No.'

Mama stares at me, frozen, dying to hear, yet not daring to put a foot wrong. Funny how I can have that effect on her when she's the one who causes all the trouble.

'Yes, and on that note, I don't want to be your plaything anymore. I'm on the site, but I can decide things for myself from now on, thank you.'

'Oo-er. Lah-di-dah. We've been told, haven't we *Ciociu*?' says Dagmara.

'Sorry Magda,' says Mama (but no apology from Dagmara).

'Are you going to tell us about it?' says Dagmara. 'Come on, you can hold court with the three of us together. Save you repeating yourself. Go on! I'm dying to know. Now I'm back with Stefan, where am I going to get all my excitement from, darling? Not me – you!'

'You have already got someone in your life then, Dagmara?' asks Mama in a 'see-Magda-it's-possible' way.

'Yes,' says Dagmara. 'Stefan. He's wonderful. I've been with him for quite a few years now. We've had our ups and downs.'

'You can say that again,' says AB, looking the other way.

'But we've always got over them, though. Haven't we, Magda?'

I don't reply. I can't.

'Haven't we?'

'Yes. You have.'

'So? Tell us then. It's so exciting!'

'Why not tell them, Magda?' says AB. 'It is amazing and unique.'

'You know already, AB? Magda, come on, you can't not say now.'

'It was Professor Paweł Borkowski off the TV,' I announce, biting into my doughnut (gorgeous, by the way. A sugar-coated golden thing, soft, doughy and with a large splodge of jam in the centre).

Mama twitches when she hears the words 'professor' and 'TV', like a rat in a lab being given an electric shock. Dagmara thinks for a second, then a light bulb comes on.

'You mean him on the telly with the crazy hair?'

'Yes, that's the one. Do you know him?'

'Magda, all of Poland knows him! You mean he's on Polishmate. com?' she squeals. *'Ciociu Bolesławo* – do you know who Magda's talking about?' Mama shakes her head but guesses it's someone big. 'He's only the computer-history-brain of Poland – oh Magda, don't tell me you had a date with our top legal eagle? I can't believe it!'

'And!?' asks Mama.

'He's very nice.'

'That's good, isn't it?'

'I guess so. We met in a pizzeria. Dagmara, guess what, he's written a chapter in a book of yours. Mama, it's about Kazakhstan, where you were. He's an expert on it.'

'Magda, I've read that book about three times,' says Dagmara. (She's much more into history, Dagmara.) 'So, what happened? Are you still with him?'

'Early days yet, early days.'

'Magda, women would give their front and bottom teeth to go out with him! If he likes you, you can't let go of him!'

'Like I said, he was nice.'

'Do you have any idea how much I'd like to have nice?' says Dagmara. 'How I crave for nice, dream of nice, long for nice ...'

'He knew all about what happened to you, Mama. Also, he says you're *w zaprzeczeniu* (in denial).'

'In denial?' she asks coldly (and clearly in denial). 'Magda, you're fixated with Kazakhstan.'

'I am not!'

'You are,' says Dagmara.

'Then you're fixated with my love life! I'm just interested, Mama – that's all. You shouldn't have gone through that. It's a black mark on your past, our past, and I'm not going to ignore it.'

'Then again,' resumes Dagmara, 'with hair like his, he should be going out with a bush, not her. Brain he might be, *Ciociu*, beau he is not.'

'Actually we were quite a good match on the hair front.'

'Then it's a start, isn't it? You've both got something in common, terrible hair. Think, Magda, you may never have another chance like this ever again!' says Mama.

'Maybe she will see him. Maybe she won't,' arbitrates AB.

'Thank you AB. Yes, I'll decide on my own.'

The niceties resume. AB opens a parcel from Mama, who has also brought her: a kilo of rice (as of course there's no rice in Poland), about twenty packets of Knorr soup (Poland is Knorr's epicentre) and two tins of corned beef from Lidl (probably from Germany, so just next door to Poland). She's also brought me another luxury parcel full of goodies, along with three pairs of massive beige tights which will be about the right size by the time I've eaten all my bars of chocolate.

'There's another type of parcel I want to show you,' says AB. 'Jacek found it the other day when he was working on the boiler.'

She produces a dented old tin, about the size of a box of tissues. Jacek found it wedged between two pipes above a ten-floor drop.

'The tin!' says AB.

'The tin?' says Mama. 'After all these years?'

'What is it?' I ask peering at the tarnished box.

'It's been teetering above oblivion since 1957,' says AB. 'Your mama gave me this tin to look after when she went to England for her visit. I remember now, I put it in the airing cupboard for safe-keeping and then when your mother never returned, I forgot it existed. At some point, it must have fallen.'

Mama prises off the lid, revealing a careful arrangement of knick-knacks which time has turned the same shade of grey. Grandma's identity papers, held together with ancient string. 'Ginowicze,' says a purple ink stamp.

'That's where I was born!' says Mama. 'But it doesn't exist anymore.'

'No.'

When Poland's borders were redrawn, Ginowicze became part of Belarus.

There's also a bundle of old złoty notes, worthless now, and a small round mirror with the silver flaked off.

'This belonged to the lady who looked after us when Mother died,' says Mama, turning it in her hands. 'I tried to track her down once. But we never found her. And this,' she says, lifting out a wooden folding ruler with intricate markings on it, 'this was Father's.'

There are also some buttons and a scrap of faded lilac fabric. Mama says this was cut from her little sister Maria's dress before she was buried. No wonder I'm fascinated with Mama's past. These objects are clues, and real. I pull out a twist of paper – some kind of plant seeds. Then there are some drawings, the paper threadbare and practically in pieces. One is of a barren landscape and one is a close-up of a woman's face.

'Dagmara, your father did these. He was such a good drawer. This one is of mother. It looks just like her,' says Mama, wiping a tear from her eye.

'Let's see,' says Dagmara. 'I want to see them – oh, they're amazing, I'm going to frame them – and keep them forever!'

'And the most prized item of all, if I can call it that…'

Mama plucks out a tiny silver ring – three tarnished silver hoops, all joined together. 'I remember this. Mother's wedding ring. She would always say these were Szymon, me and Maria. When she died, I kept it.' She clasps it in the palm of her hand, then holds it towards us. 'One of you should have it. The question is who?'

'It'll never fit on my hand, look!' says Dagmara, sticking it on the end of a finger.

'Then Magda – here – you have it, it's yours.'

I take the sweet little ring, and put it on my finger. It's a piece of family history, a real heirloom.

I rather regret our row now and try to give her a loving look. She smiles and looks pleased. Maybe it's good she has come out. She's not going to be here for long and AB's right, we should enjoy ourselves.

This old tin has been to Kazakhstan and back, like the green and brown blanket.

There we all are. AB pottering with crockery, Dagmara lost in her father's drawings and me with Grandma's newfound tiny ring. When I look at Mama, she's returned to the box, lost in her thoughts, lost in an almost child-like play.

CHAPTER 13
SEATS IN THE SKY
(*SIEDZENIE W NIEBIE*)

Dear Dagmara
Hope this finds you well. I've been meaning to get in touch.

I pause, fingers poised on keyboard. Not sure I can do this. I press delete and start again.

Dear Dagmara
How are you? It was so nice to have you over for dinner. Unfortunately, there's something I need to tell you.

Darn, this is hard. Maybe it's because emails are so formal? Perhaps I should send a text instead. No.

Dear Dagmara
There is no easy way to say this.

Deep breath. Dagmara will be livid when she gets this.

    A delaying tactic. I take the small twist of seeds we found in Mama's tin and press them into a pot of soil on the balcony.

    Long pause.

It's no good. I can't do this over email, or by text. I'm going to have to do the unthinkable and tell her face to face. I snap my laptop shut.

I have been in touch with Paweł though, to arrange another date. I sent him a message the other day but haven't had anything back. It's odd, as he seemed quite keen.

Just as I'm considering writing to Raban the Hungarian (still looking for a cooker-wife), he gets in touch:

Dear Magda
I am so sorry for not getting back to you sooner.
I have been at conferences in America, Japan and the UK *(wow)* **and unfortunately, am still involved with that Balkan case** *(impressive)*.
There have also been PhD vivas at the university, so please forgive me *(OK, you've grovelled enough. I do forgive you).*
Please will you allow me to make it up to you – soon. Maybe in the next week or two?

I immediately write:

Dear Paweł
It's so nice to hear from you.
Meeting up again would be really nice.
Let me know where and when and I'll be there. *(Sounds a bit keen but what the heck)*
Best, Magda

Sent. Crikey, I must like him more than I thought. I should have at least waited an hour before writing back so quickly. Still, at least I know I like him now. Who would have thought I'd find someone so quickly? Mama would have a fit if she knew and Dagmara would be beside herself. I'm beside myself, if I'm totally honest. All those hopeless dates have showed me the Prof is worth hanging onto after all.

I just have to wait until next week now. I know, I'll heave out Dagmara's copy of his book again and start swatting up so I'm prepared for anything.

Two hours later, as I finish page seven of his introduction, with two A4 sheets' worth of notes and about fifty new words in my vocabulary book, there's a knock at the door. It's Jacek.

'Have you been working upstairs?'

'Yes,' he says, coming in. 'You look how I feel.'

'Drained?'

'Yes. What are you up to? he says, looking at all my papers. 'Planning a lesson?'

'No. Studying. The war. For when I meet – a sort of friend.'

'Oh. Right. Interesting. Well, do you fancy a break? I've just finished and your Aunt said you were in. I thought we could go out somewhere. Anywhere – and have a nice time.'

'A nice time? Wow. I've almost forgotten what that is.'

It's true. I've almost forgotten what it is to go out with someone – and it not be on some kind of trial of either looks, character or knowledge – and just enjoy myself.

Jacek also wants to pay me back for being his 'sous-plumber'. In the past few weeks, I've helped him quite a bit as he's stripped out planks at AB's: passing him pliers, running to the hardware shop for bits of *fuga* (good word – grouting) and even holding a *latarka* (torch) as he's climbed under the floor (to think I didn't know the word for plumber once).

This little cracked pipe is fast becoming Warsaw's biggest plumbing job.

Jacek rattles off some suggestions. Old Town, the Castle, Zachęta Art Gallery.

'Zachęta?' I ask, surprised. 'Have you been there?'

'Magda – builders can like art too. And music. And theatre.'

'Sorry.'

'How about the war walks and the monuments?'

'Done those.'

'Even the Jewish ones? What about the Ghetto?'

'Give me some credit. I know what we can do.'

'What?'

'I love cafes.'

'Cafes?'

I look up out of the window to the Palace of Culture nearby, visible from the flat and golden in the afternoon sun. 'Isn't there one up there?'

Fifteen minutes later, we're approaching the entrance of the gigantic Palace of Culture in Defilad Square. I'm growing quite fond of this often-maligned monolith. Years ago, I remember coming across a group of drunks drinking beer in the esplanade. Somehow, this motley crew, who had created their own form of nightlife during the day on the street, had discovered a power point under the base of a monument and were boiling a grubby kettle to have a break from all their drinking. You won't see this outside the Palace these days. The surrounding area's been spruced up to match the new colourful, fast trams and hoards of commuters dashing past.

From the outside, the palace looks like a futuristic film set and inside, it's a self-contained metropolis. We find a hairdresser, a cafe and a few newsagents in the vast ground-floor lobby, which dwarfs the reception desk and the person on duty. Apparently, men died building this two hundred and thirty metre high palace, started in the 1950s, and there are over forty floors and more than three thousand rooms. As we walk, our footsteps reverberate, adding to the shimmer of activity in the lobby around.

The man on the desk directs us to another desk which he says, deals solely with people visiting the viewing bay on the thirtieth floor. I'm expecting something grand or at least a long queue as we walk on through, but when we find this designated area, it's just a friendly woman with a cash tin.

We get our tickets, then walk round to the lifts, our footsteps snapping against the hard floor. When the doors open, we find a man inside whose job is to ferry people up and down to the thirtieth floor. A minute or so later, we arrive on the landing of the thirtieth floor and go out into the viewing area where a gale force wind is blowing.

We make our way round, admiring Warsaw in 360 degrees. Skyscrapers, hotels, blocks of flats, the new sports stadium and leafy green squares that look like bits of patchwork. Down below, the trams look like train sets, snaking along in silence.

'What a treat you've given me, son, bringing me up here!' shouts an older lady to a man amid sounds of flapping clothes. They're the only other people up here with us. The man starts to wrestle with a mounted telescope.

'Is it what you expected?' asks Jacek squinting, his dark hair blowing. 'I didn't know what to expect!' I yell in the wind. 'Hang on a sec!'

Copying the man, I slot a coin into another telescope and everything far away suddenly becomes much closer, including my own block down the road. I cup my face around the lens with my hands, which cuts out the wind.

'Hey, I can see my flat, just about!'

Jacek takes a look and then we go inside to the cafe. Two people seem to be having a business meeting and pore over figures, so we pick a table further away from them – two electric-blue velvet chairs which remind me of psychedelic guitars from the sixties. A waitress floats over, pen and notebook in hand, and takes our order.

'This is on me,' offers Jacek.

'Thanks. They have plays and concerts on in here, don't they?' I ask, looking at a leaflet.

'All the time. I've played here quite a few times.'

'You have?' I ask, surprised.

Our coffees arrive, deep black circles of liquid with yellowish rings of foam around the rim.

'I used to play the violin,' he replies, tearing open a packet of sugar and pouring it into his cup. He holds the thin empty paper packet as if it's a bow and makes the precise and fluid movement of a violinist cutting through the air.

'I didn't know that.'

'There are lots of things you don't know about me. Anyway. I don't play anymore. Not since Marzena died.'

'Why?'

He folds his arms as if to hide his hands, hands I've seen labour away since the day we met.

'To be honest, she was the real musician out of the two of us. She could really play. Me – I was a beginner next to her. I figured that if I could never hear her play again – then I wouldn't play either.'

'I see.'

He nods, as if to a distant tune.

'In one way it's a relief,' he adds. 'Now I work with my hands in another way and life's much simpler.'

Silence falls between us and I sip my coffee, which tastes like mud mixed with bathroom cleaner.

Mundane sounds fill the grand space around us – trays clattering, the hum of the drinks machines – sounds that must be a world away from the classical sounds Jacek once helped create. He smiles, upbeat, and turns his chair to look outside.

'Magda,' he says.

'Yes.'

'I was wondering. You know you've—'

BLEEP.

My phone goes off and I can't resist but look. A message from Paweł! Would I like to go to a *vernissage* in the Old Town? In the next couple of weeks?

'Something important?' says Jacek, mid-phrase.

'No no. Well, sort of. It's this law Professor I've sort of started dating. From the university. He wants me to go to a *vernissage*. What is that exactly?'

'It's a private opening of an art collection.'

'Oh, I see. That sounds fun.'

'Is he off that site you were on?'

That sounds lovely, I hammer back, **where?**

'Sorry?' I add, only half listening.

'Is he off that site you were on?'

'Yes, he is, that's right. Sorry. That was – very rude of me. Done now!'

'It sounds as if you like him.'

'Well, put it this way. I've never really met anyone else like him before. Professor Paweł N. Borkowski – off the TV!'

'Wow. Impressive. Hence that war book of his you've been carrying around.'

'You noticed! Anyway, it's early days. What was it you were saying?'

'Nothing.'

'Tell me. Is it the job at my Aunt's? It's taking longer than you quoted for, isn't it? I can ask Dagmara for more money.'

'No no, it isn't that.'

'What, then?'

'I was... I was thinking... Maybe... How about... Could I borrow that grammar book you sometimes use at school? I've seen you with it, and it's just what I'm looking for.'

'Sure, Jacek. Why didn't you say?'

We carry on talking for hours about all the parties that must have happened up here – what ambitions were realised and what dreams were born or dashed. The distance from the streets makes the place feel locationless, as if we're suspended in the pale grey sky.

If I could play an instrument, or sing, I don't think I would stop for anything or anyone. But I haven't been through what Jacek's been through. Jacek's unfolded his arms during the course of our conversation.

I look at his hands and see they have a certain finesse to them after all.

CHAPTER 14
SKULLCAP (CZEPEK PŁYWACKI)

'**D**agmara?'
    'Hello stranger! How are we today? I just thought I'd give you a ring.'

'It's so nice to hear from you.'

I never did arrange to meet her for that tête-à-tête and weeks have passed now.

'How is my favourite British cousin?'

'Favourite? I'm your only one! Fine. How are you?'

'I'm great! What are you up to today?'

'Oh you know, this and that.'

'Are you free?'

Apart from continuing to plough through her war book (fell asleep over it last night and woke up at three with my face on pages 30 and 31), I'm as free as can be but there's no way I can see her. Not with Stefan and everything, and Paweł-*vernissage* pending.

'Er. Maybe. Why?'

'Fancy coming out? There's this place called Aquaworld. I thought you and me could go for a swim and some fun and have a girlie day out.'

'Just me and you?' I ask, thinking rapidly and suddenly wondering if this means she's split up from Stefan. 'I'm not sure.'

'Why?'

'I think I'm busy.'

'You think you're busy? You either are, or you're not.'

'Well I might go out into town and Jacek's due soon too, so I should really be around.'

'Jacek? Is he still there? What is this leak, Magda, the Niagara Falls? You can't stay in to monitor your plumber. Not if he's any good, anyway. It's the weekend.'

'It's turning out to be a really big job,' I say, wading through some cardboard boxes to make some noise and prove my point. I also want to stick up for Jacek as he's working really hard.

'So let him get on with it! Come on. You know it will be fun. Things with me are always fun.'

Actually, she's right. Dagmara is certainly one for creating drama.

'I'm also reading lots,' I say, flicking through the five hundred pages that remain. 'That history book of yours.'

'That's a bit heavy, isn't it?'

'I've got to read it some time, haven't I? You read it some time.'

'Oh, I know what this is about. That professor! You like him, don't you?'

She's right, I do really like him. But a swim is starting to sound rather nice. It's roasting outside and even hotter in.

'Oh come on, Magda! Do you want to see me grovel, is that it? Well I'm grovelling, "Please come with me, Magda!" I've been so busy drilling people's teeth that I've not had time to meet up with my own flesh and blood!'

'So what exactly is Aquaworld?' I ask, wavering.

'The clue is in the name! It's a water park with a pool, slides and saunas. It's gorgeous! It's always full of Germans, so it must be good!'

'It does sound tempting. Will Stefan be there?' I ask, all casual. I know she said a girlie day out but Dagmara does this – she says 'just you and me' and then brings him along like a pet.

'No, he's doing overtime, poor thing. It'll be just you and me.'

Overtime. Right. Crumbs. They're still together then. On the other hand, Dagmara hates Stefan doing overtime, particularly at weekends, so this bad news is good news. With any luck, she'll get really fed up of this and will end it all forever in the next couple of weeks.

'OK then, you've twisted my arm.'

'Brilliant. Get the 67 bus from downstairs – I'll be on the right-hand side. I'll get off if you're not there. See you in half an hour!'

I start to pack my swimming things. Swimming cossie, goggles, flip-flops. It's hot for early October and everyone is out.

When I get on the bus, I find Dagmara has saved me a seat by plonking her stuff on it. Outside, the avenues of yellowing trees create a golden blaze trailing. By the looks of the colourful floats on the bus, lots of other people are going swimming too.

For some reason, Dagmara is still in the superb mood she was in on the phone earlier.

'Dagmara?'

'Yes.'

'Why are you so happy?'

'I'm always happy, Magda.'

'You're not.'

She pats me on the hand.

'Stefan and I so enjoyed dinner that time,' she says with a smile. 'Yes the food was terrible – but it's about the company too, isn't it?'

This is weird. She's never this nice about anything.

I look out of the window and switch between focusing on the scratches on the pane and the shoppers outside.

'Have you got any news?' she says, nudging me. 'You must have.'

'No.'

'What's wrong?'

'Nothing.'

'You're being really quiet.'

'I'm not.'

'Anything from that Professor – or is he history, if you pardon the pun! History, professor, get it?'

'Yes I get it. No he isn't history. And he's a professor of law, not history.'

'Oooo! Magda! Well done, what a catch!!'

'Shh, Dagmara. The whole bus is looking. I'm seeing him at a *vernissage* on Sunday night.'

'A what?'

'An art *soirée*.'

'Ahh. So hence the book. Do you want me to summarise it for you?'

'Oh, would you? Not that it's not good.'

She rattles off a list, deadpan.

'Tragedy, pain, death, killing, betrayal, suffering…' she rattles off.

'Dagmara!'

'Magda, I don't want to talk about his book now! I want to enjoy today – the autumn sunshine, the trees, life in general!'

A group of yelling kids get onto the bus with more floats and rings. While I marvel at the Polish coming out of their mouths, Dagmara smiles at them, full of maternal love.

'Oh, aren't they gorgeous?'

'Dagmara, you hate children. And noise.'

'No. Deep down, I've realised that I love children very much.'

This is even more bizarre. Is she well? Has she started a course of pills which might be affecting her? She looks besotted, even with the kid that's shoving his bendy green tube into her face.

'You must really like him, Magda!'

'Well, maybe I've seen the light.'

'I'm pleased you're happy.'

'I'm pleased you're happy. Generally, I mean.'

'Well,' she says. 'Maybe I've got reason to be.'

'What do you mean?'

'Magda…'

'What?'

She's not going to say what I think she's going to say, is she?

'Calm down Magda, nothing's wrong. In fact it's good news, for once.'

Oh no. Panic's flashing through me now. What is this big news? Then, instead of answering verbally, Dagmara starts wiggling her eyebrows and looks down at her lap. My eyes follow and land on her hand. Oh no. It can't be. It is. A diamond ring, twinkling on her finger. Dagmara is engaged to Stefan!

'Yes, I'm afraid this little beauty, is why Stefan's doing overtime,' she says, delighted. 'We're getting married, Magda! Isn't it fantastic?'

No, it's far from fantastic. This is possibly the worst thing that could have ever happened. The opposite to this was meant to be happening, the opposite!

'I knew you'd be surprised. Aren't you happy? You could at least look happy, Magda. It's not every day this happens!'

'Sorry. It's just – so unexpected. Congratulations.'

'Thank you!'

Oh no, this is terrible. I feel sick to the core.

I should have told her. I should have sent that email, that text. I should have told her the night it happened, instead of letting the thing fester.

'When did he pop the question?'

'The other night. I've been dying to tell you.'

The bus screeches to a halt at some traffic lights – as if my stomach could lurch any more.

'Stefan's come up trumps. I always knew he would. Magda, are you OK? You've gone green.'

'I'm fine. It's just a bit – hot, that's all.'

'Oh I know what this is about,' she says, softening. 'Don't worry, you'll be next! I can feel it in my bones. With Le Prof, you'll see!'

'Indeed!'

I let her have her say.

Ten minutes later, we arrive. Never have I been so pleased to see a world of coloured plastic. I wasn't banking on this. A break-up, yes. Marriage, no. Once inside I let Dagmara take care of everything while I glide around, trying not to panic.

'Dagmara's getting married,' is all I can think, as I flit between the counter and a goggle stand in a tizz. Eventually, I plonk myself in a heap on a plush orange swizzle chair. How am I going to get out of this one? I've never seen her look this happy, ever.

Dagmara gets us the most expensive deal – passes that cover everything going – massages, saunas, hot stone treatments, manicures and pedicures. She also picks up two special prepaid hi-tech wristbands that let you buy food and drink without messing around with change. All paid up, a tall feline woman with a glamorous sun-kissed bun passes us some white dressing gowns and points us down a corridor. I want to pass out.

Soon, we're in the pool. While Dagmara starts clocking up lengths, I put my goggles on and have a little cry. We've a lane to ourselves and I have to hand it to Dagmara – this is one of the most gorgeous pools I've ever been to in my life. Were I not in such a state, I might be having a nice time. It's pristine and has all kinds of temperature gauges and fancy racing clocks on the walls. Poland's taken to capitalism really well. Tropical greenery and merchandise, bathed in relaxing, holistic music.

I let Dagmara swim while I cling to the edge like a barnacle. I feel as if I'm nursing a terrible boil. And we know what happens to those, don't we?

Advantages of staying quiet:
1. Will avoid black eye

Disadvantages:
1. Will have guilty conscience jabbing me forever and
2. Dagmara will marry a louse.

It's no good. I'm going to have to risk my life and tell her the truth. Better late than never. And bones do heal, don't they? Perhaps at the end of the day I'll tell her? But not in public. How about back at the flat – or while getting into a taxi that's heading for the airport?

I look at Dagmara, who's swimming like a fiend. She's in a light blue swimming costume and her black rubber skullcap makes her look like an oncoming missile as she powers through the water.

'How many lengths are you doing?' she asks, bursting out of the water.

I say any old number.

'Twenty or thirty?'

I was thinking more like five or six to be honest. She nods and pushes off again with a clip on her nose and a veil of water sloughing off her face. The next time round, she stops and joins me.

'Remember that summer in the lake?' she asks, taking off her goggles and shaking them out.

Remember? How could I forget? While she fiddles with her straps I drift back in time to 1983 when Mama and Tata and I were here on holiday in Poland once again. I was seven and Dagmara was nine.

'Do you remember that inflatable ring you had?'

'Yes.'

'I thought it was so funny!'

'I know.'

We were on a family holiday at Dagmara's home in Barlinek – well before the Polish dance competition – and we were all out in a group by the lake (in case you think Poland has no lakes, it actually has lakes left, right and centre. Last time someone counted, I think there were around nine thousand).

As Dagmara so accurately says, I had a green and orange swimming ring. I absolutely loved this ring – until the day by the lake that is. My ring was bright and shiny and it smelled of brand-new plastic. As I waded out into the water, astonished, to the adults' delight, by all the tiny fish all around me, Dagmara was already out there, swimming to and fro like a shark.

'You don't need that!' she yelled over the water.

'I do,' I muttered, paddling away.

As the adults watched me wade deeper, I remember thinking about my options: staying in with Dagmara or turning back and building a sandcastle in peace. Stupidly, I chose the former. Two minutes later, good old Dagmara was ducking me under.

'How nicely you played!' said Mama when I staggered out spluttering.

'Mama, she nearly drowned me!' I said, distraught.

'I did not!'

'Did!'

'Don't be silly. Dagmara was teaching you how to swim! Isn't that nice?'

I could have burst that stupid ring on the spot.

'Happy times,' says Dagmara, adjusting her hat. 'Fancy a race, instead of going up and down all the time? Ten lengths. Come on. I'm getting bored.'

'OK then,' I find myself saying. Where did that come from? I'm the least competitive person in the whole world. But there's just something in Dagmara that makes me want to beat her. I adjust my goggles. Stefan or no Stefan, I'd really like to win this race – and what Dagmara doesn't know is that these days, I'm quite fast too.

We set off. For the first three lengths we're neck and neck, chopping through the water at lightning speed. I'm practically giddy with the adrenaline of being quite close to Dagmara and not lagging behind. I bet she can't believe it. I inhale rapidly as I come up for air, then exhale a plume of bubbles underwater. On length number four, I actually overtake.

But what am I doing, trying to win this race? I can't beat her, with what I've got to tell her. My internal chatter distracts me and on length number five, she catches up. There's a lot of splashing and kicking and chopping of water, so she must be near. We push off together for length number six. Neck and neck but my legs feel like jelly. I could win this, I think for a moment. I push myself harder but still we're neck and neck. On length number seven, judging by the splashes, Dagmara's slightly ahead and as I turn my head to inhale a breath, Dagmara's scrunched up wet face comes up opposite mine.

Dagmara, must we always fight like this, I think as my lungs start to burn. Must you always make me mad – and win?

On length number eight, I overtake again and my foot catches against her hand but she catches me up in seconds. A final push... left arm, right arm, kick kick kick... For about ten seconds, we're side by side, slightly out of synch, the story of our lives... Just a bit further, go on Magda, go on...

Dagmara beats me by seconds. She has done it again. She tears off her goggles and catches her breath.

'You're really fast now,' she says, gasping.

'I know,' I pant. 'I know.'

It's good that I didn't win. A little later, when we get out and wander around, I feel as if an egg-timer is running out. Further on in the complex, the floor is hard but sculptured and coloured so that it looks like soft, undulating sand. This pretend beach encloses a stretch of bright turquoise water that has a wave machine creating whirlpools and miniature tidal waves. In another zone, people shoot out of different helter-skelter chutes and jump off a trio of very high diving boards.

OK Magda. No more wriggling. Tell her now, as we walk. I open my mouth but nothing comes out.

'Either we can go on the slides, try the wave machine or, we could have a sauna,' suggests Dagmara.

Darn, the moment's gone. I'm not great with saunas, but if the alternative is being shoved down a near-vertical slide by Dagmara or battling waves with her grinning nearby, I know what I'm going to choose. The sauna. There is, after all, a lot to sweat out. We cross through the bar and the music changes from pop to hypnotic.

'Let's get drinks later,' she says. 'Are you leaving your cossie out here or are you going into the changing room?' she asks, as she whips off her costume before me.

'Pardon?' I ask, staring at her naked breasts which I've never seen before.

'Are you...'

'I heard you the first time. Dagmara – it's not a nude sauna is it?'

'Of course it is, silly! What else would it be?'

'They're not like that in *Anglia*! Sorry, but I can't!'

There's just no way I'm getting undressed in front of Dagmara or anyone else. (I was a prude in primary school, secondary school and I'm not changing now.)

'Of course you can. Besides – I've paid.'

'Then I'll pay you back. You go in and enjoy yourself and I'll wait for you out here.'

'Oh come on Magda! Everyone will be naked, not just you. Just look around.'

She's right. Some more definitely naked people saunter past as if all is well – they could be out shopping for all they care. Suddenly, everyone around me is naked, including the nymph in the fountain. She's holding a shell up over her head and pouring water over her large concrete breasts.

'Are we going to wait all day?'

'Oh all right then, you win! The things I do for you!'

Without further ado I whip my cossie off like a sticking plaster and stand there naked too. 'Happy now?'

'Honestly, Magda.'

'I'm just not used to being naked in public. Who is? Even Adam and Eve didn't feel right naked – they hid, didn't they?'

Dagmara laughs.

'Magda. There's a time and place for everything.'

'Exactly. Like in your own bathroom when you're on your own!'

As I stand there getting goosebumps, I long to snap into that pose that people do when caught naked unawares.

We go inside. To my relief, the sauna's dark and nearly empty.

I sit down with Dagmara and tell myself I'm not really naked, I'm just sitting here quietly and soon it will all be over. It can be Dagmara's and my little secret and it doesn't matter that a naked man's glistening body is sprawled on the top bench in front of me and I don't know where to look.

Just then, around thirty naked people enter and fill up all the benches. An aroma session is about to start! A woman in a sarong comes in and starts ladling a perfumed concoction onto the hot coals.

Dagmara shifts closer and all I can hear is her inhaling and exhaling like a pig in labour. Her hot leg is right against mine and on the other side, someone else's hot leg has plonked itself next to me too, wedging me in like a sausage in a sandwich.

Next, aroma woman starts gyrating with a towel to get the smell moving round. Here we all are naked in searing damp heat and all I can see is this woman's body moving around and Dagmara's shiny ring catching the light from the emergency sign above.

I feel so, I feel so... very strange. The tie-dyed blue sarong – it's swirling all around me – and the smell of pine is so very strong. Dagmara's sparkling diamond is becoming a moving mass of pin-pricks before my eyes and I can't... can't... sit... upright anymore. The floor, the floor, the Prof, history, and Mama. I'm falling against the floor... against Stefan, against Dagmara...

When I come round I'm outside the sauna, covered with a dressing gown and lying on a lounger. Dagmara and aroma woman are kneeling next to me, looking worried. Is it over? Have I said it? What's happened? I look over at Dagmara, who looks normal. I can't have told her.

'She's waking up,' says Dagmara, with doting eyes.

'Where am I?' I ask, dazed.

'Don't worry. You're all right now,' says the woman, taking my hand. 'You fainted in the sauna.'

'Fainted?'

'Yes.'

'They had to carry you out,' says Dagmara, stifling a sudden giggle.

'Who's they?'

'Two men. Four actually, as the first two couldn't manage on their own.'

'Oh great! You're telling me that four men carried me out of the sauna while I was unconscious?'

'Yep. Naked. Like a barbecued carcass.'

'It was too hot for you,' says aroma woman in a comforting voice. 'How are you now?' the woman asks. 'You look pale.'

'Fine. Can I have a drink please?'

'Of course.'

'She's British and not used to saunas,' says Dagmara to aroma woman, who leaves to fetch some water. I'm just about to say that the British have plenty of saunas too when she says, 'Don't worry about a thing *kochana*. Stefan's coming to pick us up.'

'Stefan?'

'Don't sound so alarmed. I'll get you changed and we'll take you back, safe and sound.'

'Dagmara?'

'What, petal?'

I've got to tell her. It's now or never.

Advantages of telling Dagmara now:

1. If she hits me I'm down already and
2. Seeing as I've just fainted, maybe she won't get mad?

'You can't marry Stefan,' I eventually blurt out.

'What, darling? You're all confused. Heatstroke can do that.'

'I meant what I said. You can't marry him. You mustn't.'

'What do you mean?' says Dagmara, starting to look uncomfortable.

Aroma woman has returned, but sensibly backs off upon hearing me say 'can't' followed by 'marry him', and seeing Dagmara recoil horrified.

'Something really awful has happened! And I've been too scared to tell you.'

Dagmara hits the roof in approximately one second flat.

'What? What, Magda? Tell me, what?!'

I cling onto the dressing gown for some kind of security and realise Dagmara's in nothing but her flip-flops.

'Tell me!'

'Can you put some clothes on first?"

'For goodness' sake Magda, just tell me!'

'Promise you won't be mad?'

'I can't promise if I don't know what it is? Tell me?!'

'Oh Dagmara!'

I take a big breath and immediately feel light-headed. 'The night you came over for dinner and went upstairs—'

'Yes!?' she says, horrified.

'Stefan... Stefan—'

'Go on!'

'Stefan made a pass at me! Oh Dagmara, it was so awful! I know he was drunk – but he said, "What did it matter, I didn't like you anyway" – and I said, "What's liking got to do with it?" I jumped back, rang AB – and he went to hide in the bathroom until you returned!'

Big, life-changing pause. Not dissimilar to the dividing line between BC and AD.

'I'm so sorry, Dagmara. Sorry I never told you before.'

There's another long pause as Dagmara stares at me. It's the silence before the storm, before the hurricane, before the twister of rage that I know is coming very very soon. Is she going to scream, cry, punch or throttle me?

'How dare you?' she says very slowly, getting up. 'How dare you?' she yells, booting the lounger with her bare foot while miraculously not wincing.

'Dagmara – it's true!'

'You're... inhuman. After all I've done for you! You always have to go one better than me, don't you?'

'What?'

She bursts into tears and charges off towards the changing rooms hollering, grabbing her dressing gown along the way.

There's only one thing worse than arguing in public with Dagmara – arguing in public naked. I go back to the changing room too and sit inside a cubicle, the safest place to be, staring at my feet. Dagmara, poor thing, leaves Aquaworld before me, sobbing.

It's awful, hearing her sob.

If only Stefan hadn't come to dinner. If only, if only. Once I'm sure the coast is clear, I creep out of the complex and wait for a bus home.

Oh how I miss England. To talk about the weather with a total stranger. To watch the news and understand it. To queue for something in an orderly fashion, with people who know how to queue and who won't barge in past you like they do here. I also miss litter, late trains, health-and-safety-gone-mad.

Dagmara, Poland and everyone in it are just too darn foreign.

I also need a rest from speaking Polish. I feel very English in this country, which is definitely not where I am from. I need to meet up with someone British and speak as far back in the throat as I like. Polish is all in the front. I think my facial muscles are changing. Maybe my whole face has changed shape and if I went back to England now, no one would recognise me? I want to be understood properly and not have to compromise what I mean.

I miss Mama and Tata, British food, London and its manic speed and chaos. Just the ease of how things happen. Even hassle and heartbreak is easier in your mother tongue.

I feel terrible that I've ruined Dagmara's dream. I jump onto a bus, pushing and shoving through the scrum.

CHAPTER 15
THE *VERNISSAGE* (WERNISAŻ)

The journey home takes an eternity. I stumble into the block distraught, dash past Pani Zosia's kiosk and head straight for the lifts. This morning she saw me leave bright and breezy – but now I'm in tears.

'Everything all right, Magda?'

'No, Pani Zosiu! Sorry, can't stop!'

The lift doors slide closed as a text arrives from Dagmara. She wants me out of her flat by the end of next week. Where am I going to go? And what about AB? I wasn't banking on being made homeless by my own cousin.

I hit floor eleven for AB's and wait with my head against the wall as the lift rumbles up. AB will understand. I should have told her sooner. She'll know what to do, she always knows. I hammer at her door.

'AB! AB! Are you there?'

I hear her TV in the background, Grzybek barking and the sound of shuffling footsteps growing closer.

'It's Magda!'

'Wait a minute.'

Bolts slide and keys jangle.

'What is it, *kochana*?' she says, opening up. 'What's happened? I thought you and Dag—'

'AB, everything's gone wrong and it's all my fault!'

'Child, child, what is it? Come in, it can't be as bad as all that!'

'It is!' I reply, bursting into floods of tears.

'Come on. Let's go into the lounge. I'm just making dinner. We can talk over that.'

She serves up two bowls of *rosół*, clear chicken soup with fine noodles. It's the ultimate comfort food really, but things are so bad, a bowl's not going to do it, I'm going to need a vat.

I pour out everything to AB, from the evening it happened, to Dagmara announcing her engagement – and me dashing all her hopes.

'I should have told her earlier.'

'Yes, true, you should. But wait, Magda, Stefan's the one at fault, isn't he? Not you.'

'I know but I don't think she believes me. You believe me, don't you?'

'Of course! I know what Stefan's like. So does she.'

AB pulls me into her big, rolling-pin arms.

'She knows now, Magda, that's the main thing. If she doesn't believe you, then that's up to her.'

'Why would I lie about something like this? Of all the things.'

'She probably does believe you but she's lashing out. Dagmara's like this, Magda. Emotional. Like her father, like your mother – like you.'

'Me?' I ask, on my tenth tissue.

'I'll talk to her. I don't know what it is about you two. She's always wanted to prove herself to you, hasn't she? And you her.'

'She sees me as the one who's had the cushy life, with everything on a plate. She wants me to move out. If I move out, who's going to look after you?'

'Child, child, don't worry about me, I can look after myself. Anyway, you're not moving anywhere. I'll talk to her.'

'Really?'

'Yes. I'm not scared of Dagmara. I was going to ring her later anyway. She'll listen to me. At least you told her before she got married – so it's not too late really, is it? Now are you going to have this soup, or am I going to have to have it for you?'

Feeling better, I have some. It's divine. Rich with chicken, seasoning and love. It's funny. All along, I thought it would be me looking after AB, but she's the one who's looked after me, just like she did Mama all those years ago.

'How's your hip?'

'It still hurts. But it's not long now,' she says, pointing to the calendar. A month. What have you decided to do about the professor? I haven't seen him on the television lately.'

'He's invited me to a *vernissage*, AB, tomorrow night.'

'Then you should go and enjoy that. You deserve it. You've decided that you like him, have you? Or that he deserves a second chance?'

'A bit of both. Everyone says he's this major figure, but I just see him as a person.'

'Well I'm sure he appreciates that, don't you think? And it's probably good not to put him on a pedestal. What are you going to wear?'

Now there's a question. I have no idea what I'm going to wear. I was going to ask Dagmara if I could borrow something of hers but I can hardly ask her now.

'I might have something for you Magda, if you're stuck.'

'What, AB?'

'It's in my room. I was doing some clearing out when I came across it and thought of you.'

'I take it you're not going to wear it again?'

'Not unless I lose fifteen kilos and wake up half my age one day, no.'

I go through to AB's room. I've never been in it before. The door creaks open and I'm met with sweet, faint smells of various floral perfumes and talc. Rays of sunlit dust bounce off the glass bottles on her dresser.

'Got it?' she calls, stacking the bowls away in the kitchen, filling the washing bowl with water.

She can only mean the emerald green dress hanging on the wardrobe door and a pair of shoes to match.

'It's stunning, AB! Was it yours?'

'No, my mother's. Remember how I escaped from our house and I took just one case?'

'Yes.'

'I packed it then.'

I take the dress off its hanger and bring it to my face. It smells of – time, really, and of perfume, like the room.

'I've worn it many times, of course. Are you going to put it on, or are you going to stay in there all day?'

I slip it on. I say slip, but really, I mean squeeze. It fits, just about.

'You must have been so slim, AB!' I say, putting on the shoes.

'Come in then, let's have a look at you. Ah Magda, you look absolutely beautiful!'

'Is it too tight?' I twirl around so she can see. 'Tell me the truth, won't you?'

'Of course I will, what else?'

'Does it make me look f—'

'No, it does not make you look fat. It's fitted, Magda, it's meant to be like that. And my, it's so perfect for a *vernissage*. Magda, you're going to knock this professor dead!'

'I hope not, because that would definitely make the seven thirty news.'

The next day, I hear nothing from Dagmara and nothing from Paweł. He's meant to be confirming the time and place for tonight – somewhere in Powiśle, near the river and central, so not too far away.

When I jump onto Polishmate to see if he's left a message there, I find I can't get into my account. I try searching for myself to try to get in that way. I'm still there, but oh no, my profile, it's been changed. Someone must have hacked into it and by the looks of it, changed the password too.

Dagmara!

I never changed the password when she handed over the account to me – and now she's gone in to take revenge. She's written all sorts about me, about how awful I am and mean and cruel – and the worst thing is, I can't change it.

I'll have to text Paweł and tell him not to use the site but to text me instead. And, I'll have to start to get ready for this evening. AB's shoes are just a bit too tight so I'll have to wear them on and off in the day to try to stretch them.

Before I do anything else, I must go to buy a proper pair of hair-straighteners once and for all. It's all gone quiet on the Chinese hair site front and I can't go to the *vernissage* with frizzy hair. I go back to the hair counter in the department store and the assistant looks at me with I-told-you-so eyes.

'That'll be 400 PLN please,' she says.

So far this dud hairdo has cost me:
£10 for the original dud perm
£15 for the non-existent Chinese *prostownica*
£9 for returning the Chinese dog-hair clippers
£80 for the final hair-straighteners.

Making a grand total of £114 (cue sound of jaw hitting ground). Well over double the price of an ordinary perm.

In the afternoon, Paweł texts me. A trendy gallery in Ulica Foksal which will have lots of people in it. The good news is, I'm not a bag of nerves about tonight's date like I was last time. This is the new, confident and decisive me. AB's right. I am going to look 'knock-out' in my vintage dress. There'll be art to look at and people to talk to, even if art-world people are a law unto themselves. Must get clued up on the Polish for key phrases such as 'dichotomy', 'hegemony' and 'blurring of boundaries'. I'm bound to need to use them at least a dozen times. And maybe the words for different colour hues and types of paint. This time, I really want to impress Paweł.

Before going to the gallery, I pop into Language Zone with some marking and that grammar book for Jacek. On Sunday evenings, he comes in to do odd jobs that have built up over the the past week and uses the audio equipment to advance his English. I find him in the language lab.
 'Hey, Magda!' he says taken aback. 'You're all dressed up.'
 'Yes it does happen, sometimes. I'm off to that *vernissage*.'
 'With your Professor?'
 'He's not my Professor, but yes, him. Here's that book you wanted.'
 'Thanks.'
He takes it and puts it down, then looks at my dress a little more closely.
 'What amazing stitching. And what a cut. The bow at the back and all the tiny details... Is it from another era?'

'Yes, pre-war. I'm glad you like it. It was AB's mother's. I hope it doesn't smell of mothballs. I've been airing it all day. How's the English going? We should have another lesson at some point.'

'No need. I might be getting lots of practice soon.'

'How come?'

'I might be moving to London. To work.'

'Wow,' I reply, shocked. 'That's great, Jacek. I'll be sad to see you go.'

'Yes, we'll have done a sort of swap, won't we? You here, me there.'

'Yes.'

He turns his back to return to his work and I turn to go.

To be honest, I'm quite taken aback by his announcement. Slightly gutted too, he's been such a brick. I never thought Jacek would leave Language Zone, let alone Warsaw. I've always seen him as part of the furniture. But nothing stays the same, ever.

Enough musing. I'd better hurry up, I'm going to be late. If London's what Jacek wants, great, and who am I to stop him? Anyway, I've thought for a while that he needs to get out more. He could meet someone new in London, like I have in Warsaw. He must have been looking at one point, as it was he who spotted my classified ad.

I arrive at the *vernissage* with blistered feet and shoes I'm dying to take off but can't.

The *vernissage* is Paweł's!

I thought it was meant to be one of his friends'!

Is there anything this man can't do?

The place is abuzz with women dressed in black, with outsize glamorous jewellery and heavy make-up to match. No matter, my beautiful vintage dress is unique – I look just as good as anyone else here.

I spot Paweł across a crowded room, wave, and make my way over, admiring several large abstracts of his along the way. One is a sea of dark blues, the other a sky-like expanse of greys and blacks.

'Paweł, you never told me the *vernissage* was yours!'

He pecks me on either cheek, going an instant pink.

'It's just a small hobby.'

Apart from the moody landscapes, and let's face it, what else would he paint after all those trials and essays, there are some very sensual nudes (a bit too sensual, if you ask me). When does he have time to do this, in between his international conferences, trials, news reports and now, little old me?

Tonight he's in a crisp white linen shirt without a single crease in it. I only have to look at linen and it crumples. He also has on a dapper light blue and white striped jacket. His genuinely careless, dishevelled look from the pizzeria has been changed to a carefully studied, designer-messy look. I think I spot some hair-wax and dare I say, hairspray.

'Magda,' he says, taking me to one side.

'Yes Paweł?' I reply, my eyelashes aflutter. I can't quite believe this is really happening to me. After Matt in London, and all those failed dates, I might actually have met someone – and not just anyone, one of Poland's top legal eagles, who is also an artist, writer and historian! 'You never told you me could draw and paint!' I gabble. 'I particularly love the blue one at the entrance. The way you blur the boundaries between acrylic and oil. And the sense of hegemony you achieve through the use of form – and the way you use light and dark – you manage to create this dichotomy of...'

'Magda.'

Uh-oh. What's wrong? He sounds a tad awkward.

'Yes Paweł?'

'Your dress.'

'Do you like it? I knew you would! It was my elderly aunt's mother's. I must tell you all...'

'It's split.'

'Pardon?'

'Your dress. I'm afraid it's *split*. At the back. No, don't turn around. Everyone will see.'

He sips his sparkling wine in silence, bright red (him, not the wine, but trust me, I'm catching up). One of the art world women looks over and calls hello – a boney-faced pale woman with enormous red lips and a booming voice. She and Paweł lift their glasses, chink them in the air together, then she dazzles him a smile which he dazzles back.

With my back to the wall, I feel down the back of my dress. He's right. There's a massive split around my bottom about twenty centimetres long and I can feel my underwear right through it. This once-beloved-but-now-wretched dress has survived half a century in a wardrobe. Little over an hour on me and it's falling apart. I thought it felt looser as I made my way here – but I thought it had just stretched.

'Oh Paweł. I can't believe it. I'm so sorry! It must have happened as I walked over. What am I going to do? I haven't got anything to put on or to wrap around myself. Have you?'

'Er, no. Not really.'

A terrible thought sails into my mind.

'I'm, I'm going to have to go, aren't I? I'm terribly sorry.'

'It might be... wise... yes. There are a lot of important people here and it might be a bit, well – awkward.' Nervous smile followed by a slow but sure backing off. 'I'll be in touch soon, Magda. Bye!'

Well he found that easy. He's gone, just like that.

I watch him sail off into the crowd, everyone squawking compliments his way.

'Can't we see the funny side?' part of me wants to call out.

No.

I sidle along the back wall and edge my way out of the gallery through reception, edging, edging, edging... smiling nervously along the way, edging, edging. Just my luck. The occasional nod, thanks and goodbye... edging, edging, until I'm gone, departed, out of the building.

I edge nearly all the way home, crab-like, apart from the odd time when there's no one around and I can make up distance by walking normally. I even take off my shoes at one point. Here I am, walking home in a dress that's about to fall off me and a pair of shoes that are maiming my feet.

I reach Language Zone, thank goodness – nearly home. I can't help noticing that the light's still on. Jacek must still be in there and the building must still be open. I remember I've got a cardigan in the staffroom, and given I'm approaching a busy main stretch, I decide to go and get it. The staffroom is well before the language lab, so I can get my cardi and scarper without Jacek even noticing.

In through the door, ever so quietly, and up the flight of stairs, barefoot. This could only happen to me, I think. Yikes. A creak from one of the steps. Silence. Of all the times for a dress to split, it had to be tonight on a date with Paweł.

'*Kto tam?* Who goes there?'

'Jacek, it's me!'

He emerges out of the darkness.

'Magda, I thought we were being burgled!'

'Nope. It's just me. Close your eyes, Jacek.'

'Why?'

'Just close them. I need to get past you to get something from the staffroom, and then I'm off.'

'Will you be long? I'm off now too and I need to set the alarm.'

'No. Promise you won't turn round, OK?'

'Promise.'

'Two minutes.'

Two minutes later, cardi around waist, I'm decent again and we head out of the building together. What a night.

'So. How was the *vernissage*?'

I wish he hadn't asked. I'm about to say it went well, but I know that isn't true. I've barely been gone an hour and I've arrived back barefoot, unable to turn around and humiliated to the core. He doesn't want to know anyway, he's just being polite.

'It was OK.'

'Just OK?'

'It didn't go very well, if I'm perfectly honest.'

'I'm sorry to hear that.'

He sets the alarm and seems a bit more interested.

'I mean, I like this Professor, but I'm not sure I'm good enough for him. There are things that happened tonight that I can't even begin to tell you about.'

'What, like a split dress?'

'Jacek, I told you not to look!'

'I didn't mean to – I was just looking up the stairs to see where you were going. It's not that bad.'

'It is! It was so embarrassing. He practically asked me to leave.'

'What?'

'It was his *vernissage* and I guess nothing could go wrong. Including his date. There were women there who made Giacometti sculptures look fat.'

'I'm sorry. All he needed to do was offer you his jacket and it would have been fine.'

'No no no. He couldn't do that.'

'Why not? I would have.'

'I think I've blown it. Again.'

'Well if you have, all because of a dress, maybe he's not for you, Magda?'

I decide to change the subject. I would love the Prof to be the one for me, but maybe Jacek's right, only I don't want to hear it, like Dagmara didn't want to hear about Stefan.

'I'm starving. I was expecting some proper food but there were just a few fancy canapés. I suppose that's all these gallery women live on.'

'Well I'm off to get some *pierogi*. Fancy coming? I'm going to Zapiecek in Nowy Świat Street.'

'That sounds like heaven. A meal that blurs boundaries between savoury and sweet.'

'Sorry?'

'Nothing. Just tell me about this job in England.'

He starts telling me all about it. It's linked to the work he did in July, and it'll be working in Piccadilly Circus, amongst other places. He says quite a bit more but it isn't long before I stop listening altogether.

Why?

Because along with AB, Jacek's been one of the best things about Warsaw, and if I'm honest, I don't want him to go.

VOCAB CORNER:
Dichotomy (what does this word mean anyway?) = *dychotomia*
Hegemony (for once harder to say in English than in Polish) = *hegemonia*
Blurring of boundaries = *zacierać granice*

CHAPTER 16
OPERATION (*OPERACJA*)

November 8th, the day of AB's op, the day we've all been waiting for. November in Polish is *listopad*, which means 'falling leaves'. All the months in Polish indicate what's happening with the weather.

When my alarm goes off at half past six, I'm already awake, and when I go upstairs an hour later, AB's packed and ready. She's sitting in her armchair in her Sunday best, waiting for the taxi.

'I had a terrible night,' she says.

I try to reassure her, glad I'm going in with her.

'It's just nerves. You've had such a long wait and now it's over.' Grzybek whimpers. He looks at us puzzled, wondering what the change of routine is all about. Is it another trip, and is he coming too? The taxi buzzes.

'We're on our way. Two minutes!' I yell down the intercom.

'Magda, check everything's off, will you?' says AB, getting up. 'I've checked everything a thousand times already, but I might have missed something. Bye, you,' she says to Grzybek, stooping over to tickle him under the chin. 'Magda will walk you when she gets back.'

'Your glasses,' I say, picking them up off the side.

'I knew I'd forget something.'

As she turns to take them, she sweeps the calendar off the sideboard, sending both calendar and a glass of water smashing to the floor. The crossed off dates marked off in red felt tip start to smudge and run.

'Get him out of the way!' she says, as Grzybek dances around the shards of glass. 'Red liquid, it's an omen!'

'AB, don't panic, it's not an omen. You've just knocked something over, that's all. Come on, let's go, I'll shut him in the lounge and clear it up later.'

We travel in silence. As the weeks and months have gone by, I've noticed AB has become much less mobile. Outside the hospital, she leans against a bollard while I run to find a wheelchair. With the taxi gone, it's just us two now. My first time in a Polish hospital.

I find the area with wheelchairs. Some are jammed and go round in circles. Others are as immobile as the people they're meant to help, just like in England. I find one that works and wheel it over.

'Er, excuse me.'

I know that voice.

'Dagmara, what are you doing here?'

She's in her blue dentist's outfit and fits in perfectly.

'What do you think? Where've you been? I've been waiting for you for ages and I'm getting tired of being asked things by people who think I work here!'

'Sorry. I didn't know you were coming.'

'I'm family too, you know. And I've looked after AB for much longer than you, Magda.'

I don't want an argument. Not here.

'Dagmara, if you want to help, that's fine. AB's just outside. I was going to collect her – or do you want to, if you want to be involved?'

'On second thoughts, you get her. I don't want to be doing all the dirty work as usual and pushing a heavy chair.'

I want to say something really cutting and truthful but now's not the time and besides, as is so often the case with Dagmara, my brain goes to pulp just as she finishes a sentence. Instead, I tut very loudly and go out to get AB.

AB's long grey curls blow in the wind as I wheel her across the car park. Zone C, our destination, is on the seventh floor.

'Dagmara's turned up, AB. Just so you know.'

'She's what?'

'She must have known it was today.'

AB's speechless, which is good, in a way. Dagmara gives her a hug when we get to her, and we take the lift in silence. Up and down, up and down, I'm like a yo-yo, these days.

'You can both go now,' says AB, as we enter the ward. She probably doesn't want us bickering.

'Are you sure? I don't mind waiting.'

'Neither do I.'

'I don't have a class until this afternoon.'

'Well I'm fitting a new set of dentures in an hour, but I can postpone them if you like.'

AB's had enough.

'Will you two stop it? I'm about to have an operation and you're starting to drive me insane! I love you both – just the same, but my admission into hospital is not going to become your battlefield.'

'It's her not me,' says Dagmara.

'No it isn't, it's you!'

AB flops back on the bed with a thwack and stares at the ceiling, as if she's trying to count to ten before saying anything.

'Just go, will you? And sort out your differences before I get back home!'

Dagmara throws me a haughty look and I look the other way.

'Come tomorrow, not tonight,' says AB, a little more conciliatory. 'I'll be far too dozy later on. Go on, I'm all right. It'll all be forms and questions now and only I can do those.'

We leave AB behind. As I turn around to wave, she catches my eye and manages a smile, holding up her hand.

'I'm off,' says Dagmara, sour.

'Me too. I hope she's OK.'

'She will be.'

'Dagmara, I'll text you a schedule of when I'm going to be there. So we don't need to be there at the same time.'

'Fine by me.'

She's about to walk off when I squeeze in another question.

'How are things, Dagmara?'

'How do you think?'

'Can we talk for just one minute? I ...'

But she storms off, bob swinging from side to side.

'I hope your extraction and dentures go OK!' I call.

At home, I clear away the broken glass and move Grzybek down to my flat. I didn't like leaving AB. It felt as if I were abandoning her.

Only at Language Zone does the memory of hospital, with its bright lights, beds on wheels and clatter of medicine trolleys, fade away.

Pani Dąbrowska and Pani Raszewska are back from holiday and have had a make-over, just like the office. These days they look more like fancy poodles than hibernating moths. Pani Raszewska, whose hair used to be a dyed-to-death bun, now wears it down with soft brown streaks running through. She's also on her computer at last, and by the looks of things, is having a game of online poker. Her nails make a gentle tapping sound on the keyboard as she types, like Grzybek's claws on AB's kitchen lino. Pani Dąbrowska has been transformed too. Always more glamorous and outgoing than her serious sister, her blond meringue hair now has a party-pink rinse, matched by a pastel pink two-piece suit and black patent heels.

'Before I forget – here's your photo, from your first day.'

She pulls out a black and white photo with wavy edges and slides it onto the counter. I've never had an ID photo quite like it. But it's not so much the antique look that surprises me, it's how much my life has changed since my first day. My relationship with AB and Dagmara, even Mama and Jacek – everything has changed so much in the past four months.

I sail through my intermediates on autopilot, my mind drifting back and forth between class and the hospital. I also check my phone for texts or messages from Paweł for something to do. It's been weeks now since the *vernissage* and although I've had the occasional short message which has maintained my hope, I think that's probably it.

Surely he'll have seen the funny side and it's not quite the end? It was worse for me, not him. He seemed so keen before, too.

Actually, he's got a public lecture coming up – so maybe I'll go. Partly because I'm interested, but mainly because I want to see him and take my mind off AB. I've been trying to read his book every night but I can't get into it. (Tell a lie, I read it the other night, when I couldn't sleep – and it got me off in no time.)

Next, it's beginners. They all know it's AB's big day, having been through many trials and operations of their own. In a move of solidarity, Pani Teresa has baked AB a *babka* cake for me to take in later, a dense round marble cake which, I have to say, I adore.

At two o'clock, just as AB will be going into theatre, Jacek happens upon me in the classroom, staring at the clock.

'I'm worried about her, Jacek. It's her op today. Her hip. Did she tell you?'

He nods and says she told him all about it while he was working in her flat.

'Operations are always worrying,' he says, 'even minor ones. But what you have to remember is people have these operations every day, all over the world. Do you want to go for a walk to talk about it? I'm off to London later, but have some time.'

I'm sorely tempted, as it's a beautiful afternoon. I also know Jacek will have been through similar trials himself, having lost Marzena, but I want to catch Paweł's lecture. So I thank him but decline.

I pack up and head for the University Law Department. I found out about Paweł's lecture on the law department's website. In a way, I sort of feel as if I'm stalking him, as he hasn't invited me directly. But, I do know him, it is a public lecture and I am interested in history and law (almost). Also, we haven't actually fallen out, so what could be the problem?

The lecture theatre is brimming with people and I struggle to find a free seat. Eventually, I find one about ten rows back, right by the wall. 'Hello!' I mouth to Paweł at the front when he vaguely looks my way. I wonder if he's seen me? I think he has, but it's hard to say.

He starts his lecture and I make copious notes, cross-referencing words in my dictionary. Communism this, Cold War that. It's all very interesting, it's just that – my mind's on other things.

I do a lot of doodles. Paweł, AB, plus spirals and circles, anything. When I've had enough, I lean my chin on my hands and close my eyes – so that I can concentrate on his words without being distracted

After what feels like several weeks, but is only ninety minutes, I join a queue of people waiting to see him. I feel incredibly nervous, like you feel at a job interview. What are we going to talk about? Not the *vernissage*. Perhaps about meeting up? Given the other night didn't count. I know – I'll focus on the talk, how brilliant it was and crucial and important.

'Paweł!'

'Magda...'

'That was amazing!'

'Yes,' he coughs, 'I saw you there, dozing in the corner.'

'Oh no no no no no – I wasn't asleep – I was concentrating!'

'How did you know about today's talk?'

'I Googled you. Public lectures are great aren't they? I must come to some more. I'm sorry about the *vernissage* and my dress, by the way.'

I wasn't going to mention that, but somehow it's popped out.

'Not a problem!'

'Did it go well for you?'

'Yes, thank you.'

'My aunt's in hospital today...'

I'm about to launch into my spiel when he interrupts me.

'I'm sorry Magda, but there's someone I really need to talk to.' He looks over my shoulder towards somebody coming straight at him – a long-haired brunette, with razor-shell cheekbones and feline eyes.

Right. I get it. Time to slope off. I'm doing a lot of that these days.

'Bye, Paweł.'

Bag, coat, file under arm.

'Goodbye. Keep in touch.'

He means shove off, basically.

That evening, at home, before I ring the ward, I go on Polishmate for the very last time. At first I was upset about Paweł, now I'm just annoyed. Annoyed with his arrogance and annoyed with myself. It's like Matt, all over again. To think I thought Paweł was different. I thought he was modest, shy and gentle. But he's vain, uncaring and rude.

I managed to reset my password after Dagmara hacked into my account, and I have a look at my messages. The ones from Paweł can go. Then there are all the others from my other dates, they can go too. Polishmate.com might work for some people, but it's got me nowhere.

Maybe I should start a new hobby, I think, as I empty my inbox? Crocheting or traditional Polish dancing? Or maybe join a convent?

'Ping,' goes my computer. Who is it this time? A message from that photoless guy, Michał again.

'Would you like to meet up?' says his message, short and sweet.

Before I do anything rash, I need to think about this carefully. Is short good, or is short bad? Here I am, about to leave Polishmate and this arrives. He must be online now. I have a quick look at his profile again. 'Likes culture and cafes' – just like me. But no, the way I feel now, I don't another date ever again.

'Sorry, no,' I type.

'Why not?' he replies a second later.

'What have you got to lose?'

Where do I start? My dignity? Another broken heart?

'I promise we'll have a wonderful evening.'

Pause. Wonderful? *Really*?

OK, one last try before I go to 'account settings' and 'unsubscribe'.

'Oh go on then. Why not?' I reply.

Done now. No turning back.

Seconds later he writes back, suggesting a cafe in an area called Praga, east of the river. In former years, Dagmara said I should never under any circumstances go to Praga on my own (her saying 'don't do something' usually my cue do it). In fact one time, I did go to Praga on my own, to a huge outdoor flea market called Stadium, now the new national football ground. Hundreds of stall traders from places as far away as Belarus and even Vietnam would come to the crumbling Stadium to sell their wares and try to make a dime. (Once I nearly got talked into buying a Russian fur hat but the price was exorbitant.) Today, the market has moved and the area of Praga with its pre-war and post-industrial buildings is home to many artists' galleries, theatres and clubs. To be honest, Michał's offer sounds right up my street and we arrange to meet this weekend.

Later, when I ring the ward, the nurse who answers tells me that Pani Nowakowska, AB, is doing 'just fine'. She sounds positively underwhelmed – and that's fine by me. At times like this, underwhelmed is just what you want.

Grapes, chocolate and vanilla marble cake and prune juice. It's morning and I'm at the hospital, unpacking AB's goodies. She's fast asleep. I give her a gentle nudge.

'I had such a bad night,' she groans, coming round. 'I woke up, took a lot of painkillers – but they didn't help. Then they gave me a jab. That did the trick and I went out like a light.shame.'

'Great, AB. And how do you feel now, better? I'm so glad it's over. I couldn't think about anything else yesterday.'

'Sleepy... I'm still so sleepy.'

'Well there's plenty of time for that. Take a look at this!' Whipping out Pani Teresa's *babka* cake makes a glorious, sweet, buttery smell fill the air around us.

'This little beauty is from Pani Teresa at school! Shall we have some?'

'Yes please. Ouch!' she says as she moves. 'I'm just so... sore.'

'I guess that's to be expected,' I breeze. 'You have just had a major operation. I'm glad to see your appetite's not gone.'

I start to spread out a serviette so that I can cut up the cake, but when I look up a second later, she's out for the count. What a shame. I was looking forward to a chat – to telling her the latest about the Prof and my date with Michał. But never mind, she should rest.

I have a slice of *babka* myself, leave AB's on the side, and go.

When I return in the evening, she's worse, not better. AB's in so much pain that she can barely move. Dagmara's there, quiet for once. She doesn't give me short shrift about anything.

A nurse gives AB some morphine and she drifts off, mumbling. Dagmara asks the nurse some questions. Dissatisfied, she tries to find a doctor, but there's no one around.

'Stop fussing, Dagmara.' I'm starting to have enough.

'I am not fussing,' says Dagmara. 'I've got a medical training, and what's happening is not normal.'

'Then please just calm down – you're not helping anything.'

ARE MY ROOTS SHOWING?

'Calm down? Magda! How can I calm down?'

We're left with AB's orthopaedic bed which bleeps every few seconds, and nurses breezing back and forth. I know why Dagmara's fretting. It's because she's not in control, and deep down, she's scared.

I look at AB, searching for signs of improvement and start to worry too. Maybe Dagmara's right and AB should be more alert by now? Around us, the ladies in beds nearby look on with vacant stares.

'I don't like how much pain she seems to be in.'

'Me neither.'

Dinner arrives. AB awakes and we try to help her eat, but her appetite has waned. This morning's cake is untouched too.

When a different nurse comes to change her drip, Dagmara launches into a stream of questions again and I pop out into the stairwell to give Mama a ring.

'She's in a lot of pain Mama. A lot.'

'Well she's had a big procedure, hasn't she? It's not like having a tooth out is it?'

'That's what I thought, at first. But it does seem excessive. She's all dozy and floppy. Dagmara was worried, and I am too, now.'

'Magda! Magda! You don't know AB like I do! Neither does Dagmara! She just needs to rest. She's as strong as *a rosyjski czołg*! (Russian tank). You're exhausted, I can hear it in your voice!'

Mama's probably right. Fatigue does taint things. I go back in and a few minutes later, to our relief, AB comes round. Not only that but she's all chatty and lively – almost delirious – it's as if this sleepy, pain-filled phase has passed.

It's dark when we take the tram home. I'm glad Dagmara's been with me. We look back at the hospital as it fades into the distance, trying to figure out which floor AB might be on.

'Goodnight AB, sleep well!' calls Dagmara, looking through the back pane, her hand against the glass.

We may be upbeat but I don't think AB's out of the woods yet. The last twenty-four hours have been unpredictable, consuming and long.

And yet I haven't been able to ignore that Dagmara hasn't mentioned Stefan once.

CHAPTER 17
LITTLE GIRL PLAYING
(DZIEWCZYNKA KTÓRA SIĘ BAWI)

Dagmara and I were going to take visiting in turns until AB came home. But things don't always turn out as planned, do they? Entering the ward the next evening, I'm stopped in my tracks by a doctor who leads me to a side-room.

'We've been trying to ring you,' she says, in a hurried manner. 'Your aunt's stable at the moment.'

'Stable? What do you mean, stable?' I ask, shocked. 'We are talking about Pani Nowakowska, aren't we?'

She closes the door behind us and shuffles through some notes.

'Yes, we are,' she says. 'Pani Nowakowska. I'm afraid that your aunt has had a very small stroke.'

'A stroke?'

My heart starts to race.

'It's not been a large one, it's been a very small one. Take your time, I know it's a lot to take in.'

She's right there, it is a lot to take in. It's awful, and too much. It doesn't feel real, let alone true.

'But… she only came in for a hip replacement.'

'I know. I know. Please don't worry.'

'How come she's had a stroke?'

'Well, your aunt has had the strain of long-term pain – and then there's the operation itself.'

'Is she going to be all right? I thought she was going to be coming out soon. Maybe even tomorrow?'

'I'm afraid she's not going anywhere just yet. She can move and talk – a little – but we'll know more in the next twenty-four hours. She's been saying the name 'Władek' quite a lot – is that her husband?'

'No.'

'But it is someone important?'

'Was. Still is, I guess. I don't have a number or anything like that though. There's Pani Nowakowska's niece, Dagmara, my cousin, I ought to call her.'

'It's OK, we have called her already, she's on her way. Why don't I take you to see your Aunt?' she says, standing up. 'She might not be very alert but it would be good for you to go to see her. Wouldn't it?'

I nod and follow her out of her the room, my legs moving, it feels like, of their own accord. When I reach AB's bed, she's lying there asleep, her large round body rising and falling. She looks so peaceful and as if nothing is wrong, just like she did when she'd doze on the sofa at home. The doctor leaves me.

'AB? Can you hear me?' I whisper, taking her hand. Her hand is soft and warm but there's no reply. She just carries on with her heavy breathing. I wipe her tepid face, thankful that I'm there.

'It's me, AB, Magda.'

She opens her eyes wide and looks at me, dazed.

'Magda?'

'Yes. I'm here.' I touch her arm. 'How do you – feel?'

'I don't...know.'

A large tear escapes from my eye and rolls down my cheek onto her hand.

'Don't cry, child,' she says, fading again. Her speech is slow and slurred, not full of life like it usually is. Does AB know that she's had a stroke?

'Hello,' she says with sudden certainty. *'Czy to ty, Władek?* (Is it you, Władek?)'

'It's Magda, AB. Magda. Dagmara's on her way. You're going to be all right. Can you hear me?'

'I... I... I don't seem to be moving that well. My face, and my side.'

'It's because you've been asleep for so long. Try to sit up.'

'I want to, but I can't.'

'Do you want something to drink? Some water?'

'Yes. Yes. What's happening? Oh, oh. I can't sit up.'

'Let's buzz for a nurse.'

Her face contorts with pain. I don't think they've told her anything, or if they have, she hasn't remembered.

'Wait,' she says. 'I feel different.' She lifts her left hand up and gazes at it. 'My hip hurts... Look at those flies Magda, just above the bed. Who'd have thought – flies in a hospital – it's disgraceful!'

'Flies? Where?'

I can't see any flies. I look up to where she's looking, but the wall is clear. She's seeing things. Spots, perhaps, before her eyes.

'AB. You've had an *udar*. A stroke. I don't know if they've told you, but that's why you're like this.'

'An *udar*?' she says, stunned, as Dagmara hurries in.

'Yes. Just a small one though, and see, you can talk and move, you're going to be fine.'

Dinner comes and goes again. We try to feed her a little, but she pushes it away. I try to give her the pills left near her earlier on, crushing them with spoons, but she doesn't want them either.

I ring and update Mama. There's talk of her coming over again, but we decide to wait, until things become clearer.

Dagmara and I sit with AB until visiting time is over and beyond, until we can sit no more.

'Do you think she's going to be all right Magda?' asks Dagmara, as we take the staircase down.

'I honestly don't know.'

'Magda,' she says, stopping in her tracks.

'What?'

'It's over. Between me and Stefan.'

'What?'

I turn to look at her, her face is full of sorrow. The second our eyes meet, she starts one of those juddering streams of tears that can only ever be about Stefan.

'I'm so sorry, Dagmara. I really, really am.'

'He's...he's...been seeing someone else. You were right, Magda. Everything you said about him was right! I feel like such a fool!'

'You're not a fool, Dagmara. You're not!'

She cries inconsolably.

'How could he? When we were planning our wedding!'

'I'm so, so sorry.'

'He's a scumbag! A louse! A...a...'

'Dagmara, don't. Let's not talk here. Why don't you come back to the flat with me now? You can tell me all about it.'

'Really?' she asks through smudged mascara. 'You're not annoyed with me for not believing you?'

The truth is, I am miffed, lots. But next to AB on the ward, and Dagmara's heartbreak, my upset pales into insignificance.

'I'm not annoyed. I know what I said must have been upsetting. Come on, let's go home. I'll make some dinner and you can stop over if you like. We can go to hospital together in the morning. I don't want to go on my own.'

'Neither do I.'

She sniffs and we head home.

Peace, at last. I gaze down the boulevard which sweeps through the centre of Warsaw – this big, flat, fast and moving city.

There's only one thing I've forgotten about, I think, as the tram arrives. The small matter of AB's greatest love, Grzybek. Dagmara will go berserk if she finds out he's with me. There's only one thing for it. I'll have to send Dagmara to the Chinese takeaway while I take him back upstairs and whizz around with the hoover.

Despite everything, perhaps because of everything, Dagmara and I have a wonderful evening together. Tear-stained and grief-stricken, all her defences are down and there are no wisecracks or cutting comments.

'Poor AB,' she says every few seconds, sitting on the sofa, clutching at a tissue.

'I know. Mama says she's really strong.'

'Yes. I've always said she's indestructible – like a cockroach in a nuclear blast. Magda.'

'What?'

'Do you know something?'

'What?'

'It smells a bit funny in here. Sort of musty – or mouldy – yet mixed with heaps of perfume. I can't quite put my finger on it.'

'It must be the Chinese.'

'No. Nothing like that. Like old slippers or something weird.'

'Oh, I know what it is. I burnt some toast this morning,' I reply, suddenly kicking one of Grzybek's toys that I missed under the sofa, 'so I went a bit mad with the air-freshener.'

'No no. It's not burnt toast.'

'I've been cooking English things. You know.'

'Anyway, let me tell you what happened. One day last week, I bumped into one of the other salesmen where Stefan works, and I made some comment about all the overtime they've been having. He said he didn't know what I was talking about as they haven't had any overtime in months. I said, "Are you sure?" and he said, "Yes I'm sure." At that point, I think he realised something was up as then he changed subject. Magda, Stefan was doing overtime at the weekend, and overtime in the week. And always looking smarter and smarter too – wearing clothes that I'd bought him! So one day, when he said he had some overtime, I followed him in the car and he went...he went...'

The next bit is a mixture of Dagmara sobbing and gasping for air, but I can imagine exactly where he went.

'Where, *kochana*?'

'To see another woman! In a bar! I thought maybe it was a client at first – about a car – but no – they met and kissed as I watched from afar! "I want a final bit of freedom," is what he said to me, Magda! How could he do that, how?'

'So what did you do?'

'I went up to them, slapped his face and poured his drink over his head!'

'You didn't!'

'I did! Then I said to the woman, "What do you think you're playing at, with my husband?" You should have seen her face. She looked really shocked – but I was as good as married, wasn't I?'

'You were, absolutely.'

'He isn't getting the ring back, oh no. I'm going to sell it. Get myself some nice new clothes.'

'Dagmara, you poor thing!'

I try to give her a bit of a hug as she sits on the sofa, which doesn't really work as I'm sitting on the floor. Besides, I've never hugged Dagmara in my life and it feels strange starting now.

'I believed you deep down, you know that don't you?' she says, her voice wobbling. 'That's why I was so angry – I knew it must be true. You can't lie like me,' she says, as I recall my burnt-toast-and-English-food-story only five minutes earlier. 'You're the nice one out of the two us. You always have been and always will be!'

'No. Don't say that. It's not true.'

'So now, I'm back to square one again. Nothing good ever happens to me!'

'Yes it does.'

'Name one thing. Go on.'

Long pause.

Actually, I can't.

When we go to bed, we arrange ourselves so we're lying head to foot in bed, just like old times when I came to visit. Maybe even like Mama and Uncle Szymon when they were little. I fill Dagmara in on the Prof, the *vernissage*, the lecture, everything.

'He was so wrong for you,' she says. 'I knew it from the start.'

'But I thought you wanted me to keep on seeing him.'

'I know, but you need someone like yourself, who isn't normal.'

'Thanks.'

'Sorry, I don't mean normal in that way,' she says, sensing my surprise, 'I mean someone – less ordinary.'

'Paweł wasn't ordinary, Dagmara. He was extraordinary. His brain was as vast as the universe.'

'Yes but his heart wasn't, was it? I know what it is. You need someone with a good heart.'

'Don't we all?'

Another long pause. I get up to make some camomile tea and, still wide awake, we press our faces against the balcony window, looking onto the road below, letting the steam from our mugs mist up the pane.

'I'm so glad we're talking again,' I say. It's cold and wet outside but tucked inside our snug flat, you'd never know. 'By the way, I'm having a final stab at Polishmate, and then I'm calling it quits. Some guy called Michał with no photo.'

'No photo? What's he got to hide?'

'Not sure. But he got in in the nick of time. I was just about close everything down when his message arrived.'

'Polish men, Magda. I'm through with the lot of them. They're a waste of time!'

'They can't all be bad. Your father wasn't a waste of time, was he? Neither is mine.'

I switch off the light, a full stop to my sentence.

From where I'm lying I can see the elongated shadows of the seedlings that I planted when we found Mama's tin. Positioned over the warm radiator, they've come up quickly – tiny, pale-green feathered fronds.

'Dagmara, look at what's come up from the seeds in Mama's tin. I think they're carrots.'

'You don't get carrots in November, Magda.'

'I know, but I planted them and they've come up. Isn't that amazing, after all this time?'

'I didn't think they had carrots in Siberia.'

'They must have. Mama said she stole some from a field once, when she was little. She's told me the story lots of times.'

'Really? What happened?'

'She walked past a carrot field one day and decided to steal some because she was hungry. She took a couple, then she turned back to get some for your dad, who was at school. She hid them under her armpits until she got home. When she got back to the hut, she hid them under his pillow.'

'And?'

'Grandma caught him eating them and asked him where he got them from. He said found them under his pillow.'

Dagmara squeals.

'Tata never told me that!' she says.

'At that point Mama owned up. Grandma took her by the shoulders and said, 'Don't ever do that again. Because if you do and we get caught, they'll throw me in prison and that'll be the end of you.'

'Gosh. Good job she never got found out.' Dagmara moves her legs about and fidgets. 'That must have been before she got ill and died. Grandma I mean.'

'Yes,' I reply, briefly thinking of AB, then pushing the thought aside.

'Aw,' she says, 'that's a nice story. Sad, but still nice. Magda?'

'What?' I yawn.

'I'd have stolen some carrots for you,' she says, mid-fidget.

'No you wouldn't.'

'I would! Wouldn't you for me?'

'I guess so.'

I'm touched by her expression of sibling love and decide, yes I would have done too.

Soon afterwards, her fidgeting subsides, and she falls asleep.

I continue to look at the spidery shadows of the seedlings on the wall, thinking of AB and Mama. It was the story she always used to tell me at bedtime and I never grew tired of it.

I hope AB's all right. And Mama and Tata.

A snore and a whistling sound start to come from the end of the bed. Oh dear. I'd forgotten Dagmara snores.

But I suppose I should be grateful she hasn't asked about the dog.

AB's asleep when we arrive at hospital the next day. We didn't know what we'd find.

'She looks dreadful, Magda,' says Dagmara, before she's even managed to throw off her coat. 'I didn't think she'd be as bad as this. I thought she'd be better after last night.'

'Shh – she might be able to hear you.'

'No, look, she can't hear a thing.'

She tries clapping, clicking her fingers, shouting 'AB' loudly into AB's ears. None of this works and it's only when a nurse objects that she finally gives up. We stay the whole morning, holding AB's hand. As our watch runs on, AB wakes up of her own accord. She looks at us, and past us, then finally recognises us.

'We're here, AB! Dagmara and me!'

'Are you feeling better?'

'Yes,' she says. 'What time is it?'

'About twelve,' I reply.

'In the day?'

'Yes,' says Dagmara.

'Shall I ring Mama?' I ask. 'She wanted to talk to you.'

AB nods. My fingers are like jelly and I have to concentrate to get the right number up. Mama answers after only half a ring.

'Magda! How is she?'

'Not too bad,' I lie. 'I'm with her now. Shall I put you on?'

I hold the phone to AB's ear and she bends her neck to talk.

'Bolesława,' says AB faintly. 'Are you there? Everything hurts. Everything.'

Oh dear – I thought there might be words of hope, but AB's just being honest. She slumps back, not strong enough to talk.

'Sorry, I thought you might be able to have a chat.'

'I knew she shouldn't have had that operation! I knew it!'

'Mama, I'll ring you later. When I'm at home, OK?'

We stay on, sitting and waiting, waiting and sitting. The ward and the corridor is full of movement – staff working and visitors arriving. Each patient in their own world of troubles. As lunchtime comes and goes, AB pushes me away when I try to touch her face.

Dagmara and I both decide to return to work, pledging to stay in touch. At school, I can't concentrate. I go through all my lessons in a haze.

That night, Dagmara sleeps at her own flat and Grzybek comes back downstairs with me. I cancel the date with Michał this weekend. Right now, it's the last thing I want.

As I get ready for bed, the phone rings. At first I think it's the hospital, but it's Jacek who's back from London. I hope that he'll provide me with the same positive spin on things that he did the other day – but he doesn't say anything.

At around six o'clock the next morning, forty-eight hours since AB had her stroke, the phone rings again. 'You must come in,' the nurse says over the phone. 'Your Aunt's very ill.'

I spend the whole journey wondering what 'very ill' means. To my horror, when I arrive, AB's bed isn't there. I look round wondering for a moment if I've got the wrong floor, but I recognise the decor. This is the right ward – but AB isn't here. Am I too late? Has she been moved? A nurse, one I haven't seen before, hurries over.

'For Pani Nowakowska, yes?' she whispers, sweeping me along. She leads me to a side-room where I'm joined by a hospital priest who takes my hand tightly. AB, I'm told, is in here. She has had another stroke and this time, it's serious.

'Is she – still conscious?' I ask, devastated.

'We're very sorry. She's unresponsive.'

What do you do when you hear a phrase like that? What are you meant to say? What are you meant to feel? Everything around me is falling away, like a house of collapsing cards.

The nurse pushes the door open and we enter a silent, simply furnished room. My heart crumples as I see AB lying before me. The only apparatus attached to her now is a drip and all her belongings are in a bag on the floor. Is this it? Is this all it comes to?

She lies unconscious before me, breathing loudly.

'How long does she have?' I ask the nurse.

'A day, we think. Maybe less.'

The nurse's words wash through me and over me.

'AB, AB.'

She can't hear me, and never will.

Dagmara arrives and the nurse leaves us and closes the door. I take one side of the bed and Dagmara takes the other. The priest stands at the foot and begins the *ostatnie namaszczenie* – the last rites. I've never heard them said before, let alone in solemn Polish.

'*Przez to święte namaszczenie niech Pan w swoim nieskończonym miłosierdziu wspomoże ciebie łaską Ducha Świętego. Pan, który odpuszcza ci grzechy niech cię wybawi i łaskawie podźwignie. Amen.* (Through this holy anointing may the Lord in His infinite mercy help you with the Holy Spirit. The Lord who frees you from sin, may He save you and lift you up graciously. Amen.)'

Dear AB. Tears roll down my cheeks and fall onto her hand. She can't feel them this time, or see them. Dagmara wipes her own silent tears, filled with grief.

I watch AB as her body twitches. Locks of hair tumble around her moist face. AB and I had become friends as well as relatives. She had looked after Mum when she came back from Siberia and she had looked after me. She never asked for much. She was just dear old AB. The priest leaves and I take AB's hand.

I imagine her through the various stages of her life as she lies breathing before us. They stream through my mind like meteorites hurtling to earth: AB as baby, toddler and little girl. Little girl playing, little girl hiding as the soldier comes in. The meteorites are drawing to a close now, about to finish their course.

AB and her sweetheart, AB alone.

AB whose heart was broken and AB who went on.

And now...

Her body, in pain for so long, is a mound of falling and rising juddering flesh. Memories held in every limb and joint. Each ailment, each wrinkle, each tear and grey hair, an imprint of some feeling or event.

Dagmara tucks a pillow under her hip. I never thought anything like this would happen. Wasn't I meant to come out here and have, well – fun? Even AB would agree, I think, as I remember her telling me to 'live a little' on our day out to the woods? Wasn't I here to improve my Polish and find my Polish roots? Not this, for sure?

I want to do everything I can for her until the very end. I rub her hands and her feet, her arms and her legs, repositioning them into what I think might be a more comfortable position.

I have found my roots, AB. I have. Here, with you.

'This is payback time isn't it? You looked after me and Mum – and now I'm looking after you.'

I ring Mama, and then we wait.

'I'm so sorry about everything,' says Dagmara to AB, over her fading body. 'You were right about Stefan. It's finished. Do you think she can hear me?'

'Yes Dagmara. I think she can.'

Several hours later, towards nine o'clock, AB's breathing changes. It becomes deeper and slower.

'She's going, Dagmara,' I say. 'She's going. You're nearly there, dear *Ciociu*, I whisper to AB. 'Nearly there. Goodbye. And thank you.'

I hold my breath as I wait for her final breath.

It comes. And it goes.

AB

has

gone.

I feel a rush of grief and joy all at the same time. I look at the clock to record the time, 9.02 p.m. For some reason, the words 'she's made it' keep coming out of my mouth.

Yes, she's made it.

CHAPTER 18
UNEXPECTED GIFT
(*NIEOCZEKIWANY PREZENT*)

Mama says that when Grandad died suddenly, the worst thing about it was not having a chance to say goodbye.

With AB's death, Mama's grief is more like a slow but deep wound. I can see the blow land but the pain isn't instant. It seems to develop over time and touches on other griefs. For Mama, AB's passing is a severance with her past. She's grieving for her parents, her brother, and her sister too.

As Dagmara and I work through all AB's paperwork, I discover that AB has left me her flat. She arranged it this year, not long after I arrived in the summer. I think I may even remember the day. One day, shortly after our first dinner together, I saw a man leaving her flat with a briefcase full of papers. I asked her if he was her doctor, but she said no.

I don't think she had a hunch. I think she just made the decision. I suppose she looked upon me as a daughter. Mama was her first adopted daughter, then, in a roundabout way, it was me. I can see that with all my visits to Poland over the years, AB slipped me carefully and quietly under her wing and saw me as her own.

CHAPTER 19
PLAYING CHOPIN
(*GRAJĄC SZOPENA*)

Some good things happen:

1. The original Chinese hair-straighteners finally arrive. Only four months late and no longer needed. Inside I find a pleasant surprise: a compensatory voucher code for a hundred złoty – about twenty pounds – and a beauty brochure. (Possible future purchase: electric tweezers for facial hair).
2. In other hair-news, Paweł's bird's-nest barnet is no more – he's had it entirely cut off. I've seen him on TV. Before, his unruly hair filled the screen – now you can actually see a bit more of the studio he's in when he's making his comments.
3. Last but not least, I rearranged my date with Michał – for this Saturday night!

Today though, it's Friday, and Language Zone's grand opening night. The refurbishment's complete and a new era is afoot. During the past few days, Pani Dąbrowska and Pani Raszewska have been blowing up balloons and bundling off leaflets to students to give out on the streets. All in all, around ten tons of fresh plaster must have been poured into this building next to the ten tons of junk that have been thrown out.

At eight o'clock sharp, supremely hair-sprayed, powdered and perfumed, Pani Dąbrowska and Pani Raszewska burst into the main lecture hall holding trays of food: roll-mop herrings in a sea of cornichons, rye bread sandwiches smelling of caraway and ham, and platters laden with creamy gateaux. Poles love their cake and actually, they seem to eat it at any time of day. I once saw a builder tucking into a big Neopolitan – a large cube of sponge in pink icing – at nine o'clock in the morning! For me, I'm afraid Polish cakes don't cut it like English ones. They're lighter (blander), often soaked with syrup (too sweet) and have tons of that awful coffee-flavoured butter cream they stick in everything. I should say the worst cake of all is *makowiec*, (poppy seed cake). It looks like a Swiss roll with chocolate paste in it, but really, it's a mush of sweetened poppy seeds.

As people start to tuck in, I see the hall is bustling with current and prospective students, teachers like me, and hopefully, the odd local journalist.

Pani Raszewska flashes me a rare smile and winks. More retiring than her flamboyant sister, it's not been easy for her, all this change. I told her that in some ways, offices in England try to change the other way. Adspeak would have done anything for a grand old office like theirs, complete with family armour and antique dirt.

I have a little secret. I salvaged the old flag that hung above the mantelpiece from the skip on the day it was thrown out. I couldn't let such an heirloom be cast away so brutally and thoughtlessly. Washed and pressed, I returned it to the ladies.

'Thank you for coming, and for everyone's hard work,' says Pan Tadek through a clip mic, a triple vodka in his hand.

As he speaks, I drift towards my students down the side and nod some hellos as I listen. Miles is across the room with a few of the other teachers and my elderly beginners are sitting in the corner.

Oddly though, it's Jacek who stands out most of all tonight. For some reason, he's dressed very smartly, more smartly than anyone else. He's in a dinner suit and a bow tie with a flower in his lapel.

'So let's stand and make a toast to my two aunts, to all the teachers and of course my team of builders, without whom we'd never have got here.'

Just as everyone lifts their glasses, my phone starts to ring, drat. I make for the corridor, navigating through the crowd.

As I thought – Dagmara. We're best of buddies now (well nearly) but she'll have to wait. I knock it to answerphone and let her leave one of her eternal messages while I join in with the toast. It's probably about a guy.

'Before we start our celebrations,' resumes Pan Tadek, 'I need to make an announcement. As part of tonight's launch, I have the pleasure of announcing a special performance by one of our builders. Nothing to do with, demolition...' The audience laughs and he pauses, looking around, knowing he's stirring up our interest. 'This will be a surprise to some of you, but not to those who know him well. Please put your hands together for Jacek Balon, who's going to play a piece for us on the violin!'

Everyone turns around to look at Jacek and the room bursts into applause. As the audience settles down, Jacek walks to the centre of the stage with his violin and turns to face the front. I'm amazed. He said he was through with music, yet here he is, about to give a solo.

As he composes himself, someone switches off the main lights and fades in a lone spotlight. It falls on Jacek, who has his violin under his chin and is ready and waiting. He starts to play. Not like someone who hasn't played in years – but like someone who really knows how to take up a violin and bring it to life. It's beautiful.

As I stand and listen, I think about what Pan Tadek said. I probably fall into the camp of those who know Jacek well. He's been part of my life since day one. We had the terrible lamb roast, the weeks of work on the leak and he was also there for me when AB was in hospital. I feel transported yet fixed to the spot. I can't take my eyes off his hands and his eyes that are closed with concentration. He's playing Chopin, AB's favourite composer. The funeral took place at her church – Church of the Holy Cross – in Nowy Świat Street, which is where Chopin's heart is interred. She would have loved this performance. When he finishes and bows, the room erupts into applause and a ripple of stamping resounds through the building.

As Jacek leaves the stage and makes his way towards the back, he spots me in the doorway and takes the rose out of his lapel.

'Here,' he smiles, pressing it into my hands and kissing me softly on the cheek. 'This is for you.'

Then he goes out into the corridor and vanishes. What was that all about? Was that a token, or was it – something else? What did he give me a rose for, and a kiss, in front of everyone?

I next spot him when the party's in full swing but somehow, we don't talk for the rest of the night. Whether it's because I'm too shy or he's too shy, I don't know. But whenever he catches my eye and I his, we look the other way. He's far too busy talking to people who want to congratulate him on his playing, and I'm far too busy dealing with new students.

For the rest of the evening, I keep every single thought and every racing emotion under wraps and in check, just like Jacek's rose, zipped away in my handbag. When things start to quieten down, I look for him again, but I can't see him anywhere. If I found him though, what would I say? To think he's going to leave for London soon too.

When even Pani Dąbrowska and Pani Raszewska start to pack me off with leftovers and start hovering around with a bunch of keys, I know it's time to go. I check my phone, thinking that perhaps he's texted me. Nothing. He's gone.

I walk back home swinging the rose in my hand. To my surprise, when I enter my block, there's a bunch of flowers waiting by the kiosk. Just when I thought my phase of getting flowers had gone. Multicoloured gerbera, one of my favourites. I know they're for me because Pani Zosia has written 'Magda' on them, in big letters.

'To Magda. Looking forward to this Saturday, Michał,' says the card.

I feel confused. I was excited about the date too, but now? I've Michał's bunch of gerbera in one hand and Jacek's rose in the other.

Jacek. His playing was so beautiful. And to then give me his rose and kiss me on the cheek. Did he only do it because I was by the door? Perhaps he'd have done the same with whoever was there?

That night, as I lie in bed, I can't help but mull over the scene again and again. I don't want to do anything to spoil our friendship, so the best thing is – to make light of it – and forget it ever happened.

CHAPTER 20
KAMPINOS FOREST
(*PUSZCZA KAMPINOSKA*)

All this time, I never gave Jacek a second thought, but now? I've been waiting for him to get in touch since I woke up. I've done all the tricks – switch my phone off, switch it back on – nothing. Men.

I shouldn't be like this, all double-minded, just before a date. I should be looking forward to meeting Michał tonight, not hoping that Jacek will ring. When it was a nail he wanted, or some kind of glue or special paint, he sent me texts every other minute. Now he's given me a rose and a kiss, it's all gone silent! Perhaps he regrets it?

I finish washing up, another distraction tactic, and slap my Marigolds over the sink. Nearly ten o'clock. What do I do now? I've cleaned, hoovered, washed and dried up. I've got nothing else to do.

I decide I need a break, to get out somewhere. It's a nice day for late November – I'll ask Pani Zosia if I can leave Grzybek with her and hire a bicycle – I've noticed a hostel nearby rents them out.

I could go anywhere. I could go to Kampinos, where I went with AB. That would be nice. An adventure all on my own before my date tonight. All I have to do is get on the metro and head north to the end of the line, and the forest starts there. What could be better than a blast of fresh air before my date, far away from the flat, Language Zone, and Jacek?

Instances of activity over 60 minutes while waiting to hear from Jacek

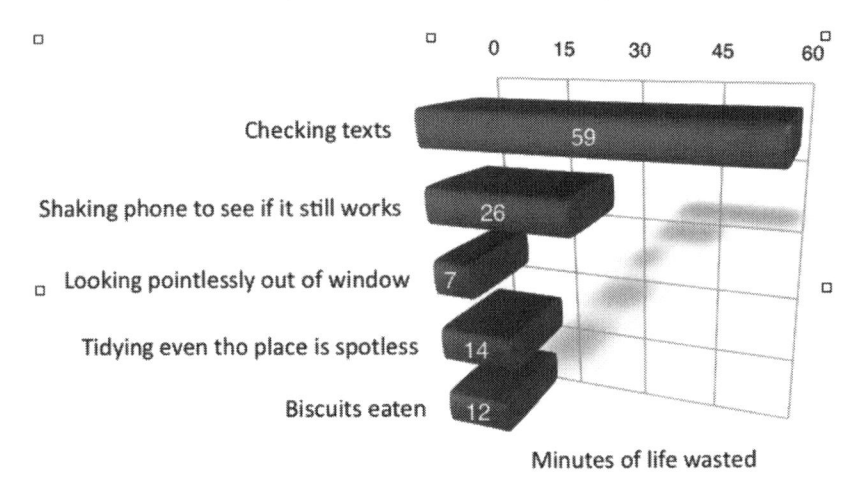

Activity	Minutes
Checking texts	59
Shaking phone to see if it still works	26
Looking pointlessly out of window	7
Tidying even tho place is spotless	14
Biscuits eaten	12

Minutes of life wasted

Warsaw's metro doesn't half make a racket but at least it's fast. I remember being here decades ago when plans to build it were under way but for some reason, had temporarily ground to a halt. Dagmara and I walked up to an enormous hole in the ground once – at least twenty metres square – with no 'danger signs' or fencing around it like there would be in England – and stared down the abyss. It was as if the Martians had landed and left a dirty great crater.

How things have changed. Now there are lines that zip north and south and east and west.

A young lad helps me into the station by whipping my bike over the barrier, then runs off for his train. As the train notches up the stations, I start to relax and gain some perspective.

I've let myself get too swept up.

I've had AB to deal with, Dagmara, Paweł – and it's all been too much.

I look at my bike and hope that it will last. Half of one of my pedals is missing. I only noticed when I set off from the hostel. I cycled the short distance from the hostel to the station but thought it was too fussy and British to go back and complain.

'What if I get a hole in my tyre?' I asked the receptionist, hoping she might have a little drawer of kits to hand out, somewhere in her desk.

'You mean a *przebicie opony*?' (puncture),' she said, correcting my Polish.

'Yes that's it!' I replied, thinking this meant that she had a stash (she didn't).

The journey north takes about forty minutes. The carriage grows emptier and emptier as the terminus approaches. When I emerge on the escalator at the last stop, dragging my bike along on the jagged steps, I'm met with a pleasing empty esplanade. Flat and endless and calming on the eye.

Just being out of the city centre lifts my spirit. I'm surprised there are no skateboarders on this big, sprawling, concrete square, or cyclists doing stunts. There would be in London. In fact there's no one at all. There aren't even any proper buildings, although they must be out there somewhere. A tall lamp post stands in the space and looks like a crotchet on a stave.

I climb onto my bike, which, I conclude, also needs oil and air, and ride around on the concrete to get into the mood. I'll need to be back for around six if I'm meeting Michał at eight. It's half past eleven now, so that still gives me the best part of the day.

A woman with a small child appears out of the indecipherable streets. The child is about seven, thin, and with a sweet heart-shaped face that tilts to one side. I ask the woman for directions to Kampinos, glancing at her staring, squinting son. She points to a long, thin, dark green strip in the distance, with a blurred top edge.

I sweep down roads, have my bones jiggled across a very bumpy stretch of gravel, then pelt like mad down a highway, stopping off for some picnic groceries in a supermarket. I ask an assistant for some help and she looks at me in a way that I last experienced twenty years ago. Maybe it's because she's seen me sweep things off the shelf just now without looking at the price, and I've betrayed myself as a foreigner with my funny English accent.

I buy some poppy-seed plait rolls, a big beef tomato which is gloriously dusty, and a big bottle of water. I'll have to balance this bag on one of my handlebars.

Shortly after I leave the store and as I'm cruising along a highway towards the forest, it starts to pour. Drat. I never brought a waterproof.

Or anything really apart from money and my phone. The last thing it looked like this morning was rain, never mind a deluge.

Eventually, I find shelter under a makeshift veranda in an old lady's garden who's selling *pierogi* from her garden shed. I've never come across a pensioner in catering before, let alone one who's set up shop in a ramshackle hut. She's nimble, but has one shoulder higher than the other. She looks as if she's had the same clothes on for years, and her hair is tied in a small knot on top of her head. Soaked to the bone, I buy some tea and she points me to a table under a roof of corrugated plastic.

The rain eases and large droplets of water drip down from the roof in a curtain of beads.

Behind me is a vast expanse of trees – Kampinos. As the sun breaks through, the old lady waves me off down a dirty track, and nods and laughs when I ask if it's the way.

'Look out for the coloured signs on the trees!' she calls. 'Black and blue are short routes, red and white are longer!'

Before I leave civilisation completely, I check my mobile, a small amount of battery and not much signal. Oh well. No messages from Jacek, or anyone else for that matter. I haven't listened to Dagmara's message from last night – but it can't be that important as she hasn't rung back.

I roll down a long muddy path and start to loosen up. Even my bike feels sturdier now, as if it's come into its own. I find a tree with a short route, blue stripe painted on it, just as the old lady said, and I sail down it, inhaling the fresh forest air. There's no one else around, which is rather strange for a Saturday. Hyde Park would be packed but here there's no one. I can feel the cobwebs blowing away! Then the earth turns sandy – not the best surface for cycling but no matter – and it's also completely silent. All I can hear is my own breath, not even a bird – what a tonic.

Another blue stripe. After that, it's, well – tree after tree after tree. All of them huge, at least fifty feet high, and all identical. They're shedding their leaves, making the branches more prominent. They stand out of the trunks at right angles, a bit like arms, pointing in different directions.

I hurtle along, not going as fast as I'd like to, but with the poststorm winter sun licking my face through the branches, my cycling pace working up a breeze. Another blue stripe. I could do with a map really, but no matter. I will trust in this simple colour-coded system.

Half an hour or so goes by without any change in the landscape. Still no people, but I don't mind. I'll stop to have a hot chocolate at some point at one of the refreshment kiosks. Not that I've seen any yet – it's just trees and trees.

Suddenly, a black painted tree appears, which is odd, as I don't remember ever veering off the blue. Perhaps the paths have joined? I roll down a gentle hill and spot some kind of small wooden hut further down and two cyclists reading a map. This is more like it! An information point, at last, with a nice loo tucked round the back too, I hope. From what I can see, these cyclists are very well kitted out (unlike me) – luminous clothes, streamlined helmets, bicycle pumps and compasses.

'Excuse me! Is this the blue track?' I call, my plastic bag banging against my front wheel and my half-pedal slipping. They look up towards me surprised. 'Sorry to bother you,' I jabber, 'it's just that I was on the blue track, but now it's changed to black.'

They look at me as if I'm from another planet. I get that a lot – either it must be my British-Polish accent or because I'm on my own. They look me up and down in my jeans and fleece, and stare at my supermarket bag which is wet and slightly torn. Then they let me look at their fancy laminated map which I wish was mine. I can see where I am – on the southern edge of a vast expanse. Vast.

'Just keep going,' they say, pointing down the track. Generally speaking, I find Poles are terrible at giving directions, so if ever lost in Poland, do not ask anyone, find a map.

'Where, down there?' I ask, so there can be no doubt.

They nod.

'You couldn't look at this pedal could you?'

As they produce a spanner from their bag of tricks, I think about how great it would be to join them on their bike ride. I could amble along behind them quietly, if ambling fast is possible.

Ten minutes later, I'm off on my own again and the track turns red. I'm starting not to like this, it's starting to give me the heebie-jeebies. I've gone from blue to black and now to red. Also, the path is forking, if not splitting into three.

I look behind me and ahead of me – it all looks the same and the two well-prepared cyclists have gone. I can't turn back as I could get lost, but which way now – and more importantly, where are all the cafes? Warsaw has got Starbucks now, and once they get in, they pop up everywhere.

I take a swig from my water bottle and take the most established track, cursing the sand and my split pedal which, although tighter, is still slipping from my foot. For a split second, the thought, 'This isn't fun,' sails into my head but I push it back out in a sort of valiant, don't-be-daft-you're-only-panicking way. This outing has been designated fun and a contrast to the city. (That said, I would really like some coffee and a muffin and some Wifi.)

I look this way and that. I cycle for another thirty minutes and start to do that thing where you know full well you're panicking but daren't admit it. Instead of finding a cafe or quite simply, something different to look at, there are more and more trees, just like before.

I look at my watch. It's half past one. I'll have to get out of here reasonably soon. I don't want to be here when it's dusk or dark, sunset is not long after three at this time of year. I look at my phone. No signal. Ahead, I see what I think is a board with a map on it in the distance but when I reach it, it's a portrait of an elk with explanations about its antlers!

I strike my pedal downwards and feel an utter *idiota* (berk). Then, a bit further along, when I do come across a map, there is no 'you are here' sign on it. What were they thinking of?

As if being lost (I'm admitting it now) isn't bad enough, a wind gathers pace out of nowhere, and blows gusts through trees. Now, everywhere around looks like forest, but sounds like the sea.

Fifteen minutes or so later, after wondering if this is a cruel joke Kampinos National Park is playing on me, and I'm not really stranded in a forest but on camera on live TV, I come across one of the cemeteries that AB mentioned with an official-looking house at the side. Great, a cemetery, for dead tourists, probably. But perhaps someone here can help.

I grind to a halt. If my ears aren't fooling me, someone is hoovering. I follow the sound until I find the source. Sure enough it's a man with a hoover, clearing up leaves from in between the graves.

I throw my bike down and run up to him, bedraggled, with leaves stuck to my trainers and the most desperate face I can muster.

'*Przepraszam*,' I beg. 'I'm sorry to disturb you, but how do I get out of here? Is there a bus stop? I'm lost!'

'Follow the road,' he says. Nothing more elaborate, just that. Then he turns and walks off with his electrical garden appliance. Is that it?

'You mean this road here?'

'Yes,' he says, fading away.

'Anything more precise maybe?'

'Just go down there.'

He motions vaguely and looks at the leaves stuck to my shoes, viewing them as potential litter, presumably. Before I know it, a posh limo arrives and he's gone to meet whoever's inside. A man and a woman get out and they all go into the official-looking building while I stand and stare. I look at my bike on the ground, which looks how I feel: totally conked out.

I try my phone again, just one bar. I know, I'll call Dagmara. She'll get the search parties out. First, I listen to her message from the other night. Oh no. She's heading for Gdansk this weekend and do I want to come? Yes, I want to come. Anything but be here, lost in a cemetery in a sprawling forest. I could cry. Why didn't I listen to it earlier? Because of obsessing about Jacek, that's why. I can't ring her in Gdansk now, what can she do from there?

I could ring the school – but it will be closed now. I could ring the Prof and concoct some story about being stuck in a cemetery in Kampinos – and maybe make it sound like historical research. Still, what would he do?

I don't want to, but I'm going to have to ring Jacek. I don't care how it looks, it's urgent. I ring and ring and ring but he doesn't answer. Desperate, I message Michał that I'm lost in a forest and might not make it, and then my signal peters out.

'No!' I yell upwards into the trees, staring at my phone. AB would have killed me for not having a map.

There's only one thing for it. Get back on my bicycle and go the way the man suggested. I cycle on a reasonably smooth road for about ten minutes, quietly determined. If that limo got here, there must be an exit somewhere, surely?

Suddenly, the road ahead forks, and again, and there are no directions. Just as I'm about to go back to the cemetery, another cyclist whizzes past.

'Stop!' I yell, unrestrained and desperate.

The cyclist does stop, to my surprise. He screeches to such a halt I think he's going to go flying over his handlebars. He stops about twenty or so metres away and gets off his bike, which he then leans carefully against a tree. It's very fancy, the kind champions can lift with a finger. He's tall, broad and a hundred percent muscle. What's slightly odd is that he doesn't look over, he focuses on straightening up his bike. Perhaps it's a prized possession? There's no one around apart from us. I must be crazy. I've stopped a stranger while all on my own and in the middle of nowhere. I look him up and down, trying to read his character. He's wearing those special cycling shoes, some black Lycra cycling shorts and a Lycra top.

'One minute,' he says calmly. 'I'm coming.'

'Please don't be a murderer,' I think, terrified and taking a sharp breath. His legs are like cedars, hairless and sinewy and his feet are about twice the size of mine. He walks over in silence, winding his MP3 cord around his hand, about the same thickness as my neck.

'I'm lost!' I stammer, trying to sound together. 'Is...is this...the path for central Warsaw?'

I sound petrified, I can hear it in my voice. He's in his late fifties, but young-looking for his age, with fine lines around his eyes. What, what, is going on in his mind? On the one hand I'm pleased he's stopped, on the other hand scared to death. The man is getting close now and my strength is all but gone.

'You need to turn left,' he says, as if it should be obvious. 'Then get the bus.'

'A bus? There's a bus stop nearby?' I ask, ecstatic with relief.

'Yes.'

'Do they take bikes?'

'Yes they do.' Then he asks the million-dollar question. 'Are you alone?' he asks, putting his hands on his hips.

'Sort of,' I quiver, grasping my handlebars.

'Well, the stop's about twenty minutes away. That's how long it takes me, anyhow.'

I watch him take off, hope he hasn't hidden behind a bush, then set off myself. I pass through a village with barking dogs and boys playing football and after that, there's a winding road which spirals upwards like a corkscrew.

As dusk falls a bus stop appears in the distance. Hurray! Hurray! I'll never go cycling in a forest again! No Starbucks, no tarmac...no map! I've been such a fool! Still, I think, no one need ever know apart from the two sensible cyclists, hoover man and MP3 powerhouse man. Best of all there's a bus that says 'Warszawa' on the back!

Terrified it might start up and leave, I muster a final burst of energy and cycle over as quickly as I can. It's empty, apart from the driver. Fantastic, at last an end to this awful outing.

I clamber off the saddle, hoping I never have to get on it again, and go up to the driver's window. He has his nose in a paper.

'Excuse me please, can I get on?'

I turn the front wheel in the gravel to try to make some noise.

'Excuse me. Please can I get on?'

Still nothing. I'd better knock. I'm just about to lift my hand, which happens to be stuck in the shape of a claw from clinging to my handlebars for so long, when he points to my bike and shakes his head.

'What?' I ask, horrified.

Surely he doesn't mean...no bikes?

'You don't take bikes?' I stammer.

He nods his head.

So far, he hasn't uttered a word but has made himself very clear.

'But...but, someone told me you did!'

He shakes his head and goes back to his paper.

'You have to!' I yell, starting to crack. 'I'm lost! I don't know the way back to the metro – and it's dark!'

Some bikeless people appear and get on fine, even though one has an enormous pram and three screaming children. Then, to my horror, the driver starts up the engine and leaves, just like that. The whole Polish thing is over in about a Polish minute! He does a large, majestic, pointless arc across the square, and pulls out onto the road, with everyone on board staring at me as the bus spews out a perfect trail of smoke.

'I'm going to report you!' I yell in English to no one. 'To the Ministry of... of... Transport!'

If I survive, that is.

And then it dawns, why didn't I just leave the bike and get on? I could be sitting on the bus now, on the way back to Warsaw. I could have paid for the near-ruined bicycle that was unfit for purpose in the first place – and that would have been that.

I look at my phone. Still no signal. I try to ring Jacek again as sometimes, dialling can make a signal come. Nothing – and nothing from Michał either who – if he's got my message – must think I'm mad.

So much for my date tonight.

So much for my relaxing day out of the city.

To rub salt into the wound, I could be in Gdansk with Dagmara now, laughing at all her outrageous jokes.

A little further on, I spot a sign.

'Warsaw 36 km.'

My heart sinks into my feet. Cycling back is going to take me hours along the hard shoulder of a motorway.

I look back towards the forest which is one large, black mass filling the horizon like an inkblot. Evening is here and at least I'm not in there. Crestfallen, cold and exhausted, I cycle along the road in a wiggly line, probably looking as if I haven't a care in the *świat* (world).

Shortly afterwards, I stagger into a petrol service station to buy a fizzy drink. Then, my phone rings – it's Jacek!

We've all seen it. Exhausted victims being hauled to safety on TV after some madcap expedition has gone horribly wrong. Depending on what extreme stunt they have got involved in, victims are either filmed hanging helplessly from a rope underneath a helicopter, looking wearily into camera, or walking away in embarrassment with a bandage around their head.

One hour, two Cokes and a cheeseburger later, Jacek arrives in his white van. I feel like a runaway dog that the car pound has finally caught up with. I hobble over, weary and dirty, and he swings my bike in the back.

'How on earth did you end up here?' he asks, his breath steaming in the air.

'On the metro. Then through the forest.'

'Forest?'

'I just thought it would be nice,' I reply.

'Did you have a map?'

I can barely look at him.

'No.'

'Magda, you went cycling in Kampinos without a map?'

I hang my head in shame. 'Correct. I had no map, no plan, no puncture kit, nothing. An old lady told me the way, then two properly kitted-out cyclists helped me, followed by a gardener and a six-foot cyclist who I thought was a murderer. I was going to take the bus but the driver said bikes weren't allowed.'

'Magda,' he says, softening, and relieved. 'Why doesn't this surprise me? Come on. Hop in. You're safe now.'

'I'm so glad you rang,' I reply, almost in tears.

It's pitch black and freezing by now but Jacek's van is warm.

'You're lucky to be alive. Kampinos isn't a paddling pool, you know. It's an ocean. What were you expecting, cafes and nice paths?'

'That's exactly what I was expecting.'

I glance at the dashboard – the clock says six. At this rate, I might still be able to meet Michał. We sit in silence for the first part of the journey. I swing between thinking how much my thighs and buttocks are throbbing and wanting to lay all my cards out on the table. Ask him about last night, about everything. I can't. I should ignore what happened and focus on this date.

'Did you enjoy last night?' he asks all of a sudden.

'Er, yes,' I reply, all casual. 'You gave a brilliant performance.'

More silence. There's just the sound of the indicator as he overtakes some cars and the murmur of his radio.

'What made you take up the violin again?' I ask, staring out of the window into total darkness. 'You said you wouldn't.'

'It was just the right time.'

'You should play more.'

I want to say more – that his playing was magnificent – that it was amazing to listen to him – but I also don't want to.

Back in the city centre, Jacek carries my bike back to the hostel while I wait in the van. The pedal did fall off in the end.

Five minutes later, and we're back at the flat and I flop on the sofa.

'You look terrible,' says Jacek.

'Thanks.'

'That bike was ready for the rubbish tip.'

'Just like me then.'

It's wonderful to be horizontal and safe and not pedalling anymore. For some reason, I feel strangely complete, staring at the waves of Artex on the ceiling. My feet like a pair of balloons.

'You look traumatized.'

'I know. The worst thing is, I'm going out tonight.'

'What, in your state?'

'I have to,' I reply. 'It's a date and it's arranged. I don't play around with people's feelings, Jacek.'

He nods, embarrassed, and glances at his rose which is resting in a glass next to Michał's bunch. He messaged me before Jacek arrived and I messaged him back to say we were back on. I fish a dress out of the wardrobe.

'I don't know what I'd have done without you, Jacek. Thank you. But I have to go and get ready now – if you don't mind.'

I need to have a shower and then hobble for the tram. I can't stand Michał up now, and besides, my near-death experience will make for brilliant conversation. (I'll choose how I'll angle it, of course, I'll make myself sound brave and adventurous, not a blinking fool.)

'What tram is it to Praga?' I ask, as he's about to leave. 'I'm going to a cafe.'

'Magda,' he says, looking as guilty as anything. 'Let me give you a lift. I'm going that way anyway.'

I should say yes. Another short trip with him won't do any harm. I'll get ready, look a million złoty so he knows what he's missing, then go to meet Michał.

'OK. Thanks Give me five minutes.'

I emerge from the bathroom, transformed from vagabond to gorgeous date.

'What are you doing tonight?' I ask, as we set off. 'A night out with the lads? A concert?'

'I'm just going home. I've got a lot to do.'

'Arranging London I suppose? I know when I moved out here, there was so much to do.'

Thank goodness I didn't say anything. He's doing nothing tonight but still hasn't suggested we see one another. The rose and his kiss were nothing after all – a flight of human fancy.

At least I know the truth now. I can forget everything and focus on tonight. Jacek drops me off outside the café just before eight. I watch his van trundle down the street and turn off down a side street.

The things to think are:
1. I'm not in that forest
2. I'm about to have a date and best of all
3. I'm about to consume a very large quantity of cake

The cafe is fabulous – these Poles, with their whacky interior design. Red carpet on the walls, dressed up shop mannequins in expressive poses, feathers adorning the light bulbs above and one-off wooden tables with tea-lights in water. Funnily enough, there are vases of single gerbera dotted around, all in different colours just like the ones Michał sent. This guy's got style – he's matched them up especially.

I look round but he can't be here yet – everyone else around me is in small groups or couples. I sidle my way into an empty table set for two by the window, and a waitress with psychedelic white eyeliner comes to take my order – a large hot chocolate with a flake and extra cream. (I must have worked off at least five thousand calories through cycling so no matter, none of it will count).

Eight o'clock comes. And eight o'clock goes. Don't tell me he's late.

I check to see if there's a section around the back that I've missed, but there isn't. Eight fifteen comes and is followed by eight thirty. Have

I got the wrong place? The wrong date? I check my messages but there's nothing.

Here we go again. He can't be coming. As if I haven't been through the mill and back already – I've now been stood up after nearly dying in a forest. I call over the waitress and order a big fried pancake on top of my hot chocolate.

Big sigh. Annoying? Yes, but after a day like today, it's best to take this philosophically. Maybe my attempt to meet this guy was never meant to be. Yes, my hot chocolate goes really well with my brown and cream dress and I look a picture, but maybe I was just meant to be here on my own tonight, drinking hot chocolate and eating ice cream and pancake.

At eight thirty-five, when my stuffed pancake with a lit sparkler stuck in the top more than makes up for being stood up, I hear a car pull up, out of sight, in the quiet road outside. A car door slams and footsteps approach. Not dainty footsteps, such as stilettos. Heavier footsteps, those of a man in a hurry. Michał? Not now, surely? I was rather looking forward to blowing out the sparkler on my own.

It isn't Michał though. It's Jacek, and for some reason, he's back. I thought I recognised the slam of his van door. Also, he isn't in his work gear. He's shaved and changed. Perhaps he's checking on me to see if I'm alright before he goes out to meet his date. Or maybe…

Hang on a minute. Hang on.

He comes in and sits down, a smile lighting up his face. A penny the size of a manhole cover is starting to drop very loudly in my head.

Is photoless Michał… Jacek?

Jacek who knew to suggest a nice cafe, who messaged me only when he knew it was off with the Prof… who was so shy in the van he didn't know what to say, and who drove to a motorway to find me!

The silver-eyed waitress breaks into our bubble for a second, bringing a second fork, then vanishes again.

'Jacek?' I ask over the crackle of the sparkler.

'Yes.'

'Are you Michał?'

'Yes.'

'It was you…'

'All along! I'm sorry I'm late. I had a cyclist to drop off you see. She'd gone into a forest thinking it was a park. And then I had go home to get ready myself. Like I said, I had a lot to do!'

I bury my face in my hands and start to laugh. The gerbera, they were from him!

'I'm sorry I didn't ring yesterday. I wanted to wait until tonight and surprise you. Then when I saw all your missed calls – and got the message you were lost...'

'I thought I'd imagined last night!'

'No, I just didn't know what to say. I nearly told you in the flat but when you were determined to go out, I knew I had to wait. And I'm not going to London. How could I, with you here?'

The sparkler goes out and he leans over and kisses me on the cheek.

'My second kiss in two days. So. Am I welcome? Shall I stay?'

'Yes,' I reply, passing him a fork, 'stay.'

CHAPTER 21
HAVING BUTTERFLIES
(*MAM TREMĘ*)

It's funny. You search for a treasure all your life and you find it's been there all along.

Dear Polishmate
I'm writing to inform you that I no longer need my account, as I have now met someone. He subscribes to your service, although that's not how I met him – I knew him before. I am cc-ing him in, along with Dagmara Szymańska, the holder of my account, as I know you need her authorisation to close it.
With thanks
Magda Mikołajczyk

Dear Polishmate
I am writing to ask you to close down my account, as I have now met someone. She subscribes to your service, although that's not how I met her – I knew her before. My username is Michał1 but my account is in my real name, Jacek Balon. I am also cc-ing her in – Magda Mikołajczyk.
Jacek Balon

Jacek proposes, and my answer is 'yes.' We've had our courtship: an English lesson, a never-ending plumbing job, a violin concert and a forest rescue mission. He pops the question one evening at my flat, when we're looking at the sunset and watching Balcony TV. An elderly man helps his elderly wife take in their washing.

'We should get married,' he says as we look out.

'Yes. I think we should.'

CHAPTER 22
FILLED WITH RICE AND MINCE
(NADZIEWANE Z RYŻEM I Z MIĘSEM)

I'm meeting Dagmara for lunch in the same place where we met on my first day in Warsaw, six months ago.

She's late as usual, but I don't mind. I've got lots to think about and a wedding to plan.

I flick through the menu. My Polish has improved so much. I can manage with the Polish one these days. Today, lunch will be on me, no matter what Dagmara says. I look at the starters, just like before. I won't be having the lard again, that's for sure.

I have two bits of news for Dagmara. I'd like her to be my bridesmaid and I need to tell her Grzybek's living with me in the flat for now, until I move into AB's.

She's here. She knocks on the window near my table and mouths hello, steaming up the glass. She's in a white fur hat, a red swing coat and she sports a pair of grey suede boots with buckles around the rim.

'*Kochana*, what a wonderful idea, an engagement lunch! Congratulations! I always knew Jacek had his beady eye on you,' she says, leaning over to kiss me. Her lips are cold against my cheek.

'Really?'

'Yes. I mean, whoever heard of a pipe taking weeks to replace? I could have re-plumbed the whole of Warsaw in that amount of time!'

She sits down and gets comfortable. A waitress appears with a notepad and sees we haven't chosen yet.

'Today's on me,' I smile, passing her the menu. She acquiesces with a nod. We choose two Kir Royals, two portions of *rosół* (chicken soup) followed by *gołąbki* – cabbage-leaf parcels the size of a fist, filled with rice and mince.

'So when did he join Polishmate?'

'When he realised I was on it. After our dinner. But the trouble was, he was too shy to go on it as himself, as we'd already met by then.'

'So for him, signing up just led to endless torture, as he saw you go on all your dates!'

I never thought of it that way, but yes – my dates with Paweł – he knew about them all.

'Go on then, tell me all about it, and don't miss out a thing. Now is not the time for censorship.' She leans her head on her hands, which have rings on every finger but her wedding finger. 'Did he go down on one knee? Did you cry? Did he swear undying love?'

'Not exactly.'

I tell her everything – about the rose and the kiss and the rescue and the cafe in Praga.

'Oh Magda, it's like some kind of reverse, anti-romance fairy tale!' she says, dabbing her eyes with a tissue. 'Which could only happen to you, you daft British thing! Just think if you'd come to Gdansk with me and not nearly killed yourself in Kampinos? We might never be sat here, talking weddings. What does Mama think? I bet she's told the whole of Doncaster, *nie*?'

'Probably.'

I think back to my call with Mama. The spider plant by the phone came tumbling down and there was a thwumping noise which could only be her plonking herself down onto her bad-news chair (only this time the news was good).

'Are you going to go over to introduce him to them?'

'Well Mama's already met him, remember, when she came over.'

'Oh yes. What about Tata? I bet he's sad he's losing his girl.'

'I guess so,' I reply, thinking of Tata and his soft, gentle face. 'But if I'm happy, he's happy.'

'So, let's see it then!'

'What?'

'Your ring! There you are, hiding your hand away, come on!'

'I'm not hiding anything.'

'Magda! she gasps, grabbing at my hand. 'There's nothing there!'

'I haven't got an engagement ring, Dagmara.'

'Why not?'

'I don't want one.'

'Oh Magda, why do you have to always be so weird about everything?'

'What do I need a ring for? I'll get one when we get married, won't I?'

'There's no way I'd ever say no to a ring off anyone. Anyway, I know you're still working through your English ways. *Gratuluję, kochana*! (congratulations, darling),' she says, lifting up her Kir. 'You're going to become a true Pole now, being married to Jacek. You've gone from being a half-baked British Pole to slowly emerging as a fully blown one.'

'Thanks. I'll take that as a compliment.'

She guffaws and we chink and sip our Kirs, and then our bowls of *rosół* arrive. Ah, I love this soup. Golden baubles of oil float on hot clear liquid covered with smithereens of parsley.

'Now Dagmara, some practicalities.'

'Actually,' she purrs. 'I've got something to ask you.'

'What?'

'I was thinking... of getting you some *lekcje gotowania* for your wedding present.'

'Cooking lessons?'

'Magda, you can't feed Jacek on beans on toast forever. Remember this as you prepare for married life: "Polish man cannot live by bread alone." He'll have needs, if you know what I mean. And by that I mean breakfast, lunch and dinner.'

'Dagmara, I can cook.'

'No Magda, I'm sorry. I don't mean to be rude, but that lamb you made. You nearly killed us! It still haunts me today. Even Stefan left some. That's like a dog saying no.'

'Well you can't cook either,' I reply. 'What did you ever make when I came to visit? Chinese takeaways.'

'He's closed down, that other Chinese chap,' she says. 'Because I'm no longer in the area, keeping him in business.'

'Dagmara, there's something else I need to talk to you about.'

'Oh hang on just a sec *kochana*, I need to text Luigi.'

'Luigi?'

She takes out her phone and starts punching at the keypad.

'That's my other news, Magda.'

'What?' I reply, wondering how on earth I'm going to mention Grzybek now. He's probably lying on her silk cushions as we speak.

'I've met someone – an Italian – called Luigi!'

'Luigi?'

'Yes – he lives in Pisa,' she says, bursting with pleasure. 'Pee-za!' With any luck, I'll be there soon too.'

'How did you meet him?'

'*L'uomo italiano*! Like Polishmate, but in Italy. I've decided to go for a foreigner, Magda, like you. Who knows, I could be moving to Italy. Arrivederci Warsaw. This city Magda – ugh. Sometimes it looks like dirty dishwater.'

I let her talk a while and slurp my soup. Sometimes Dagmara needs to get all her drivel out, and then she's OK.

'Anyway. What were you going to say? You were going to tell me something before I so rudely interrupted. What's the matter? You've gone all quiet.'

'Well...'

'You're not pregnant, are you?'

'Dagmara! Of course I'm not pregnant. Two things. Firstly, would you be my bridesmaid?'

'Would I? I thought you'd never ask!'

'And secondly...'

'Yes...'

'It's Grzybek.'

'What about him?' she says, turning pale. 'Oh Magda, please don't tell me he's...'

"fraid so. He's... he's...'

'I was wondering about him...'

'He's in the flat with me. Don't worry. It won't be a problem when I move into AB's.'

'Magda...'

Dagmara's unspoken wish: she'd always wanted to have Grzybek put to sleep.

CHAPTER 23
THINGS THAT HAPPEN WHEN YOU'RE GETTING MARRIED
(RZECZY KTÓRE SIĘ ZDARZAJĄ KIEDY OGŁASZASZ ŻE WYCHODZISZ ZA MĄŻ)

1. **People want to know your future husband's surname and if you're going to take it**
   Jacek's surname is Balon – granted, not one syllable, but easy to say. Yes it means balloon, and yes I'm going to take it.

2. **Every woman you know is obsessed with your wedding dress**
   'Planning your wedding has done wonders for my web skills,' Mama trills down the phone one day. 'I know who do nice wedding dresses Magda! 'Marks & Spencer.'
   'I am not getting my wedding dress from M&S. And you're wrong, they don't do them.'

'They do. At least I think they do – let me see. You've got such a wonderful figure – just like a vase.'
'Don't you mean hourglass?'

3. **Your mother becomes obsessed with where you're having your reception**

    'Mama, I've got something to tell you. We're getting wed in Kraków.' (Cue thwumping sound in the background).
    Long silence, followed by:
    'Kraków Magda? What's wrong with Doncaster?'
    'We want to get married at the salt mine in Wieliczka. You know, the World Heritage Site? A winter wedding will be gorgeous there.'
    'But there are mines in Doncaster, Magda.'
    'Yes, but they're coal Mama, not salt.'
    'But what about the buffet, and the party, and the JOURNEY!'

4. **You have to decide where you're going to live**

    'You're going to live out there, aren't you Magda? Come on, spit it out.'
    'Yes Mama, we are.' (Cue more thwumping).

5. **Everyone wants to kiss you**

    Even strangers.

6. **You start having to say 'we' instead of 'I'**

    Another big change. I now feel like the Queen.

7. **You have to know your own mind**

    'Dagmara?' I ask, as she tries to zip me into some far-too-small designer wedding dress in some fancy boutique.
    'Yes?' she says, huffing and puffing. 'You know you're going to have to eat like a *królik* (rabbit) for the next few weeks.'
    A flash of inspiration.
    'I know.'
    'What?'

'I know what I'm can wear. AB's green dress! It needs mending – but it fits me and I like it.'

'Be careful Magda, if you wear green, go easy on the jewellery, or you'll look like a *choinka* (Christmas tree).'

8. **You have to think carefully about your wedding photos**

    In previous decades, a newly wed Polish couple would look so miserable on their photos, you'd think it was the worst day of their lives. This is because Poles are conditioned not to smile on photos. These days, that's no longer the case, with wedding photos anyway. In fact, I think people have gone slightly the other way and have photos taken in the most outrageous of poses. I recently saw a photo of a bride tied to a (real) train track and her husband saving her. And another one of the happy couple with a sunflower between their teeth! (Note to self, must hire British photographer).

9. **You sometimes question your sanity**

    Why oh why did I make Dagmara chief bridesmaid?

CHAPTER 24
THEN THERE'S THE DAY ITSELF
(NO I NADSZEDŁ TEN DZIEŃ)

'Pani Mikołajczyk?' calls a young man up the path, flinging open a door. A shaft of light falls onto the pitch-black track. He must have heard our limo arrive and come out to meet us.

'We're here!' I call. 'One minute!'

Dagmara and I have arrived at Wieliczka salt-mine. It's cold and dark and everywhere is under a thick blanket of snow. All being well, Jacek and everyone else will already be in situ, two hundred metres underground, inside a chapel carved entirely out of salt.

'It doesn't look like a mine,' says Dagmara, hurrying, as our car rolls away. 'Although, look up there, there's a big iron wheel with a pulley. If that isn't a mine, I don't know what is.'

What a sight we must make, hoisting up our dresses underneath a starlit January sky, clambering through deep powdery snow, Dagmara in a dress that I can only describe as a Barbra-Streisand-esque-panto-outfit, and me wrapped up in a fur coat and boots.

'Oh no!'

'What?'

'My green shoes, Dagmara, I've left them in the car!'

We look back, but all we can see is an empty dark road and some deep tyre tracks.

'What am I going to do?' I say, lifting up my fur ankle boots, looking at the sodden soles.

'You'll have to borrow my shoes,' she says. 'Once we're at the chapel, we'll swap and I'll go barefoot. I've got a long dress so no one will know.'

'I can't wear those! They're orange.'

'Orange goes with green. Everyone knows that,' she says (in her orange and green dress).

'Pani Mikołajczyk?' calls the voice again. 'Is everything – all right?'

'Yes! Just coming!'

Dagmara and I scramble up along the pavement and the man guides us straight into a lift. Not a normal lift, but the original miners' lift, which has criss-cross bar iron doors so that the hewn walls of the salt-shaft show through! We glide down, listening to the smooth mechanism of pulleys and chains. The air starts to change, becoming cooler and purer and a few minutes later, we come to rest with a gentle thud. The man pushes back the doors and we enter a dimly lit tunnel made entirely out of rock salt.

'Have you been here before?' asks the man, leading us quickly.

'Never, but I've always wanted to.'

It's incredible. A proper ancient salt mine. The rock salt walls are held up by big wooden beams and the salt isn't exactly white, but grey and opaque. Occasionally, there's a brilliant white cauliflower-shaped encrustation in the join of the beams.

'What are they?'

'Salt that's bubbled to the surface and then solidified again. This way please, ladies,' he says, opening a door into another tunnel. 'It isn't far now,' He takes us past some life-size salt-statues and through some grotto-like areas, then up a flight of steps, where, finally, we reach another door.

'Through here you will see Chapel Kinga.'

His voice, excited and brisk until now, has become a whisper and I can hear everyone talking on the other side. He opens the door and Dagmara and I go through to a balcony above our gathering.

The view is breathtaking. Even Dagmara is lost for words. A peek over the edge and there are all our guests, in the most unique chapel I've ever seen. Hewn by several generations of miners and entirely out of rock salt. It's not rough or misshapen like it is in the tunnels, but intricately detailed. Spectacular salt crystal chandeliers hang from the ceiling. The floor's salt, the altar's salt, the crucifix is salt, even Jesus is salt. The font, the walls and the two huge flights of stairs on either side are salt too, as is a towering statue of the late Polish Pope.

'Shall I let your father know that you're ready?' asks the steward.

I nod, speechless and excited, almost forgetting about my soggy boots. Dagmara prods me.

'Oh Dagmara, I wish she were here!' I say, as I slip on her high heels.

'AB?'

'Yes.'

'Me too, *kochana*, and my mum and my dad. AB spotted something about you and Jacek, didn't she?'

Jacek. I open my eyes and find his face in the crowd. He's beaming and my nerves melt away. Looking at his suit, his shoes, his tie, it could be anyone standing there. It's only when I happen upon his face that I realise that it's him.

I see our guide escort Tata out of the chapel upstairs so he can walk me down the aisle.

'Magda?' says Dagmara, stopping me in my tracks. Her face for once is pure and at rest.

'What?'

'Our parents. And AB. They were children of the war, weren't they?'

'They were.'

'War fruit, I call them,' she says, with a little laugh. 'It's a miracle our family made it, isn't it? That you and I are here.'

'*Tak* (Yes), it's true.'

'Magda I know we haven't got on always. But I'm so happy for you.'

Tata slips through the door. Not a hair out of place and his suit and tie is immaculate.

'Ready Magda?' he asks, shedding a tear. He gives me a final hug.

'Ready.'

I take him by the arm and have one last look over the balcony.

As I peer over, Jacek looks up and spots me. He smiles and blushes, his eyes sparkling, and starts to wave. Within seconds everyone else is looking up and waving too.

People start to take their seats and the noise increases and subsides.

We have a flight of about fifty steps down and as Tata and I take the stairs with Dagmara behind us, people's faces grow nearer and clearer.

Viv from Adspeak has made it – she's next to a small crowd from Language Zone. Next are Jacek's parents and his relatives.

And finally, Mama, bless her. I love her so much.

I walk across the floor and down the aisle past the rows and rows of faces. Everyone's eyes are shining.

'*Już się zaczyna!* (It's starting!)' says someone.

'*Jak pięknie wygląda!* (Doesn't she look beautiful!)'

In my head, or perhaps from everywhere around, I hear AB whispering loudly, her dear old face bursting with smiles.

'No, *dawaj Magda, dawaj!* (Go for it Magda!)'

I'm standing at the front now.

Deep breath, Magda.

Jacek takes my hands and I start to tremble.

CHAPTER 25
LEGACY (DZIEDZICTWO)

It's February. It's been three weeks since we got married and four months since AB's funeral. I'm in Wilanów Cemetery in Warsaw, standing by AB's grave beneath a sycamore tree. A thin cloud hangs in the grey sky, ends upturned, like a simple brushstroke. The rust-coloured earth, white with frost, crunches beneath my feet.

Jacek's here too. He's gone to visit Marzena's grave.

'I married him AB,' I say towards the stone. 'Did you know I would?'

The cemetery is quiet but dramatic. I look around, burrowing my head into my scarf. They do elaborate graves, the Poles. Different shapes and sizes, packed tightly together, with lots of candles and flowers.

As I look around, I see elderly women tending them. They stoop over with cloths and bottles of water, as if cleaning these graves is an extension of their housework. Perhaps it's easier to care for the dead?

'Magda!' calls Jacek.

I look to where he is, about ten rows down.

'What?'

'Over here!'

He's looking at a headstone.

I make my way over, weaving through the graves, thinking he wants to show me Marzena's grave or the grave of someone famous.

But it's Władek's grave. AB's first love whom she lost in the war.

Władek Czyżewski. Born February 21, 1923, died September 10, 2004.

'It's him, isn't it?' he says. Jacek knows all about Władek. I told him what happened as we cleared AB's flat and came across some photos. Some had been signed by Władek, others had been written on by AB.

'It must be,' I reply, staring at the letters, embossed in gold.

'Do you think she knew he was here? Look. Their plots are in line.'

I look back towards the sycamore tree.

'She said not. I guess we'll never know.'

Dear AB. Her face was so alive.

As I sort through her belongings, I see that her dresses and coats still carry the shape of her body.

I will carry her shape too.

As we do with all of our relatives.

Thank you for reading

Did you enjoy *Are My Roots Showing?*

If you did, I'd be delighted if you could take a moment to share your comments on Facebook or Twitter

Please keep in touch by adding your email to the subscribe option at www.karolagajda.com – I won't share your details with anyone else and I won't email too often!

I'd also love it if you could review the novel on Amazon
or at www.goodreads.com